Coming

on

Christmas

Gardens

THE MULTI MILLION BESTSELLING AUTHOR

HOLLY MARTIN

CHAPTER 1

❄

'I've found one.'

Alex looked up from making her daughter's packed lunch as her sister, Immy, burst in through the back door brandishing a square box in her hand. Immy's scruffy little black Skye terrier, Jacob, ambling in at her side was clearly nowhere near as excited as his owner.

Immy yanked her hat off, her red hair tumbling out in a cascade of curls, her pale, freckly cheeks flushed with cold or excitement. She bit the ends of her snowflake-patterned gloves to remove them as quickly as possible and then reverentially laid the box down on the table as if it was a prized treasure.

'You've found what?' Alex asked. Judging from Immy's excitement it had to be a cheque for a million pounds, which quite honestly couldn't have come at a better time; they had bills coming out of their ears.

'A bauble.'

'Oh.' Alex frowned in confusion before the penny dropped. 'Ohhh.'

Zara's packed lunch momentarily forgotten, she hurried over to look at it. Since the start of December these exquisitely hand-painted baubles had been popping up all over the little seaside town of Lovegrove Bay and no one knew who was painting them. With only one week until Christmas, it had become the talk of the town with people desperate to find one or find out who the mystery bauble painter was. Or 'St Nick' as they had called themselves. Each one was completely unique and came in a lovely little presentation box, with a little gift tag attached that simply said, 'Keep, re-hide or gift to someone else. Love St Nick.'

Alex looked through the clear lid at the iridescent white bauble nestled on a layer of red tissue paper. This one was beautifully painted with a pair of roller skates. They had gold stars painted on the side and pink wheels with purple laces. The skates were surrounded by holly leaves, berries and pine cones and more sparkly stars. Zara would love this. She had been roller skating ever since she was three years old and practically lived in her skates when she wasn't at school.

'That's beautiful,' Alex said.

'It really is. I found it in Christmas Gardens. We'll have to ask Quinn if he's seen anything suspicious. I wonder, as it was near Christmas Cottage, whether it might be one of the elves doing this.'

As far back as Alex could remember, the cottage on

Christmas Gardens, Quinn's home, had been used as Santa's house for the weeks leading up to the big day. About a week before, although no one knew the exact date, a team of elves, or people from the town, would transform the outside and inside of the cottage into something magical. The children of the town always got a big kick out of seeing it the next day knowing the elves had visited overnight and that shortly after Santa would be arriving.

'Maybe,' Alex mused. 'Although that might be too obvious. Lots of people go through Christmas Gardens.'

'Well, who do you think is doing this?' Immy asked.

'I don't know.' Alex thought about all the artists who worked alongside her at the Wonky Tree Studios, woodworkers, mosaic artists, clay. 'None of the artists at the Wonky Tree Studios paint anything like this. Rose paints landscapes not stuff like this and she is denying it's her. And I know most of the artists at the craft market on the village green and none of them do anything like this either.'

'It's a shame the artist isn't more visible,' Immy said. 'Hand-painted custom baubles like this would sell very well. Imagine asking the artist to paint your favourite hobby or your pet or your favourite place and then getting something like this. People would love it.'

Alex nodded. 'They obviously like the mystery and I think it's such a lovely idea to give this to people for them to keep or pass on to someone else. What will you do with yours?'

3

'Photograph it and share it on the Lovegrove Bay Facebook page and then give it to Zara of course. There's no one who loves roller skating as much as that girl.'

'Don't you want to keep it?' Alex asked. 'You were so excited to have found it a few moments ago.'

'Yeah, of course I'm excited. Loads of people have found one so far. I feel like I've found Willy Wonka's golden ticket now I have one too. But Zara will love this and I will get just as much joy giving it to her as I did finding it in the first place.'

Alex smiled at that. She loved her sister. But Immy was so much more than that, she was her best friend. It had been just the three of them growing up, Alex, Immy and their mum. When their mum had died when Alex was eighteen, it had brought Alex and Immy closer than ever. Alex had supported Immy after her horse riding accident which had caused brain trauma and when Alex's husband, Liam, had died, Immy had moved in with Alex and Zara to look after them both. In the months after Liam's death, it had been so much easier having someone to talk to about everything; her guilt, her feelings surrounding his death, Zara's grief, Immy had been there for it all. That sisterly bond wasn't like anything else and, more than anything, Alex wished she could do something to thank Immy for everything she had done for her.

'It is funny that the illustrations seem to be tailored to the people who find the baubles or at least someone close to them,' Immy said. 'Mrs Kendall found one with a black cat wearing a Santa hat and she has four black cats. Mr Malik found one painted with chess pieces and his son loves chess. Miss O'Connor found one with a kingfisher on it and everyone knows her next-door neighbour Bob, an amateur twitcher, has been searching for a kingfisher for months.'

'I don't know. If St Nick wanted to do a bauble for a specific person, why not just leave it outside that person's door rather than hiding them in parks and woods, on the beach, or around the town?'

'True.' Immy went to the fridge and started preparing Jacob's breakfast. 'Although a few people have found them outside their door. Not specifically on their doorstep or in their garden but on a nearby bench or on the garden wall, so maybe some of the baubles are meant for certain people.'

'That's true,' said Alex. 'I've been asked to write an article about it for the local paper, it's such a heart-warming Christmas story, perfect for this time of year, but maybe I could make it more of an investigative piece and try and find out who it is.'

'Ooh yes, I like that idea, although the mystery of it does make it more exciting. There's a huge part of me that wants to know who it is but I'm not sure I want to ruin the secret either. It's like Santa, I never really wanted to find out the truth about him, I even cried when Mum told me.'

'Yet you kept the magic alive for me.'

'Of course I did,' said Immy. 'I could see how happy it made you, leaving food out for the reindeer, a mince pie for Santa – when you saw the snowy footprints across the lounge you used to squeal with excitement. I couldn't take that away from you.'

Alex smiled at that.

'But enough about that for now. Are you ready for your date today?' Immy asked.

Alex pulled a face. 'No, but I don't think I'll ever be.'

She sighed. After Liam had made her life a living hell for the last eighteen months of his life, she had been desperate to finally move on after he'd died but something had held her back. She knew Violet and Quinn were part of it. She adored Liam's mum and brother and she never wanted to do anything to hurt them. She also worried how Zara would feel about having a new man in her life. Whoever she ended up with had to be right for Zara too, someone who would love her as much as Alex did. But it was more than that holding her back. There was fear of falling in love and putting her trust in someone else after Liam had let her down so spectacularly. And there was guilt that moving on and falling in love would mean benefitting from Liam's death. She carried enough guilt over his death not to want to add to it. But it had been four years since he'd died and Immy had decided that it was time Alex started dating again. Over the weekend, Immy had sat with her and helped her create an online dating profile. And since then Alex had received messages from several men, and she was meeting one of them for coffee at lunch that day. She felt a bit sick at the thought.

Immy was watching her closely. 'I know you're nervous, and rightly so after the hell Liam put you through,' she said. 'But you're a wonderful person, you deserve to find happiness again.'

'I am happy,' Alex protested. 'I have you and Zara, a job I love, I live in the most beautiful part of the world. I don't need anything more than that.'

'I think you'd be a lot happier having a hot man take you to bed.'

The thought of that made her stomach clench with need, although whenever she thought about sex, there was only one man she could imagine that with.

As if Immy had read her mind, she smirked. 'This dating malarkey would be a lot easier if you just told Quinn how you feel and let him take you out on a date instead.'

And there was the crux of it. How could Alex even think about dating someone else when she was head over heels in love with Quinn?

'He doesn't feel that way about me.'

'He's round here every day,' Immy pointed out.

'To see his niece.'

'He moved here to Lovegrove Bay shortly after meeting you at Liam's funeral.'

'To get to know his niece and spend time with her.'

'He moved his art studio into the Wonky Tree Studios when you moved in there.'

'Well, that was because the arrangement that Luke and Flick were offering was such a good deal.'

'His studio is next to yours.'

'There isn't a lot of space there.'

Immy gave her a look. The truth was there had been many times when Alex had questioned whether Quinn saw her as more than a friend: the way he looked at her or touched her felt like something more than just platonic. But she had kissed him once, a few years ago, and he'd stopped her. If he'd changed his mind about how he felt, surely it was up to him to make his move. She couldn't keep putting herself forward and getting rejected.

Upstairs, she could hear Zara singing in the shower. Her daughter loved having a shower and always used way too much soap so the shower cubicle looked like she'd had a bubble bath, but Alex figured too much soap was better than not enough. According to Zara, some of the boys in her class were really stinky.

'I can't date Quinn,' she said, returning her attention to Immy.

'Why the hell not?'

She bit her lip. Dating Quinn, if he even felt that way about her, would be huge and significant and life-changing. There was no way it could be anything casual and she wasn't sure if she was ready for something like that, not after what happened with Liam before he died. But there was another reason.

'You know why,' Alex said, quietly.

Immy sighed. 'Because you have stupid misplaced guilt over Liam's death.'

'He would still be here if it wasn't for me. It's my fault he died.'

'He died because he drank a bottle of whisky and then got in his car and drove into a tree. You have nothing to feel guilty about.'

Alex winced at the blunt summing up of Liam's death but then Immy had never liked Liam and she liked him a hell of a lot less once she found out how bad it had been in the eighteen months before he died.

'It's still my fault and if Quinn ever found out, he would never speak to me again. I couldn't cope with losing him too. I could never have a relationship with him and not tell him the truth about his brother's death. I should have told him years ago but I was always too scared to. But if we were together I'd have to do it, I couldn't live with the lie.'

'You're making it into a much bigger deal than it is. You need to let go of this guilt. Liam was an adult, he made his own choices. And Quinn will understand that.'

Alex shook her head, knowing he would hate her. If it wasn't for her, his brother would still be here.

She heard Zara come out the shower and knew she had to divert the conversation. She didn't want Zara to hear about her dad drink driving or Alex's inappropriate crush on Zara's uncle.

'Look, I'm going on dates like you wanted, let's just leave Quinn out of it. I highly doubt he is even an option. So let's focus on today instead. I wore a dress.'

Alex did a little twirl, trying to change the subject. 'Is it OK?'

'You look lovely,' Immy said.

'Is it too much for a coffee?'

'No, it's pretty.'

'I didn't know what to do with my hair.' Alex ran one of her red curls through her fingers. 'I thought I might put it up but I'm useless at stuff like that.'

'Come on, sit down, I'll do it.'

Immy took off her coat, revealing a brightly coloured dress that had polar bears ice skating all over it. Ever since her brain injury Immy had decided that life was too short to live her life for other people. She didn't wear dark sensible clothes anymore, she wore every colour of the rainbow, she wore dresses with frogs or cows or narwhals playing on them. She dyed her hair a multitude of colours, she quit her job as an accountant and opened up a very successful sweet shop in the town. She'd taken up scuba diving, painting, pottery and learned how to play the saxophone. She was the very definition of reinventing yourself. Immy was a firework and Alex only hoped that one day she would find a man worthy of her. Immy had been at this dating malarkey for a while now but had yet to find anyone she wanted something serious with, which didn't give Alex any hope that she'd find her happy ever after either. Not that she was really looking for that.

Immy started work on Alex's hair, reminding Alex of how they'd spend hours playing with each other's hair when they were kids. Immy had always had a talent for creating beautiful braids or twists when the best that Alex could manage was a messy bun.

'What are you nervous about?' Immy said, expertly sweeping, twisting and scraping Alex's hair.

'I don't know, conversation running smoothly, awkward silences, making a good impression.'

'Of course there'll be awkward silences, you don't know each other, but just keep asking him questions. In my experience, men like nothing more than talking about themselves. And you don't need to worry about making a good impression. You are a wonderful, brilliant, kind, funny person and any man would be lucky to go on a date with you. If they can't see that, then there's something wrong with them.'

Alex smiled. 'OK, then what if the conversation flows really well, what if we just click and the chemistry is off the charts, what if we end up…' She paused in case little ears were listening. 'Doing the horizontal tango?'

Alex couldn't even begin to imagine going to bed with someone she'd just met. She wasn't judging anyone who did that, but for her, intimacy went hand in hand with an emotional connection. There was no way she could have that with a man she barely knew.

'What's the problem with that?' Immy said, her hands moving swiftly across Alex's head.

'It's been a really long time since I've done… the tango.'

'All the more reason for you to get back on the horse.'

'But what if I've forgotten which bits go where? What if I'm completely useless at it?'

'It's like riding a bike, you never forget.'

'Which is it, a horse or a bike?'

Immy laughed. 'Look, don't be scared off by it. You deserve to have some fun. Having a one-night stand is hugely liberating.'

'How many one-night stands have *you* had?'

'One and it was amazing.'

'Why don't I know about this?'

Alex knew about all of Immy's exes – they talked about everything.

'I was always dating men looking for Mr Right, someone I could one day fall in love with and marry, just as I imagine you will be looking for that when you date,' said Immy. 'I was never looking for something casual. I'm still not. But Quinn had taken you and Zara to London for the weekend so Zara could see the dinosaurs in the Natural History Museum and it just sort of happened. It was one of those incredible, unexpected, brilliant nights and I don't regret it for one second.'

'Wait, that was three weeks ago, the weekend when you were supposed to have a date with that loser Ethan. You said he never turned up?'

'No, he didn't.'

'So who was it?'

There was a pause before Immy spoke. 'Xander.'

Alex swivelled to look at her sister in shock. 'Xander Wild? As in Max's brother? Quinn's cousin?'

Immy turned her head around so she could continue working on the up-do. 'Yes, the very same.'

'But… you hate him.'

'Hate is probably too strong a word. I'm… frustrated by him.'

'So how did it happen?'

'He was there when Ethan stood me up and, instead of being a jerk about it, he was really nice and one thing led to another and he came back here. He was insatiable. We must have had sex six or seven times throughout the night. It was like he couldn't get enough of me. I have never felt so adored, so revered in my life before. It was utterly wonderful. And then I woke up the next morning and he was gone. I texted him to say thanks for the best night of my life and he never replied.'

'What a dick.'

'Ah, that's Xander all over. He only ever does one-night stands. He hasn't had a relationship with any woman since his wife died. And he has his daughter Etta to think about. I knew very well what I was getting myself into. But the point is, maybe it was so good because we both knew there were no strings attached, no commitments, no broken promises, just one night of fun and we both walk away unscathed. After what Liam did to you, I can understand you being scared of commitment or a long-term relationship again, but it doesn't have to be that. I think you'd enjoy the dates a lot more if there are no expectations of something more or something meaningful. Then there can be no disappointments.'

Maybe Immy had a point. It didn't need to be something serious. Alex still couldn't imagine sleeping with a stranger but she would love a kiss, a wonderful, passionate, stomach-clenching kiss, with someone who wasn't Liam.

Her thoughts turned to Quinn again and what it would be like to kiss him. She blushed as she tried to push those inappropriate thoughts away.

'OK, all done,' Immy said.

Alex stood up and looked in the mirror, admiring the plaited halo of hair around her head. It looked lovely.

Alex gave her sister a kiss on the cheek and then rested her head on her shoulder. 'You're a star, thank you.'

'You're very welcome. But you don't need pretty hair to impress the right man. Any man worth his salt will instantly be bowled over by how wonderful you are, regardless of what you're wearing or what your hair is doing.'

Alex smiled and moved back over to Zara's packed lunch, shoving in a couple of clementines and closing the lid. She went to the kitchen door and shouted up the stairs. 'Zara Seren Campbell, you better get your butt downstairs right now or I'll gouge your eyes out and feed them to the rats.'

Zara loved the threats, every morning there was a new one and the gorier they were the better. Alex heard her daughter laugh upstairs. Alex swore Zara had been waiting until the threat was dealt before coming downstairs.

A few seconds later Zara came running downstairs in her school uniform, which was already showing signs of being outgrown, her nose buried in a book as soon as her feet touched the bottom stair.

This book was about an evil uncle coming up with a several different ways to kill off his nieces and nephew in order to get the inheritance. Alex sometimes worried about some of the darker themes in the books Zara read but apparently lots of kids at school were reading the same ones so she tried to be cool about it. Alex tried to remember what kind of book she was reading at Zara's age. She'd liked the Famous Five, Secret Seven and, while Enid Blyton never bumped anyone off, there were some hairy scrapes the kids got themselves into so she supposed this wasn't really that different. At seven years old – or nearly eight, as Zara liked to tell anyone who asked – she had a reading age of someone a few years older. She was also wise beyond her years.

Sometimes Alex could have very mature conversations with her about very adult topics, like the environment or things that were happening in the news, and she was so knowledgeable about wildlife that she'd often taught Alex things she hadn't known. It was so easy to forget Zara was only seven but then she'd get excited about making cakes with sprinkles or Santa coming and Alex remembered that, behind all that maturity, she was still a little girl.

Zara sat down on the bottom step to pull her boots on, while still reading the book on her lap.

With her dark hair and sky-blue eyes, Zara was

looking more and more like her dad every day. Alex wondered whether Zara saw that when she looked in the mirror and whether it made her sad. She hadn't even turned four when Liam had died and Alex didn't think Zara had really understood to start with – she hadn't even cried. When she'd been told, she'd just nodded and went back outside to play in the garden. It had only been after a week or so that Zara started asking when Daddy was coming home and Alex had to explain that he never was. And that was when the tears started. Zara had adored her dad. But the grieving process didn't last long. Apparently in younger children, they just dealt with it and moved on.

Alex often wondered if she should do more to preserve Liam's memory, other than the photos that were displayed around the house. Maybe she should talk about him more, play the videos of them together more often. But the eighteen months prior to his death had been difficult to say the least and when she remembered him she remembered that, rather than the happier times. She never wanted to say anything negative about Liam to Zara so she avoided talking about him at all and she felt guilty about that. Although her guilt stretched far beyond that. The night he died, they'd had a massive row and he'd stormed out, drunk, and half hour later he'd crashed his car into a tree. She'd never told anyone apart from Immy about that because she knew they would point the finger of blame at her. And she knew that was part of the reason she never wanted to talk about him. What would she say if Zara asked how her dad had died? But thankfully, Zara didn't talk about him either so it hadn't come up.

Alex felt bad for Liam that his daughter never missed him. But then maybe Zara didn't need her dad because Quinn, Liam's older brother, was round the house every day. He was such a massive part of their lives.

Right on cue, there was a knock on the back door and, when she turned round, Quinn was letting himself in. Her heart leapt at the sight of him as it always did. He had Liam's looks in a way, dark hair, blue eyes. Although Quinn's eyes were more the colour of the sea than the sky, with hints of green and gold. Sharing the same facial features, they were undoubtedly brothers but Quinn definitely carried that hotter older brother look. The look he gave her made her stomach clench with desire. It was as if he wanted to do rude and wonderful things to her. Well, that was what she liked to tell herself he was thinking, which was a harmless little fantasy. He'd always looked at her with that intensity that made her feel weak, when clearly it meant nothing. He'd never showed any sign of having feelings for her while she was completely in love with him. In fact, she'd tried to kiss him once a few months after Liam died and he very kindly but firmly turned her down. Sadly, it didn't change how she felt. She knew it was completely inappropriate as he was Liam's brother but she couldn't help these feelings.

'Hey,' Quinn said, staring at her as if she was the only person in the world. If only that was true. 'You look… beautiful.'

'Oh. Thank you.'

'Hi,' Immy said, dragging Quinn's attention away from Alex. He gave Immy a wave. Immy's dog, Jacob, who was also in love with Quinn, scrabbled round him with excitement as if he hadn't seen him in months. Quinn bent down and scratched between his ears.

Alex pushed away romantic thoughts because she'd be mortified if he ever found out about her feelings for him. 'Morning, did you want a tea or coffee or juice?'

Alex knew he wouldn't say yes to a hot drink as he wouldn't have time to drink it if he was going to walk Zara to school. Although that technically wasn't what happened when he and Zara left the house together, he just 'happened' to be going the same way. Zara was desperate to walk to school on her own, just like her friends did, and so Alex had said yes and Quinn had conveniently turned up every morning on his way past their house heading towards the main town, explaining that the school was on his route. Zara hadn't cottoned on yet to what they were doing, she was just happy to spend some time with her favourite uncle.

'Yeah, apple juice if you've got it. I haven't got long. I have to go into town to collect some more metal.'

'I see I didn't get offered any juice,' Immy said.

'Because you live here, I'm pretty sure you're capable of getting your own juice,' Alex laughed, but she got out three glasses anyway and poured one for her sister and one for Zara.

'I bought you these,' Quinn said, offering out a small

box which she recognised immediately as being from Sweet Escapes, the bakery near Christmas Gardens.

Alex let out a soft gasp, knowing what they were before she'd even opened the box. She took it and reverentially opened the lid. The smell of the apple custard Danishes hit her and it was pure heaven.

'Oh god, thank you,' Alex said, picking one up and taking a bite. She closed her eyes in bliss. It was so sweet and delicious. She loved these so much. For some reason Sweet Escapes didn't make these every day, so when they did, Alex always grabbed herself a box, if they hadn't already sold out. Sometimes she missed out.

'Oh, you know the way to a woman's heart,' Immy said. 'You propose to her while she's eating one of those and I guarantee you she'd say yes.'

Quinn laughed. 'Surely it wouldn't be that simple.'

Alex nodded as she continued to eat.

'They really taste that good?' Quinn asked.

Alex's eyes widened in shock. 'You've never had one?'

'I'm more of a savoury person. Give me one of their sausage rolls or steak slices and I'd be asking you to marry me too.'

'Their steak slices are lovely but this is the best thing I've ever tasted.'

'That's high praise indeed.'

'Here, just take a bite.' Alex held one up for him.

He bent his head and took a bite, his eyes on hers as he did so, and she suddenly realised how intimate this was. She felt like she needed to take a step back out of his space but she couldn't. All she could think about was reaching up and kissing the crumbs off his lips.

'Mmm, this really is good,' Quinn said, reaching out to take another bite and his lips grazed her fingers.

Her breath caught in her throat. His tongue slid out to catch the crumbs and she watched it, completely entranced. He'd missed a crumb on the corner of his mouth and without thinking she leaned up to wipe it away. Her eyes widened in horror as she realised what she'd done.

'God, I'm so sorry, I don't know why I did that.'

'It's OK.' Quinn's eyes were still on hers in that way he had of looking deep inside her.

'She does that to me all the time,' Immy said. 'I think once you're a mum, you're a mum to everyone.'

Alex stepped away but Quinn was still watching her.

Zara walked into the kitchen, her nose still buried in her book, though she was now wrapped in her coat, body warmer, and scarf, her purple pompom hat sticking out from her pocket.

'Hey Rocket,' Quinn said, calling her the nickname he'd given her because she was always speeding around on her skates.

Zara's face lit up at seeing her uncle. She gave him a big hug, which he returned, then diverted her attention back to the book again.

'Zara, I have something for you,' Immy said.

Zara lowered her book momentarily and eyed the box with interest. 'What is it?'

'Come and see.'

The book was finally relinquished, Zara's curiosity getting the better of her, and she moved over to take a look.

'Whoa, you found one,' Zara said, her eyes lighting up. 'Where?'

'In Christmas Gardens.'

'By Santa's house?'

'It was right outside,' Immy said. 'And no, it hasn't been decorated yet.'

'Maybe they really are from Santa Claus,' Zara said, in wonder. 'It's beautiful.'

'Of course it had to be yours with the roller skates painted on it.'

Zara took the lid off and touched the painted skates lovingly. 'But you found it, you should keep it.'

'No, St Nick clearly says keep, re-hide or give to someone else. It's yours. Definitely.'

'Thank you so much.' Zara hugged her aunt.

Immy smiled. 'Now if you find one with my beloved Skye terrier on it, then you can repay the favour. I've never seen anything with a Skye terrier on so I will be over the moon to get a bauble if you ever find one.'

That gave Alex an idea. Maybe if, through her investigations for the local paper, she was able to unmask St Nick, she could offer to pay him to do a Skye terrier bauble for Immy as a thank you for everything she had done for her. She suddenly had a new incentive to find out who he was.

'I will, but no one could capture Jacob's cuteness.' Zara bent down to stroke Jacob's head.

'I don't know, this St Nick is a pretty talented man,' Alex said.

'Or woman,' Zara said. 'It could be St Nicola.'

'It could,' Alex agreed, although in her mind she was pretty convinced it was a man, only because she didn't think a woman would give herself a masculine pseudonym. But maybe she was wrong.

Quinn leaned over Alex's shoulder to look at the bauble, his hand holding her back so casually he probably wasn't even aware he was doing it, but every cell in her body responded to his touch.

'I bet it's a woman,' he said. 'It's too… whimsical to be a man. A man would just paint a pair of skates. A woman would add purple laces and stars and pretty holly leaves and berries. And a woman pays attention to little details, like knowing purple is your favourite colour. Men are rubbish at stuff like that.'

'You think St Nick painted this just for me?' Zara said, her eyes sparkling with excitement.

'There's only one roller skating queen in this town, St Nick must have known this would make its way to you.'

Zara's smile spread across her face.

Alex checked her watch. 'Well, I hate to break this up, but Zara, you have to get to school.'

She watched Quinn and Zara down their juice in one big gulp.

'I'll come with you, I have to pick up the metal before nine,' Quinn said, moving to the sink and quickly washing up his and Zara's glasses. 'Mr Bellamy gets very upset if we turn up after nine.'

'Seems like a funny way to run a shop,' Zara said.

Alex suppressed a smirk. Her daughter was so bloody smart.

'I agree,' Quinn said. 'But I'm too scared to tell Mr Bellamy that.'

Zara started walking towards the back door with Quinn.

'Hey, what about my kiss?' Alex said.

Quinn immediately turned round and placed a kiss on her cheek, which caused Zara to burst into giggles and Alex's heart to race.

She cleared her throat and when she spoke she tried desperately not to sound like that simple kiss had affected her. 'I meant from my daughter.'

'Oops,' Quinn laughed, winking at Zara.

Zara, still laughing, wrapped her arms around Alex and leaned up to give her a kiss. Except she didn't have to lean up as far as she used to, she was growing so tall, just like her dad.

Alex gave her a tight hug. Her little girl was growing up and in a few years she probably wouldn't let her mum do this so she had to make the most of it now.

'Mum, I'm going to be late,' Zara said, her voice muffled as her face was pressed against her dress.

Alex quickly let her go and with a wave Zara and Quinn left.

'I have to go too,' Immy said, pulling on her bright purple coat and wrapping her big red scarf round her neck twice. 'I have yoga tonight but I could pick up a takeaway for us on the way home?'

'Sounds perfect.'

With that Immy walked out the door, leaving Alex alone. She reached up to where she could still feel Quinn's lips on her cheek. She had liked that way too much and the worrying thing was she was pretty sure Quinn had seen her reaction to it too.

CHAPTER 2

❄

Alex walked towards the Wonky Tree Studios a short while later, as tiny flakes of snow swirled through the air. It definitely felt like it was cold enough to have a winter storm but right now the snow wasn't even settling. It would be nice if they had some proper snow for Christmas Day but that was a few days away yet. Knowing the British weather they'd be having some kind of heatwave by then.

The Wonky Tree Studios was a large house on top of the hill overlooking Lovegrove Bay, earning its name from the wonky tree that stood next to it, bent at such an angle it looked like it had been caught in a hurricane. The tree was currently covered in lights and various ornaments made by the artists who worked in the house.

The house was an art studio where ten artists, working in various different mediums, made and sold their goods. She and Quinn each had a studio on the second floor. The third floor held a café with the most amazing cakes and a gift shop that sold, among other typical gift shop wares, all the things anyone would need to try their hand at their own arts and crafts. On the top floor lived the owners, Luke and Flick.

Alex walked inside and immediately the warmth of the house swallowed her. Most of the artists were here already, getting ready for another busy day. She spotted Luke, one of the artists and the owner of the house, and his wife Flick talking very excitedly about something. She had become quite close with the two of them since she had started working at the Wonky Tree Studios, especially Flick who worked in the gift shop, upstairs. Alex and Quinn had joined them for dinner sometimes too and the four of them always got on really well. Alex waved hello and they gestured her over.

'We got one,' Flick said, her face alight with happiness.

Alex spotted the bauble in Luke's hand as she walked over. 'Oh wow, Immy found one this morning too.'

'What did she get?' Luke asked.

'A pair of roller skates. She gave it to Zara, she loves roller skating and practically lives in her skates.'

'It does seem that St Nick is creating these baubles for specific people, or at least in the hope that they find their way to specific people,' Flick said.

'What does yours have on it?' Alex asked.

Luke and Flick looked at each other and Flick shrugged. 'We might as well show her, it's only just over a week away.'

Luke nodded. 'We're not telling many people right now. Quinn knows and Flick's nan but we wanted to wait until three months, which would be on Christmas Eve. We also thought we'd wait until after Christmas so people didn't feel obligated to buy us baby-related Christmas presents.'

Alex stared at them. 'You're pregnant? Oh my god, congratulations, that's such wonderful news.'

She hugged them both.

'I'm so happy for you.'

'Thank you,' Flick said. 'We're obviously over the moon. But this is the bauble that was left for us.'

Luke showed Alex the bauble and she saw a pair of knitted yellow baby booties surrounded by holly leaves and berries had been painted on the side. It was beautiful.

'So we think we know who St Nick is,' Flick said excitedly.

'You do?'

'Flick thinks she does, I'm not so sure,' Luke said.

'Well, who do you think it is?' Alex said eagerly.

'I'm not sure it's a good idea to expose them,' Luke said. 'If Flick is right. Not when the mystery of his or her identity is what makes this so exciting for everyone. They've done an excellent job keeping it a secret and we don't want to ruin it for them.'

'I promise not to tell anyone,' Alex assured them.

'Not even the local paper?' Flick asked.

'No, I promise. I agree the mystery of who it is makes this whole thing so much more special. I actually want to ask whoever it is for a specific commission, well not for me but for Immy, so I definitely want to keep them on my side.'

Flick nodded. 'OK, I trust you. You've never been one to spread gossip.'

'Oh hell no, I hate gossip and I'd hate to be at the centre of it. If St Nick wants to keep his or her identity a secret, I'm guessing they probably don't want to be the centre of attention either.'

'OK, I think it's Quinn,' Flick said, quietly.

'Quinn?' Alex said, probably a bit too loudly.

'Sshhh!' Flick hissed, looking around, although no one was around this early.

'Sorry,' Alex whispered. 'What makes you think it's Quinn?'

'If St Nick specifically painted this for us then it has to be one of a handful of people we told that we were pregnant, and only Quinn lives in Lovegrove Bay.'

'It can't be Quinn,' said Alex. 'He's a metal artist, he's not a painter.'

'Can't he be both?' Flick said.

Alex weighed that up. Flick had a point, although she'd known him for four years and had never seen him paint anything.

'See, I don't think it was Quinn at all,' Luke said. 'It was Quinn who gave it to us, he said he found it outside so presumed it was for us. If he was St Nick, wouldn't delivering the bauble by hand be a bit obvious? It's more likely that St Nick heard that Rose has just had a new granddaughter or, knowing how many people come through here on a daily basis, maybe he left a generic baby-related bauble knowing that someone would have a new baby in the family somewhere and so it would find the right home anyway.'

'See, that does make sense,' Alex said. 'There are probably several generic baubles that weren't meant for a specific person at all but would fit several different people. Like painting a bauble with a chocolate bar on it – I bet there are hundreds of people in the town who love chocolate.'

'I suppose,' Flick said, obviously slightly deflated as Alex and Luke popped her bubble of excitement.

'Is there any other evidence that it's Quinn?' Alex said.

'Well, no, I suppose not.'

'OK, so let's put a pin in him for now. I'm not saying it's not him, but let's see what evidence we can gather, for and against,' Alex said.

'That's probably very wise,' Luke said, rubbing his wife's back, consolingly.

'And it is a beautiful bauble,' Alex said. 'You're very lucky.'

Flick's face lit up again. 'It is beautiful, isn't it. It will take pride of place on our tree.'

Alex smiled. 'I was talking about the baubles this morning with Immy. Whoever it is has so much talent. This kind of thing would sell very well here in the studio, especially if people could buy custom baubles for their loved ones.'

'We said the same,' Luke said. 'We'd love to get the

person on board here at the studios, even if they were only here as a pop-up from October onwards, although I think Christmas ornaments sell well all year round. But I'm not sure how we can find out who it is to offer them the opportunity and retain the mystery that's so important to them at the same time.'

'We could get an assistant to run the shop side for them so they were never visible to the public, but at least they would get some recognition and payment for their work,' Flick said. 'Or I could just sell the baubles in my gift shop.'

'That's a good idea,' Alex said. 'Although, if they are doing hiding them secretly rather than selling their baubles, they probably like the gifting side more than the money.'

Luke nodded. 'True, but I'd still at least like to offer them a place here, they can decide whether to take it.'

Alex nodded. 'Right, I better get to work.'

She waved goodbye and went upstairs to her studio, her mind whirling with all the possibilities of who it could be and whether it could be Quinn. A lot of people would know that Zara loved roller skating, but how many would know purple was her favourite colour? Not that many. Probably only Quinn, Immy, Quinn's mum Violet and a handful of Zara's friends. But still that was hardly conclusive evidence against Quinn. And when would Quinn have got the time to paint all these baubles? He was at the studio all day making his metal monsters and several of his evenings were taken up with social activities: rugby, his pub quiz night, even his kayaking club that met every week in the winter to practise in the local pool. On his free nights he was mostly round her house, watching movies and cosy crime TV shows with her and Zara or playing board games. The baubles would take a lot of time. And they were so different from his metal work, such delicate paintings seemed a million miles away from bending and shaping metal. It couldn't possibly be Quinn, could it?

But then if it wasn't him, who was it?

Alex wrote occasional feel-good pieces for the local paper, *The Lovegrove Lighthouse*, and she had been intending to write an article about St Nick and his generous gifts. She could use her role to try and find out who it was, not to out him or her to the town but purely for her own satisfaction of solving a mystery. She and Quinn often watched *Midsomer Murders* and other cosy mysteries together and they loved trying to work out who committed the crime; this would be no different. Plus she wanted to be able to offer them the opportunity of working here and maybe persuade them to do a bauble for Immy.

She pulled out her phone and logged into Facebook under *The Lovegrove Lighthouse* page where she posted nice, heartwarming stories from time to time. She quickly threw up a post.

Who is St Nick?
Since the beginning of December beautifully painted

baubles have been mysteriously found all over Lovegrove Bay, with instructions from the equally mysterious St Nick to either keep, re-hide or gift to someone else. So many of us have received these gorgeous baubles yet we have no way to thank the person who took so much time to paint them. Everyone wants to know who St Nick is.

*The Wonky Tree Studios would love to find out who it is as they would love to offer him, or her, studio space to paint and sell these exquisite baubles. Maybe we can work together as a community to find them. If you've found a bauble, where did you find it? Do you live near where baubles have been found, have you seen anyone suspicious hanging around late at night? Do you have CCTV or Ring cam footage of any mysterious people who might be St Nick? If you have any information, no matter how small, that might lead to us finding out who it is, then please message **The Lovegrove Lighthouse**.*

While we have no intention of revealing publicly who St Nick is, unless they wish it, hopefully we can persuade them to sell their art in the Wonky Tree Studios next year and then anyone who has not been lucky enough to get a bauble this year might be able to buy a custom-made one, if St Nick is willing to take commissions.

*And if you are St Nick and would like to get in touch, anonymously, please do message **The Lovegrove Lighthouse**. We'd love to hear from you.*

There, that should work. Alex didn't want St Nick to feel like it was a witch hunt, not after their incredible generosity. And no matter what happened, if she found out who it was, she would respect their need for privacy and not reveal their identity to anyone, but she really hoped she could find out who it was, especially because talent that special should be celebrated. Getting St Nick to work in the studio, even if their identity remained unknown, would be a big boon for the Wonky Tree Studios and she wanted to be able to do that for Flick and Luke after all their help over the last year or so.

She switched on the lights in her studio and looked around. Her little hobby of making paper sculptures out of pages of a book was something she loved doing. She never, in her wildest dreams, ever thought she'd be doing this kind of thing full time and have her own studio selling her sculptures. And that was all thanks to Luke and Flick.

She had around fifty smallish sculptures on shelves around the room but she knew that half of those would be sold by the end of the week so she was constantly having to replenish the shelves. At this time of year most of her sculptures were Christmas or winter themed and a lot of them were built inside clear plastic baubles. There were also several that depicted scenes from favourite movies that were always very popular. She turned on the fairy lights that adorned the shelves, and the lights on the little Christmas tree in the corner, decorated with paper sculpture baubles.

Alex sat down and started work on a sculpture that depicted a scene from *The Polar Express*.

She had been working at the Wonky Tree Studios for

around eighteen months now and she loved it. Her sculptures sold well and, while she was never going to be going on any world cruises anytime soon and had to supplement her income by doing illustrations for children's books and the occasional article for the local paper, she wouldn't want to do anything else. She adored the creative side but more importantly she wanted to do this for Zara because she wanted to show her that she could follow her dreams, have a job she loved, be who she wanted to be. Alex wanted Zara to see her mother going to work and doing something she loved.

And working at the Wonky Tree Studios had the added bonus of working alongside Quinn every day. She had been in love with him pretty much since she first met him. She felt guilty even acknowledging that since she had been married to his brother and even more guilty because the first time they met was at Liam's funeral.

When she initially met Liam they had hit it off instantly, within six weeks they were living together and after four months, he asked her to marry him. And that was when she realised he was estranged from his family. Whenever she'd brought up his family before, he just muttered something like they didn't get on and changed the subject. She hadn't realised they didn't get on to such an extent that they wouldn't even come to their son's wedding.

Alex had been in two minds whether to even let them know he had died because they cared so little for him, but she had and invited them to the funeral and that was when she found out that he'd never told them about her or Zara. They had a three-year-old grand-daughter they didn't even know existed. They'd arrived at the funeral and Alex had been fully expecting to hate them, but Violet and Henry, his parents, had been utterly lovely and when Quinn came over to introduce himself and offer his condolences he had given her the biggest hug that made her heart ache. It had been a long time since anyone held her like that. With the guilt asso-ciated with Liam's death and all the stress of the previous year she'd ended up crying against his chest. He'd shuffled her into a secluded corner of the hotel where they were holding the wake and simply held her tight until the tears had passed. It was so sweet and kind that she might have handed over a tiny piece of her heart there and then. He had been there for her that day and he had showed up almost every single day since then and every time he did she fell for him a little bit more.

She'd become incredibly close to Violet over the last few years, and after Henry died, that bond had grown stronger as Alex invited her round to dinner fairly regu-larly so Violet wasn't alone. Now she felt as close to her as she had to her own mum.

She still felt sad for Liam that he'd never see his daughter grow up, she felt sad for his family, his cousins who all missed him terribly, and his mum especially who talked about him all the time. She felt sad for Zara who wouldn't get to see her dad again. But now, four years later, she felt cautiously optimistic about her future and couldn't help feeling horribly guilty about that too. With Liam gone maybe it was time she started looking for that someone who could fill the hole in her heart, the one he'd ripped open eighteen months before he died. Although nervous about her upcoming dates, she couldn't help feeling a little bit excited about what might happen. Somewhere out there might be the man of her dreams.

Her thoughts immediately turned to Quinn.

It was too simplistic to think that Quinn would step up and declare his love for her when he'd never showed any signs of having feelings for her in the past. He was in their lives because Zara was his niece and he loved her and because he and Alex had become really good friends but it was never going to be anything more than that.

Just as she was cutting out a snowflake shape for her sculpture she noticed movement by the door and looked up to see Quinn leaning against it, watching her.

'Hey, did Zara get to school OK?'

Quinn nodded. 'I walked her right up to the gate. But you know she's going to get wise to this soon.'

'I know, I'm just banking on the part of her that loves spending time with you outweighing her cleverness, at least until she's eighteen.'

Quinn laughed. 'I don't think there's much chance of that but I will show up every day to take her to school until she figures it out.'

'Thank you.'

'I'll always be here for you. For her,' Quinn quickly amended.

'Being there for her *is* being there for me.'

'I'm here for you too.'

'You always have been.'

'No, I mean, whatever you need, whatever you want, I'm your man.'

'Anything?'

'Of course.'

Alex considered telling him she wanted one night of hot passion. It had been so long since she'd been with a man, she'd almost forgotten which bits went where. She felt herself go hot just at the thought of him kissing and touching her in that way.

He moved closer and she could smell his citrus scent. 'What are you thinking?' he asked, softly.

She would die if he knew what exactly she had just been thinking about. 'Oh, nothing.'

'You can tell me.'

She frantically wracked her brain for something. 'Oh, it's just the toilet doesn't flush properly, the shelf in the bathroom keeps falling down and the kitchen sink keeps clogging up.'

He stared at her and then a smile spread across his face. 'Consider it done.'

'No, I don't need you to take care of that for me, I can get someone in.'

'It's no bother.'

She sighed. 'I lead a glamorous life.'

'It's hard doing everything on your own. And you don't have to.'

'I'm not alone, I have Immy.'

She would forever be grateful to Immy for moving in with her and Zara after Liam died. She'd always been close to her sister and when Immy had brain trauma after falling off a horse, Alex had looked after her. Alex knew moving in with her was Immy's way of repaying the favour. A few days after the funeral Immy had turned up on her doorstep asking to move in, claiming that her landlord had doubled her rent and they'd cut her hours at work. But Alex had known Immy was doing it for her. It was a good job too – she would never have been able to afford to stay in her house by herself.

'You and Zara could have moved in with me,' said Quinn. 'I'd have looked after you.'

Alex shook her head. 'I love having you in my life, Zara adores you and I appreciate everything you do for us so much, but I would never want you to feel obligated to us, to help us or keep coming round. I wouldn't want to be a burden to you.'

'You could never be a burden to me.'

'It's very kind but I come as a package, and Zara comes with a lot of books, toys and games. She loves arts and crafts, everything she makes or paints has copious amounts of glitter on it. Believe me, that stuff gets everywhere.'

Quinn grinned. 'I'm already finding glitter for most of the year after Santa leaves. She'd be right at home.'

'And how would it look when you bring home a

woman, and she finds you've already got another woman and child in situ?'

'I don't have too many women at my house and if I did I'd just explain I have a lodger.'

The thought of sitting in his lounge while he brought another woman home and took her upstairs to his bedroom made Alex's stomach turn. Of course she knew he had girlfriends, there was a period of time when he seemed to have a different one each week. But it was one thing knowing he was sleeping with other women – being there while it was happening would be another kind of torture.

'And what happens when I bring men back to yours, you'd be happy with that?'

His face darkened. 'What?'

'I've decided to start online dating. It's time I got back on the horse.'

'You… you're dating?' Quinn said, his voice rough.

'Yes. Well, I just filled in the online application over the weekend. I have coffee with a man at lunchtime. Immy thinks I need a one-night stand, apparently they are very liberating.'

'I don't think that's a good idea,' he said through gritted teeth.

She felt her eyebrows shoot up in surprise. 'What? Why?'

Quinn ran his hand through his dark hair. 'Because…'

He clearly didn't have a reason other than his loyalty to Liam.

'It's been four years,' Alex said gently. And it would have been much sooner than that but she had held off out of respect for Liam's mum, who would probably never get over the loss of her son and understandably so. But her marriage had been over long before he'd died, she certainly didn't have any loyalty to Liam. But Quinn and his family didn't know any of that. It was hard enough telling them their son and brother had died, she didn't want to tell them he'd been a complete and utter arsehole for the last eighteen months of their marriage. They'd never spoken about the reason why Liam was estranged from his family either. What was the point of dragging up past hurts?

'I'm well aware how long it's been since my brother died,' Quinn said.

She stared at him in surprise. Was he angry? She'd never seen that side of him before so she didn't know what it looked like.

He shook his head. 'Sorry. I'm just... What about Zara? I don't think it's good for her to see a parade of men coming through the house.'

Alex folded her arms across her chest. 'A parade of men? That makes it sound like I'd be sleeping with a different man every night. Is that what you think of me? Besides, sleeping with a different partner every night sounds much more like you than me.'

'What does that mean?'

'I remember working at The Frog and Lettuce, you had a different woman with you every time you came in there.'

'That was… a long time ago. And has nothing what-soever to do with this.'

'*This* is coffee with one man.'

'You just said you're looking for a one-night stand.' Quinn was scowling. 'What if it progresses into something more? Will you be bringing him back to your house, sleeping with him in the room next to Zara's?'

'What I do in the privacy of my own house is nothing to do with you.'

'I love her and I worry about her.'

'I do too and I would never do anything to upset her or cause her harm.'

'I don't know if she is ready to have a new dad in her life.'

'Who said anything about that? You're being ridiculous. What's the real reason behind all this? Do you honestly expect me to dress in black and live in mourning for the rest of my life?'

'No, of course not. I just hoped you would talk to me about this first.'

'Why?'

'Because… I want you—'

Just then a customer walked in and started looking around at Alex's sculptures.

Alex gave the woman a winning smile before turning her attention back to Quinn. She lowered her voice. 'You want me to do what?'

He shook his head. 'We'll talk about this later.'

'There's nothing to talk about, I'm going for that coffee.'

Quinn let out a grunt of frustration and stormed out of her studio.

She stared after him in shock. That was the first time she'd argued with Quinn about anything. He was always so laid-back and easy to talk to. She'd kind of hoped he would be happy for her, cheer her on, give her some advice. It had been a long time since she'd gone on a date.

Should she have given him some prior warning? But surely he must have expected her to start dating at some point? She sighed and shook her head. If she hadn't been feeling guilty before, she certainly was now.

CHAPTER 3

Quinn was making one of his cutlery monsters. Every one was completely different, made from knives, forks or spoons, or other kitchen utensils, all with different facial expressions, they were very popular. This one looked particularly angry though, reflecting his mood perfectly.

He sighed. He wasn't really angry at Alex. Of course she'd want to date and move on with her life, she wasn't going to be mourning his brother forever and he didn't want her to. But he'd really thought she would talk to him about it first. They talked about everything.

He'd wondered for a long time when she would be ready to date again. She'd been so upset after Liam's death and understandably so: she'd lost her husband, the father of her child. So when she'd tried to kiss him about two months after the funeral, he'd stopped her because she was emotional and vulnerable and he would never want to take advantage of that. But he'd be lying if he said he wasn't tempted. He had fallen for her so fast and so hard and he hated himself a little because of that. She was his brother's wife and although he hadn't spoken to Liam for over five years prior to his death, he still owed him some loyalty.

But as time had gone on and his feelings had grown stronger and he and Alex had got closer, that loyalty hadn't seemed that important anymore, though it was still part of the reason he held himself back. He'd tried to gauge when would be a good time to tell her he had feelings for her and that he wanted to be the one to take her out on a date. He'd decided to do it at Christmas and had been planning what to say ever since making that decision.

But it wasn't straightforward. Would she feel that dating him was too close to home or disloyal to Liam? And what if she didn't want to date him, would that make things awkward when he came round to see her and Zara? And how would it feel to come round to see Zara, and Alex was with another man?

And that was the crux of it. Quinn wasn't angry with her for wanting to date, he was annoyed with himself because he felt like he'd missed his chance. He'd waited too long to make his move and, while coffee today was unlikely to end up being the big love story, if she and this man hit it off he'd always be kicking himself for not telling her how he felt.

He couldn't exactly march back in there and declare his feelings because now it would look like he was saying it just to stop her from dating.

But regardless of what happened he needed to apologise. He had no right to react like that. He needed to react like a friend. Venturing into the dating pool after so long was likely to be a daunting experience and he needed to be there for her.

He'd let her calm down first while he worked out what he was going to say.

His mum suddenly appeared at the doorway, all big smiles and happiness. Quinn adored his mum, she had always been his and Liam's biggest cheerleaders growing up so it had broken her heart when Liam became estranged from them, even if there was a part of her that had known it was for the best.

When his brother and then his father died, Quinn and his mother had become closer than ever. He was all she had left, which was why she had opened her arms and her heart so widely to incorporate Alex, Zara and even Immy into her life. At four foot seven, his mother was exactly two feet smaller than him but although she was tiny she had the biggest heart and looked like a storybook grandma with her gold-rimmed glasses and curly white hair. She was at her happiest knitting jumpers for her family or making cakes for them. But she was a formidable force when she needed to be. If someone crossed her, then they definitely knew about it.

'Hello, my dear,' his mum said, coming over to give him a big hug despite it only having been a few days since the last time he'd seen her. He hugged her back equally as hard.

She pulled back and he placed his hands on her shoulders. 'How are you doing?'

He knew this time of year was hard for her celebrating another Christmas without her husband. She always loved Christmas and having lots of people round to celebrate but he felt like the last few years she'd been putting on a brave face or hiding behind all preparations for Christmas Day so she wouldn't have to think about Henry. Whenever it got to this time of year, he thought her happiness was a little bit forced but this year she was glowing.

'I'm doing good, really good,' Violet smiled. No, not smiling, she was beaming.

'You look really happy, is there something in particular that has put a smile on your face?'

'No, no, everything is fine,' Violet said, her voice high with… nerves? Anxiety? There was something going on. 'Does a woman need a reason to be happy?'

'Well, no, I guess not but—'

'I've brought you your Christmas jumper,' Violet said, deftly changing the subject as she rooted around in her bag.

She pulled out her knitting masterpiece triumphantly and held it out so he could see the design. Quinn was by now an expert at showing his enthusiasm for her jumpers, but this one was going to take all of his acting skills as he had no idea what it was supposed to be. Some kind of animal maybe. Were those antlers on its head? But if it was a reindeer, this one had six legs.

Maybe it was a stag beetle, those pincers could be mistaken for antlers, at a push…

'I love it,' he said, hoping he hadn't taken too long to try and decipher what it was. 'Definitely my favourite so far.'

'Come on then, put it on.'

He pulled it over his head and looked down to see that one side was definitely longer than the other. He quickly put his hand in his jeans pocket to hide that from her, bunching up the jumper as he did so.

'It fits perfectly.' If perfectly was having enough room for Alex to share the jumper with him. Although that thought was pretty perfect.

'It looks great on you, right, must go and give Alex hers.'

She turned and started to hurry out.

'Mum.'

She turned back.

'Are you sure everything is OK?'

She smiled brightly. 'Everything is tickety-boo.'

She hurried out of his studio and he frowned. Something was definitely up, not least because he'd never heard her use the phrase tickety-boo before.

❄

Alex was trying to concentrate on making a paper sculpture of a child building a snowman when she saw movement at the door. She looked up to see Violet walking in. She would often pop in and see Alex at work and of course she was round the house a lot visiting Zara. Alex loved her. It was funny to find out she and Henry had been living in the next town for the first half of Zara's life. Alex might have walked the streets with Zara and walked straight past them without even knowing.

'Hello, my dear.' Violet came over and gave her a kiss on the cheek. She always wore the most amazing, brightly coloured dresses and clothes. She walked with a cane and had a prominent limp on her left side, but even the cane was a different colour every day. This morning's one was red and white stripes like a candy cane. 'I've finished knitting the Christmas jumpers for you.' She fished in her bag and pulled out a purple one which had to be Zara's. It had a kangaroo on it, Zara's favourite animal, wearing a Santa hat. At least Alex thought it might be a kangaroo. Violet's knitting was particularly bad and her animals were wonky, inaccurate and looked like they had been knitted by someone who had never seen a picture of the subject before. This kangaroo might even be a crocodile or maybe a camel.

'Zara will love that, thank you so much,' Alex said. And that was the truth: Zara would get a big kick out of this and would happily wear it, if only for comedy value.

Violet smiled as she dug out the next one, a bright blue one with what appeared to be a dog on it. Alex guessed it was a poor attempt at a Skye terrier, also wearing a Santa hat, but honestly it could have been a gorilla or maybe a platypus.

'This is for Immy.'

'It's gorgeous,' Alex said, suppressing a smile.

Violet dug in her bag for the last one and Alex held her breath with nerves and a little dash of excitement about what would be on hers. It was always a treat to see what kind of jumper she would get from Violet for Christmas. Violet pulled out one that was a bright Barbie pink and on the front was... well, to be honest Alex wasn't sure what it was. There were droplets of water coming out the top of the thing and it kind of looked like it might be an aubergine emoji, which most people knew represented a penis in text messages. She half squinted her eyes as she tried to work it out. She was pretty sure Violet hadn't knitted her an aubergine emoji Christmas jumper, even if she didn't know the alternative meaning behind it.

'Do you like it?' Violet said eagerly.

'I love it,' Alex said. 'It's wonderful.'

'I thought I'd do you a whale as Quinn said you loved that whale and dolphin watching trip he took you and Zara on in the summer.'

It was a whale! Now Violet had identified it, it was obvious. OK, it wasn't obvious at all but there were some similarities.

'Thank you, that's really sweet.'

'Well, let's see if it fits.'

Alex pulled it on and tried to suppress her laughter as she looked down at her aubergine or whale themed jumper. 'This is... amazing.'

'I'm so pleased you like it. Anyway, I must dash. I promised my neighbour I'd help her feed her tortoise this afternoon, the little bugger is quite vicious and we have to wear welding gloves to feed him.'

'Violet, before you go, I wanted to talk to you about something,' Alex said. She hadn't been sure whether to mention the dating to Violet or not, especially as the chances of finding the man of her dreams from an online dating site were slim to none so it would probably never amount to anything. But she didn't want Violet to find out accidentally. Judging from Quinn's reaction to it, it was certainly something she should have mentioned to him, not just launched it at him as a fait accompli, so she wanted to do that for Violet.

'What's that?'

'I have… signed up to an online dating app. I'm meeting a man at lunch for coffee.'

Violet's face fell and she looked utterly heartbroken. 'Oh.'

Alex bit her lip. 'I'm sorry.'

Violet forced a smile on her face. 'You don't have anything to apologise for. I knew at some point you would start looking around for a new man. You're funny, sweet, beautiful. Does Quinn know?'

'Yes, he wasn't happy about it either.'

'No, I don't suppose he was, silly boy.'

Alex frowned in confusion.

Violet put a hand on her shoulder, clearly putting on a brave face. 'You should have some fun. Just make sure you pick someone nice for Zara.'

'She will always be my priority,' Alex said. 'And I'm

not looking for someone to be Zara's new dad, Liam will always be that.'

Violet nodded and when she spoke her voice wobbled. 'I should go. I hope you have fun today.'

With that Violet hurried from the studio leaving Alex feeling like the most awful person in the world.

❄

Quinn walked into Alex's studio a while later with his big apology planned in his head. She was wearing one of his mum's Christmas jumpers. He was just trying to work out what was on her jumper when he saw she was crying as she tried to build one of her paper sculptures. His heart dropped into his stomach.

She spotted him and put her hands up. 'If you've come to shout at me again then can it wait? I'm really not in the mood.'

He moved over to her and immediately enveloped her in a big hug. She wrapped her arms around him and cried against his chest.

He was suddenly aware of a customer walking past Alex's studio door looking in at what was going on so Quinn quickly shuffled her backwards into her store-room and shut the door behind them.

Alex looked up at him in confusion. 'What are you doing?'

'I don't want anyone to see you like this.'

She nodded and put her head back against his chest again and he held her tight, stroking her hair.

'I'm a horrible person,' Alex said.

'No you're not, not at all, you're one of the kindest, loveliest people I know. And I had no right to say those things to you before. You're a brilliant mum to Zara and I know she will always be at the forefront of anything you do. I was completely out of order and I wasn't angry at you, I was annoyed with myself.'

'What does that mean?' She looked up at him.

'It… doesn't matter. But I'm sorry if I hurt you.'

She leaned her head against his chest. 'You didn't hurt me, I was pissed at you but you didn't hurt me.' She sighed. 'Your mum came round. I told her about the date.'

He winced. 'What did she say?'

'She was utterly lovely about it, unlike some people,' she looked up briefly to give him a mock scowl. 'But I could tell I broke her heart.'

He stroked her back. 'We spoke about it once, about how she would feel if you started dating again. I think she's scared of losing you and Zara.'

'That will never happen. Zara loves her and I do too. She will always be a part of our lives.'

'I think she knows that really but I guess it hurts to see you move on when she will never be able to get over Liam's death.'

Fresh tears filled Alex's eyes. 'I think that's why I feel so horrible and guilty about this. I feel like I'm benefitting from Liam's death. I get to finally move on, fall in love again, maybe get married again one day, and I wouldn't be able do any of that if Liam was still alive.'

He frowned in confusion. 'I don't understand.'

'I know.' She sighed. 'Our marriage was over probably eighteen months before he died.'

'What? I thought you were happy together.'

'We were. Very happy. But then his best friend died.'

'Tom?'

'Yes. He had a heart attack while out jogging.'

'Shit. I didn't know. Christ, I wondered why he wasn't at Liam's funeral. Those two were always as thick as thieves. I'm guessing Liam didn't take it well.'

She looked at him in confusion. 'You know, don't you?'

'That he was an alcoholic, yes.'

She stared at him with wide eyes. 'I… I didn't. He never drank, not even on our wedding day, but he never said he had a problem with it, just that he didn't like the taste or the hangovers.'

Quinn shook his head. 'We were never a big family of drinkers, the occasional glass at celebrations, but Liam went off to university and, just like all his friends there, he was drinking every single night. I didn't think much of it, he was a student, that's what students do. But when he left university and was still getting stupid, blind drunk every night, I started realising he had a problem. He went to work with raging hangovers, or called in sick if he couldn't get out of bed. He lost more jobs than I can count. He started drinking in the mornings to help combat the hangovers and it was just a very fast slippery slope into full-blown alcoholism. He was an ugly drunk as well, always getting angry and rude. He got into so many drunken fights, he was always sporting a black eye or a bruised lip. We tried getting him into rehab or to attend Alcoholics Anonymous, but he refused to go, saying he didn't have a problem. He didn't want help. He got so good at hiding it too, he wasn't staggering around obviously drunk. Sometimes you could have normal coherent conversations with him and we thought maybe he wasn't drinking all the time, but we could smell it on him all the time.'

He sighed, pushing his hand through his hair. 'But the straw that broke the camel's back was when he picked Mum up one day. I can't remember where they were going, but she asked him if he had been drinking and he flat-out denied it. She got in the car and a few minutes down the road he crashed it. Mum's leg was completely crushed – pretty much every bone in her leg was shattered, which is why she walks with a cane now. He was five times over the legal limit.'

'Oh my god,' Alex gasped.

'Well that was it. We all had a massive row with him, told him he needed to sort out his life and he wasn't welcome back in our lives until he'd given up the drink for good. He stormed out and we never saw or heard from him again. There was a part of me that thought we could have done more to help him, but he had to want our help and he never did.'

'I presume the accident was the thing that shocked him into changing,' she said. 'When we met he was sober, never touched a drop, he was lovely and we got on so well. He was a good dad to Zara too.'

'I bet you helped him more than you know. The first few years of becoming sober are always the hardest, but in you and then Zara he found a reason to keep fighting that temptation.'

She nodded. 'But when Tom died it was like a switch went off in his head. It was like you said, he was drunk every day, he lost his job and we needed that money. He had his gardening job but it wasn't enough. But he was horrible and nasty all the time, always belittling me, always criticising everything I wore or what I did. Surprisingly, the only time he was nice was when he was with Zara – there was something about her that reached the old Liam that we loved. One time, he snapped at her and made her cry and I told him if he ever did that again I would take her and leave him. He apologised and said she was his world and he'd never do it again and he never did, well not to her. But he was always nasty to me. Every single day. Like you, I tried to get him some counselling, tried to get some help, but he wouldn't have it. I'd never let him have sex with me when he was drunk and so he went out and slept with another woman and then came home and gloated about it. I knew then and there that our marriage was over. I packed a case and told him I was leaving and he sobbed like a baby, promised me he'd never do it again, which as far as I know he didn't. And there was a part of me that knew I couldn't leave him. He was depressed, grieving, sick – he needed my help, not me walking out and leaving him.'

'Then you're a braver and more compassionate person than I am.'

'I just kept hoping that one day he would wake up and choose us rather than the whisky or the beer. I hoped that the Liam I married was still in there somewhere. I didn't think we could ever go back to how we were, there was too much damage to our relationship for that, but I stayed because I wanted to help him.'

She sighed and Quinn stroked her hair. Knowing she still had more to say, he kept quiet, giving her the space to talk, but inside he was furious. How could his brother have treated Alex like that? The mother of his child, the woman he supposedly loved with all his heart. Despite his betrayal and nastiness, she had stayed to help him and Liam had still treated her like shit.

'I wanted out so badly,' Alex went on. 'But I was always worried what he would do. Not to me, but to himself. He was so sad and so angry and nothing I did or said would change that. After he cheated on me, just to hurt me and gloat about it, I just couldn't love him anymore. I cared what happened to him but I couldn't foresee a time when we would ever be happy together again. I started to resent the life I had with him but I couldn't see how I could ever move on. I missed having a loving partner, I missed that companionship, I missed kissing and cuddling with someone, and I did wonder if I'd ever have that again. And now he's dead and I have the freedom I so desperately wanted. I can move on with someone else and I feel so guilty that his death means I can finally have that.'

Quinn pushed the hair from her face. 'You're a good person. You deserve to find love and I think Liam would have wanted that for you.'

'Really?' she sniffed.

'Yes, he loved you, he would have wanted you to be happy.'

Alex stared at him and then let out a heavy, shaky breath. 'I think you're right.'

He stroked her back. Although she was no longer crying, she was still holding him and he had no intention of letting her go either.

'So you can finally let go of this guilt,' he said. 'Liam, the old Liam that was sober, would never have wanted you to live your life in guilt and regret. He would have hated that he made your life so miserable, he'd want you to be happy.'

She nodded. 'We talked about it once, before his life fell apart. You know, one of those silly conversations you have, what would you do if I die. He said he wanted me to find someone else if he died,' she smiled. 'As long as they weren't hotter than him.'

Quinn laughed. 'That's typical Liam.'

'I teased him and said, do you have any hot brothers. He said you were way hotter than him, hence why he never introduced us. Then he said if we ever met, we'd hit it off like a house on fire and we do. Then he grew serious and said if he could choose anyone for me to marry and be a dad to Zara after he died it would be you.'

Quinn felt the breath knocked out of him. Liam had

all but given his approval for him to ask Alex out. So maybe it was time he let go of the guilt of betraying his brother too.

'And it's true, you have been wonderful for Zara, she adores you,' Alex went on. 'I'm so glad we met.'

'I am too.'

'But while Zara is obviously a priority, I'm not just looking for someone who fits with her, I want someone for me too.'

Was she discreetly trying to tell him that she wasn't interested in him?

'What is it you're looking for?'

'And there's the big question. Love of course, the can't-sleep-can't-breathe kind of love, with someone who feels that way about me too. Someone who is kind but makes me laugh.' Alex bit her lip. 'Sexual chemistry is important.'

He felt his eyebrows shoot up.

'I know, I know. It shouldn't be a factor. There are more important things than that. But I want someone to make me feel alive. It has been so long since I've been kissed, the kind of kiss that makes you see stars, that gives you butterflies, that leaves you breathless. And while I'm doing this online dating to ultimately find love, get married again, have the happy ever after, there's a part of me that just wants one heart-stopping kiss.'

'You… want to be kissed?'

Alex nodded. Her eyes cast down to his lips and his heart leapt. She wanted him to kiss her. It would be so easy to bend his head and kiss her right now, something he'd wanted to do for years. Every single part of him wanted that but he couldn't do it. Not here. She was upset and emotional and he didn't want to take advantage of that.

And did she just mean a kiss or did she mean something more?

His stomach rolled at the thought of her sleeping with some man, desperate to have that connection with someone, and him not treating her with the care and respect she deserved. Quinn could give her that but it obviously wasn't completely selfless. But could he really have no-strings-attached sex with the woman he was in love with? And what happened if he helped her back onto the horse for her to ride into the sunset with someone else?

Suddenly there was a knock on the door and they leapt apart as if they'd been doing something wrong.

'Is anyone going to serve out here?' called a voice Quinn recognised instantly as belonging to Elizabeth, Lovegrove Bay's biggest gossip. She was certainly going to get a big kick out of seeing them in here together.

Alex stepped up to him and gave him a kiss on the cheek. 'Thank you.'

'For what?'

'Being lovely as always.'

'I'll always be here for you, for whatever you need.' Quinn dipped his head and looked at her meaningfully.

Her eyes widened. 'I, umm… should go.'

He nodded. 'Are you OK for me to tell my mum about Liam?'

'Yes of course, if you think it's appropriate. I wouldn't want to upset her with this. I wanted to tell you this before but I didn't see the point in upsetting you all further.'

'I feel like she should know.'

She nodded. 'OK.'

'Excuse me!' Elizabeth shouted outside.

Alex slapped on a big smile and stepped out of the storeroom. He followed her out and watched Elizabeth's eyes light up.

'Thanks for helping me with that shelf, Quinn, it's been wobbly for ages.'

'My pleasure.'

'I'm sure it was,' Elizabeth muttered. 'Wobbly shelf, my arse.'

Quinn smirked and left them to it. He had thoughts of his own he needed to process.

CHAPTER 4

❄

Alex was on her way towards Sweet Escapes where she was going to have her date. Tiny flakes of snow were dancing through the air and fairy lights twinkled in the windows of houses and shops. Everything just looked so much happier and magical at this time of year.

She was glad she'd finally been able to talk to Quinn about what had happened between her and Liam in the months before his death. She should have told him and Violet before but she hadn't wanted to hurt them with tales of Liam's bad behaviour. But at least Quinn now knew that her dating was more than just moving on, it was a need to heal after all that hurt.

She couldn't tell him about the night Liam died though, that was something else altogether. It didn't matter that Quinn and Liam had been estranged at the time, she knew he still loved and missed him. Quinn was her best friend and she couldn't bear the thought of losing him or Violet. If they knew what had happened the night he died, they wouldn't want anything to do with her.

But what if something happened between her and Quinn, as unlikely as that seemed? If they were together she would have to tell him the truth then.

There had been a moment when they'd been standing in the cupboard and she'd felt sure he wanted to kiss her. God, she wanted that so much. If Elizabeth hadn't turned up when she had, would they actually have kissed in her cupboard or was she seeing what she wanted to see?

Suddenly, someone called out to her from across the street. She looked over to see Violet hurrying towards her, her cane clicking across the cobbles as she crossed the road.

'Oh Alex dear, I'm glad I caught you.' Violet joined her, slightly out of breath. 'I wanted to say how sorry I am for making you feel bad earlier when you told me you were dating. I had no right to do that.'

'Liam was your son. Of course I understand that you'd be upset that I'm moving on. I expect it seems disloyal to him.'

Violet frowned and shook her head. 'My feelings about you dating have nothing to do with Liam. It's just that… I love you and Zara so much, I don't want to lose you.'

'And we love you too, nothing is going to happen to take me away from you.'

'You don't know that. If you get married again, how will your new husband react to you hanging around with your dead husband's mum and his brother? Quinn especially would lose out, you two are so close and I can't see any man putting up with that.'

Alex hadn't even thought of that. 'Well, he would have to put up with it. Quinn is Zara's uncle, you're her nan. No matter what happens you will always be a part of our lives.'

'I hope so. But I want you to be happy again. After everything Liam put you through, you deserve to find love and happiness again.'

'Quinn told you.'

'Yes, and I can't help feeling responsible. If we had got him the help he needed instead of cutting him off then it would never have happened.'

'He had to want to change though and he didn't. I tried to get him help too and he didn't want to know. There is only so much we can do.'

Violet nodded. 'That's true.'

'Also, Quinn told me what happened to make you cut him off,' Alex added. 'There was a limit to what you could withstand.'

'Yeah, there was,' Violet said.

'I get it, I really do.'

'But that's why I think it's so important you start dating again, regardless of my concerns. You stood by him for eighteen months when every day was a living hell, you didn't leave.'

Alex played with the frayed edge of her sleeve, knowing that wasn't exactly true.

'You deserve to be loved again,' Violet went on. 'I

want someone for you who will love you and adore you and treat you with respect and kindness always.'

'That sounds perfect, although I'm not sure I'm ready for something serious again,' said Alex. 'Not yet.' Although she had told Quinn she was looking for that big love story, in reality that felt like a step too far right now.

'I totally understand that, it's hard moving on after a serious relationship. I was married to Henry for fifty-six years, I never thought I'd move on with someone else. But now…' she suddenly trailed off.

Alex cocked her head, her eyes widening in surprise. 'But now?'

'Oh nothing. You better get to your date, you don't want to be late. Where are you meeting him?'

'Sweet Escapes.'

'Oh lovely. Max has just started working there,' Violet said, referring to Quinn's cousin. 'I think he's sweet on Cleo. And it just so happens I'm on my way there to meet a friend, but don't worry, I won't be in your way.'

Alex frowned. Having her mother-in-law in attendance at her first date wasn't exactly how she had planned it.

'I'll go on ahead so it doesn't look weird if we arrive together,' Violet said.

It was definitely going to be weird, whether they arrived together or not.

Violet hurried off and Alex saw her disappear inside the bakery.

She bit her lip. What was she doing here? She wasn't sure she was ready to date again and she definitely wasn't looking for something serious. She wasn't ready to put her trust in someone again after what happened with Liam. And what if Violet was right and it did get serious and they didn't like that Quinn was always hanging around? Beyond the fact she was head over heels in love with him, he was also her best friend. They saw each other every day, they hung out together and watched movies and cosy crime shows, they went on days out together, with Zara and sometimes Immy, they'd even gone on holidays together. She simply couldn't imagine not having him in her life. But if she wasn't looking for something serious that only left something casual and she wasn't sure she wanted that either. The thought of sleeping with a man she barely knew made her stomach turn.

Still, she was here now so she might as well go in.

She took a deep breath and stepped inside Sweet Escapes. Violet was already at the counter just taking her coffee. She gave Alex a big theatrical wink which if her date was there he would undoubtedly have seen. Fortunately there was no one who looked like him waiting at any of the tables.

Alex waved at Cleo Knight, the owner, and Max Wild, Quinn's cousin and Cleo's new assistant, who were working behind the counter. She was nervous about this date so she'd arrived a little early so she could take a few minutes to calm herself. She'd never been on a proper date before so she wasn't exactly sure of the etiquette. She went to the counter to order herself a drink and wondered if she should order Dave one too. Although she didn't know what drink he liked, it didn't seem right to buy herself one and not get one for him. Hot chocolate seemed safe. Surely everyone liked hot chocolate.

'Hey Alex, what can I get you?' Cleo said after she finished serving the last customer.

'Two hot chocolates please.'

'With cream, marshmallows and a flake?'

'Oh sure, why not.'

Cleo ran it through the till as Max started making them and Alex leaned forward to talk to her. 'Cleo, I'm on a date. If he's awful, I might need you to save me.'

'I'm on it! We need a code or a signal. I know, if I see you playing with the tassels on your scarf I'll run over and tell you your house is burning down or something.'

Alex laughed. 'Perfect, although maybe something a little less dramatic.'

'Got it.'

Max came over with the drinks. 'And if he's a weirdo and you don't feel safe, scratch your chin and I'll come over and physically remove him.'

Alex grinned at the thought of Max tossing someone out on the street. He was easily big enough to do that too, he was built like a house. She liked Quinn's cousin. He had six of them. The Wild brothers. All big man mountains who were ridiculously handsome. Some of them lived in this area or the next town, but she'd met all of them at Violet's Big Christmas Day Lunch every year where almost all of Quinn's extended family were in attendance. Xander, Max's brother, worked here in the town too, much to Immy's annoyance, although maybe it wasn't so annoying after all considering Immy had now slept with him. Alex wondered if Violet was right and Max had a soft spot for Cleo. She watched them for a moment as they moved around each other. There was a definite spark there, like a secret hanging in the air between them, but was that spark just from two friends working well together or was it something more?

'Is it going to be awkward having a date with your ex-mother-in-law in situ?' Cleo muttered.

'A little,' Alex said. 'I love her dearly and she says she's OK with me dating again but I'm not sure I need her this close to the action.'

'Leave it with me,' Max said, cracking his knuckles. 'I'll ask her to make some changes to her famous Christmas Day lunch. That should set the cat among the pigeons.'

Alex laughed, knowing Violet's Big Christmas Day Lunch, as it was called, was sacred. No one was allowed to mess with the recipes.

Max walked over and engaged Violet in conversation, simultaneously blocking Violet's view of the rest of the café with his enormous frame.

Alex picked up her drinks and then carried them over to a spare table in the corner, sitting facing the door so she could see Dave when he arrived. At exactly one o'clock, the time they'd agreed to meet, he walked through the door. At least she thought it might be him. But it looked like an older, hairier version than the one she'd seen in his photos. She waved tentatively and he came over.

'Alexandra?'

'Alex, yes hi.'

To her surprise Dave offered out a hand to shake. It felt very formal but what did she know, she wasn't used to this dating game. Maybe that's what people did on a first date. She shook it and gestured to the seat in front of her.

Over his shoulder she saw Violet peering round Max and giving Dave the once-over and whatever she saw clearly didn't meet with her approval. But as much as she loved Violet, she didn't need her approval for who she should date. Although it would be nice.

'I bought you a drink,' Alex said, cheerfully.

He looked at it distastefully. 'Oh, I'm not sure whether to drink that or get a knife and fork and try and eat it. I think I'll just stick to a glass of water.'

He went to the counter to order a water and Alex plucked out his flake and quickly ate it before he came back. She wondered if it was too early to start playing with the tassels of her scarf.

He came back to the table and sat down, eyeing the hot chocolate with some annoyance. 'I thought for a moment you'd brought your daughter to our date, which would have been an instant dealbreaker.'

Alex frowned in confusion. 'Dealbreaker? How so?'

'Well I don't like children.'

'Then why would you agree to date a single mum?'

'I presume the kid will be with her dad at least half the time, which would leave us in peace.'

She didn't like the disdain in his voice. 'Her dad's dead so no, she's with me all the time. Apart from when she's at school or with friends.'

'Oh.'

She was surprised that he didn't offer his condolences but he was clearly trying to work out how this unwelcome child would impact on his chance of getting lucky. Maybe she should start bringing Zara on dates, then at least she could weed out the men who didn't like children right from the off. Except she wouldn't want to expose Zara to people who didn't like her.

'But you can get babysitters or... have you thought about boarding school?'

Alex rubbed her head with a sigh. She'd heard of the expression you have to kiss a lot of frogs to find your prince but, while she certainly hadn't been expecting to find her prince on her first date, she hadn't expected him to be such a slimy toad either.

'Excuse me for a second.' She stood up, picking up both hot chocolates and moving over to the counter. 'Cleo, can I get these two to go?'

Cleo's eyes widened. 'Is the date that bad already?'

'Yep.'

Cleo quickly poured the chocolates into two takeaway cups and passed them back. Alex turned back to Dave who was watching her in confusion.

'My daughter is my entire world so this clearly isn't

going to work.' She pulled her coat on and wrapped her scarf round her neck. 'But I wish you good luck.'

She picked up her chocolates and started walking out but Violet stopped her.

'Is everything OK?'

Max glanced round at Dave, looking like he wanted to physically throw him out without even knowing the reason why.

'He's not right for me,' Alex said.

'Oh, I'm sorry,' Violet said, not looking remotely sorry.

'It's OK, plenty of fish in the sea,' Alex shrugged but inside she was disappointed. 'I have another date tomorrow night. Pip. We've actually chatted quite a bit, he seems really nice.'

'Oh,' Violet said, unable to hide her disappointment. Then she forced a smile back on her face. 'Good luck with it.'

Alex took her hand. 'Whatever happens, it will be OK. I promise.'

Violet nodded.

Alex said her goodbyes and left. She drank both her hot chocolates on the way back, they'd be too cold to give one to Quinn by the time she'd walked up the hill to the art studios. But as she walked along, she checked her phone. She had a notification from the dating app and a private message on *The Lovegrove Lighthouse* Facebook page. She checked the dating app first, wondering if Dave was messaging to apologise. She opened it up and saw she had a message from another man called Oliver.

.   .   .

Hello, I saw your profile and you look nice. Would you like to meet for dinner tonight at Alberto's, say seven thirty?

She had a quick look through his profile to make sure there weren't any obvious red flags before she replied. He seemed nice too, very outdoorsy. Zara was staying at her friend's tonight, which meant Alex had a rare night alone so why not. She hesitated before she replied because dinner with people who didn't know her was always a tiny bit awkward but it was best to be honest than reap the consequences later.

She hit the reply button.

That would be lovely, I'm looking forward to meeting you. Just so you know, I have an allergy to shellfish, so I just have to be careful what I eat.

She paused as she thought then added:

Sometimes even being in close proximity to someone eating shellfish can set me off. And I'd rather spend the night talking to you and getting to know you than spend half the night in the toilets being sick.

.   .   .

She hit send. Thankfully her allergy to shellfish wasn't life-threatening but if anyone at the same table as her had some on their plate she would be physically sick for hours after. She had often kept quiet about it, not wanting to put anyone out, but after enduring several meals where she had spent most of the night in the toilets, she now told people upfront. Quinn always said she had to advocate for herself so she did.

She checked her other notifications from the dating app to see she had another message from Pip. Some of the men who messaged her were like Oliver and wanted to go straight to the date to get to know each other, while others, like Pip, took the time to get to know her before meeting and she liked that.

She opened up his message which was in reply to her previous one and read it.

I loved Back to the Future too. What kid didn't want their own flying skateboard? It is funny though that so many of the future technologies we see in Back to the Future 2 we now see today, smart watches, smart glasses, video calls, self-driving cars. They were clearly way ahead of their time. But still no flying skateboards. What invention would you like to see in the future?

She smiled. Pip was a bit of a geek and she liked that. She also liked that he wasn't trying to hide who he was, that he was happy to talk about stuff like this with her, rather than pretending he was interested in something else.

She quickly sent a reply.

We have so much cool technology nowadays: those smart glasses that can translate anything, in any language, virtual reality headsets and games you can play in your own home. The café near where I work even has self-heating butter knives. But in Star Trek if you're not well, you lie on one of those medical beds and they do a full body scan in seconds and they can find out exactly what's wrong with you. Imagine going to the doctor with a headache or a backache and instead of dismissing it and sending you away with two paracetamol, you could get this scan straightaway and find out exactly what's wrong. All the cancers or diseases could be spotted very early so we could get treatment, that would be amazing. So that's what I'd like, one of those in every doctor's surgery in the country.

She sent the message, clicked out of the dating app and opened up the private message on *The Lovegrove Light- house* Facebook page, wondering if someone had a lead to help her find St Nick. She stopped dead on the street corner. The message was from St Nick himself. Or at least someone claiming to be him.

Hello Sherlock – or should I call you Barnaby?

She smiled at that. She loved *Midsomer Murders*. Although most people in the town would know that. They had filmed part of an episode there once and she had won herself a small walk-on part after they had done a *Midsomer* quiz and she'd got every question right. Getting a photo with the actor who played DCI Barnaby had been the highlight of her year. She loved all cosy mystery shows like that and loved being able to spot the clues and try and work out who had committed the crime.

She carried on reading the message.

So you want to solve the mystery of who I am? It won't be easy. I've very carefully covered my tracks. But if anyone can work it out, it's you. To make it easier, I'll give you a clue every day until I give the last bauble on Christmas Eve. If you haven't solved it by then, I will disappear forever. If you figure out who I am, I'll paint a custom bauble for you, anything you like.

While I appreciate the offer of selling my baubles at the Wonky Tree Studios, making money from them was never my intention. Nor would I ever want to take commissions. I love the joy of giving without ever wanting something in return. I also get to choose what I want to paint. Taking commissions would take away some of that joy.

OK, time for your first clue. Painting isn't my real job – if you're looking for someone who paints, you won't find me there.

Snowy hugs,

Alex couldn't help smiling as she reread the message. She loved this challenge and she loved that someone would do this for her. She was sad that St Nick didn't want to set up a shop in the Wonky Tree Studios as that would have brought in good business to the studios which in turn would have helped everyone else. But she did understand his reasons. Maybe, once she unmasked him, she could talk to him about sharing his talent with more people, but ultimately if he didn't want to do that she would respect it.

She couldn't wait to tell Quinn about this. She practically burst back into the Wonky Tree Studios a few minutes later and ran up the stairs. He was working on a cute little monster wearing a metal Santa hat. He looked over at her with a smile but it soon fell off his face, his shoulders slumping as if in defeat. She frowned in confusion.

'I take it the date went well,' Quinn said.

'God no, I got out of there as fast as I could.'

He moved over to her, concern filling his eyes. He put his hands on her shoulders. 'Did he hurt you, are you OK?'

She smiled and reached up to stroke his face. 'No, but you need to stop being so lovely. You set the bar impossibly high for other men.'

'You know the answer to that then, date me instead.'

'Oh, if only life was that simple,' she said lightly.

'It can be.'

Her heart ached at the thought, but he was just being nice, he didn't actually want to date her. She glanced down at Quinn's Christmas jumper, which was obviously one of Violet's creations. She hadn't had a chance to look at it properly earlier. She frowned in confusion.

'What is that supposed to be?' she pointed to the Picasso-style creature with arms and legs seemingly everywhere.

'I have no idea but I couldn't exactly ask for fear of hurting her feelings.'

'It looks like roadkill.'

Quinn laughed and glanced down to her jumper. He cocked his head as he tried to work it out. 'Is that… an aubergine emoji?'

'Oh my god, Quinn, I thought the same. Dave, my date, probably thought his luck was in when he saw me turn up in this. I might as well have a flashing sign that says I love penis. Violet said it's supposed to be a whale, because I loved our whale-watching trip.'

He burst out laughing. 'That's not a whale.'

'It's supposed to be.'

'What did Dave think of it?'

'He was too busy scowling at my hot chocolate with all the trimmings to notice my offensive jumper.'

'What's wrong with a hot chocolate with whipped cream?'

'Exactly.'

'Well, did you at least get your kiss out of this date?'

'Eww, no. Pretty much the first words out of his

mouth after he sat down were that he didn't like children. He asked if I'd thought about boarding school so we could get rid of Zara and I left after that.'

'Good lord. What is wrong with some people?'

'Well, at least I found out now before I wasted any more time with him.'

'True.'

'And when one door closes another opens. I have dinner tonight with a man called Oliver, he wants to take me to Alberto's.'

'Oh nice.'

'And before you ask, I've already told him about my shellfish allergy.'

'OK, good. I think Max is working tonight, he'll make sure the kitchen is careful with your food.'

'Alberto's always do. They take very good care of me. Let's just hope Oliver is better than Dave. It can't get any worse, can it?'

Quinn looked doubtful and then seemed to force a smile on his face. 'I'm sure it will be fine. So is Oliver the reason you came in here smiling like a Cheshire cat?'

'Oh no, I don't know anything about him to smile about a date with him. I did get another message from Pip, though – I'm seeing him tomorrow night and he seems really nice – but no, I'm excited because I got a message from St Nick.'

His eyes widened in surprise. 'That's … amazing. I saw your post on Facebook, I did wonder if anyone would respond.'

'No response from the public yet but I wasn't

expecting St Nick to reply. He's set me a challenge and I'm so excited about it. He even called me Barnaby, here look.' She fished her phone out of her bag and passed it over for him to read.

He took a few moments, his eyes scanning over the words. 'This is really cool.'

'I know. I mean, the clue is pretty useless. The fact that he said he doesn't paint isn't much to go on, he could be a policeman, fisherman, accountant. But this challenge is right up my street. I'm even more desperate to find him now.'

'Why do you want to find him?' Quinn asked.

'To solve the mystery for one,' Alex replied. 'But I really want to thank him, not just for Zara, but for everyone who has received a bauble. And I was chatting to Luke and Flick and we really think that a talent like that should be celebrated and that those people who haven't received one should have the opportunity of buying one.'

'It's very different thing though, selling them rather than giving them as gifts. He already says he doesn't want to do that.'

'Yeah, I get that,' said Alex. 'But as he has offered to do a custom bauble if I guess who he is, I'm desperate to figure it out.'

'What would you get done if you could?'

'It wouldn't be for me, it'd be for Immy. Just as a little thank you for everything she's done for me over the years. I'd get one with Jacob on it. Most people have never even heard of a Skye terrier before so you never see it on decorations or any other dog paraphernalia. She would be over the moon to finally get something with a Skye terrier on it.'

'And what would you get done for you?' Quinn asked.

'Good question. Probably a whale that doesn't look like an aubergine emoji.'

Quinn laughed.

'What would you want on your bauble? If you could choose?' Alex asked.

'I've never thought about that.'

'There must be one thing you'd want more than anything,' she prompted.

'Oh, there's definitely one thing I want more than anything. But I'm not sure how to encapsulate that on a bauble.'

'What is it?'

He shook his head. 'It's hard to put into words and stupidly I've wanted to say those words out loud for several years and now it's probably too late.'

'It's never too late to go after your dreams.'

'Well, maybe I'll share those dreams with you on Christmas Eve, providing you're not engaged to some amazing hot guy by then.'

Alex laughed. 'I don't think that will ever happen, especially if Dave is representative of the calibre of single men out there. But what has that got to do with your dreams?'

Quinn smiled. 'I guess you'll have to work that out as well.'

She frowned. 'Are you worried that me being with someone else will affect what we have? Is that why you were sad when you thought I was happy because of my date? I told Violet you don't need to worry about that. You two will always be a part of our lives.'

He chewed his lip as he clearly thought how to reply. 'If you find the man of your dreams, and marry him, I will be happy that you're happy but this...' he pointed between the two of them, 'will change. How could it not? No man is going to be happy with us hugging, me coming round your house every day, us going on holiday or days out together. Maybe they'll be OK with me taking Zara out for the day but not this.'

Alex hated to admit he was probably right and she felt sick at the thought. She simply couldn't imagine not having Quinn in her life.

'Well, I'm sure we don't have to worry about that for a long time yet,' she said. 'I don't honestly know if I'll ever be ready for marriage again.'

His face softened. 'After what Liam did I'm not surprised. But if you one day fall in love with the *right* person, I hope you'll change your mind.'

She wasn't sure that was likely but she decided to change the subject before Quinn started digging into what her dreams were. Because *he* would be at the top of every list.

'Leaving our hopes and dreams aside for a moment, do you think I should reply to St Nick?'

'Oh yes, the more you get to know about him the more chance you'll have of guessing and winning that custom bauble. Ask him everything, let's see what he comes back with.'

'OK,' said Alex. 'He says he'll only give me one clue a day but I guess I could ask him some generic questions and see if he answers.'

'Worth a shot.'

Alex saw someone walk down the corridor towards her shop. 'I better go. I'll show you my reply later. Maybe we can work together to work out who it is.'

'Sure thing.'

She paused as a new thought occurred to her. 'Do you think I should publish his reply on *The Lovegrove Lighthouse* Facebook page, open up the challenge for everyone to try to find him? That way everyone gets a chance at the custom bauble not just me.'

Quinn immediately shook his head. 'If he wanted that he would have replied to your post more publicly, not sent you a private message. He even addressed the message to Barnaby, rather than the readers of *The Lovegrove Lighthouse*. This challenge is specifically for you so go for it.'

She smiled at that. 'Why would he want to do the challenge just for me?'

He shrugged. 'Maybe he likes you, or maybe he just wants to do something nice for you. I wouldn't read too much into it, just enjoy it.'

She nodded, waved goodbye and headed back to her shop.

CHAPTER 5

❄

Alex looked at the paper bauble she had just finished making with a lone reindeer standing on a small hill. Something simple like this was almost as popular as the more elaborate designs. She glanced around her studio: a quarter of her stock was already gone and she was trying to make more and capitalise on the last-minute Christmas rush. She nibbled her lip while she thought about what she could make next.

Her thoughts turned to St Nick. It would be lovely if she could give *him* a bauble instead as a thank you for all his kindness and generosity. But what could she make for him that was specific to him in the same way his baubles were specific for other people? She needed to know more about him even if she didn't know who he was.

She grabbed her phone and reread his message. She hadn't had a chance to reply yet as she'd had quite a lot of customers since she'd come back from her disastrous date.

She quickly typed out a reply, wondering if he would give her any more information as she had already used up her allotted clue for today.

Dear St Nick,

I can't tell you how excited I was to receive your message today. I'm definitely up for the challenge. As you addressed me as Barnaby, you already know I love a good mystery. Are you a fan of cosy mysteries? If so, do you have a favourite TV show or book?

I also want to thank you personally for Zara's beautiful bauble. She was over the moon with it. Not only did it capture her love of roller skating but her favourite colour too. Not many people would know that. I think that kind of eye for detail would make you a great detective too or at least an amateur one like me.

So what do I know about you so far? You live in Lovegrove Bay, and with a population of around five thousand people I bet I can narrow that down quite significantly. You talk to a lot of people and you really listen to the answers. How else would you know that Mr Malik's son loves chess or that Mrs Kendall is a keen entomologist? I speak to her quite regularly but we've never spoken about her love of insects before. I don't think I've ever seen someone so excited to receive a bauble with a beetle painted on the side. So your job probably brings you in contact with a lot of people. Perhaps you are a milkman, a postman, a hairdresser, they always talk to their clients, or perhaps you work in a shop that sees a lot of footfall.

And I do think you're a man. I think a woman would sign the gift tags with a female nom de plume, something like Mrs Claus or Elf Holly, not hide behind a male pseudonym, but maybe that's just me.

Would you like to confirm or deny any of these things?

I do think you are incredibly talented and so very kind. You have brought joy to so many people and I want to thank you for that. Whatever happens at the end of this challenge, your anonymity is safe with me.

Warmest wishes,

Alex (Barnaby)

She read it through wondering if it was too many questions and assumptions but it was worth a try to get closer to unveiling the truth. She pressed send. Then she noticed she had a reply from Pip. Opening it to see what he said, she smiled to see that he had replied to her message about inventions for the future.

An all-seeing medical bed is a lovely thing to want for the future and says a lot about the kind of person you are. I'd still like to see a talking car like Kit from Knight Rider. What does that say about me?

By the way, I've phoned ahead to the Rhubarb and

Crumble to let them know of your shellfish allergy for tomorrow night and I've asked if we can be seated in a quiet corner to try to avoid any cross-contamination from other customers. They said they've got just the spot for us.

Pip x

Alex smiled at how thoughtful that was. Conversely, she hadn't heard a peep from Oliver since she'd messaged him about her allergy earlier that day. Possibly he was busy and not had time to reply but now she had a niggle of doubt about dinner that night. Some people could be arseholes about her allergy, she just hoped that Oliver wasn't going to be one of them.

❄

Alex left her house later that night and made her way down towards town, passing through Christmas Gardens on the way. The cottage where Quinn lived looked cute as golden light spilled from the windows. As two of the elves, she and Quinn were due to decorate it two nights from now, transforming the outside into something wonderful. It was one of her favourite nights of the year.

Quinn had moved to Lovegrove Bay shortly after Liam's funeral and Alex knew that was so he could spend more time with Zara. He'd managed to get the house on Christmas Gardens for very low rent because for the month of December it was always taken over by

Santa, the elves and as much Christmas paraphernalia that you could throw at it. Quinn wasn't even allowed in the house during the day once Santa had arrived. During the rest of the year, Quinn had full use of the whole house but once Santa arrived he was relegated to the rooms upstairs. The elves had been surreptitiously decorating the ground floor of the house over the last few weeks but the children didn't know that as the outside was still normal-looking right now.

Christmas Gardens was a large village green surrounded by a little white picket fence which had already been festooned with beautiful garlands of holly, berries and pine cones. Quinn's cottage stood proudly in the middle of it. From September or October onwards it was also the place where all the children of the town would take their letters to Santa and quite often Quinn would get knocks on the door from little kids wanting to know if Santa was home. He'd always tell them kindly that Santa was in the North Pole and he was simply looking after the house for him until he arrived.

Alex cut through the gardens and walked by the house wondering if she'd catch a glimpse of him. She stopped when through a gap in the curtains she could see him, almost completely naked apart from a towel wrapped round his waist, soaking wet clearly having got out the shower as he talked to someone on the phone. He had the most amazing body. Of course she knew that because she'd felt it whenever he gave her one of his wonderful hugs, but she'd never seen it in all its glory before. It was toned and muscly and utterly captivating,

86

she couldn't drag her eyes away. She followed the path of one of the droplets that traversed his chest and down across the hard plains of his stomach and suddenly had an overwhelming need to lick those droplets off. She snorted with laughter at the thought of marching in there and doing just that and what his reaction would be. She turned and hurried on before he caught her watching him.

Christmas Gardens was kind of at the back of where the main shops started, heading towards the seafront, and it wasn't long before she reached the main part of the town. Almost every shop and every house was already decked out in Christmas splendour, making her feel excited for the big day. She loved Christmas, the decorations, the movies, the food, choosing the right presents for her now extended family.

Christmas Day would normally start with just her, Immy and Zara, but sometimes Quinn was there. They'd open the presents, play some games and then all make their way over to Violet's for the Big Christmas Day Lunch. Despite Violet's poor knitting skills, her cooking was to die for.

There were always lots of other relatives there too. Last year she'd met Max for the first time, as he'd been in the process of moving to the area. He had several jobs around town, always popping up in places where you'd least expect. So it was no surprise when she pushed open the door at Alberto's that he was there, serving behind the bar.

She waved at him as she unwrapped herself from her coat and scarf. He came over to talk to her.

'Is that your date?' Max said, gesturing to a guy seated at one of the tables.

Alex looked over and saw the man thankfully looked exactly like his photos. She waved at him and he waved back, although he didn't smile.

'Yeah, Oliver.'

Max pulled a face.

'You know him?'

'Unfortunately.'

'Oh god, is he that bad?'

'Well, maybe I just caught him on a bad day, but he was rude to Cleo at Sweet Escapes and there was no way I was standing for that.'

Alex let out a little sigh. Everyone had a bad day now and again and, while she couldn't abide rude people, Oliver deserved a chance at least. She would go over there with no judgement or preconceived ideas about him.

'Well, let's see what he has to say.'

'Just give me a wave and he's gone,' Max said.

She was just about to wander over when she spotted someone who looked like Violet at one of the tables at the back, but she was hiding behind one of the menus. She was with someone, although the restaurant was quite dark and Alex couldn't make out who it was.

'Is that Violet?'

Max looked embarrassed. 'Umm, it might be. I can neither confirm or deny it.'

'Is she here spying on me?' Alex said, taking that as a yes.

'No, I don't think so, she's having dinner with a friend.'

Alex peered over again. 'A male friend?'

'I'm sure there's some kind of client confidentiality that forbids me from talking about other customers with you and, if there isn't, I'm damned sure there is some kind of aunt confidentiality, as in I'd get a clip around the ear for talking about what she's doing here with you. So I'm saying nothing.'

Her eyes widened. 'Is she… on a date?'

Max's eyes widened to comic proportions. 'I don't know why you'd think that.'

'Well, she's with a man and you're not allowed to say anything and she's hiding from me which would kind of make sense if she doesn't want people to know she's on a date.'

'I think those things are circumstantial at best.'

She opened her mouth to ask more questions but Max mimed zipping his lips closed and throwing away the key so she didn't. 'You know I'll find out.'

'I'm sure you will but not from me.'

'That's fair enough. Right wish me luck.'

She plastered on a smile and walked over to the table. 'Hello, I'm Alex.'

'Oliver.'

Oliver didn't stand up, didn't even offer out his hand to shake like Dave had, although that was probably a bit too formal. His eyes were hard as if he was already angry. Alex checked her watch to see that she was five minutes early so it couldn't be that he was cross that she was late.

She sat down, already feeling uneasy.

Just then a man and a woman rushed past on their way out of the restaurant. The woman had her face wrapped in a scarf as if ready to face the Arctic so it was hard to tell who it was but the sweet apple-smelling perfume the woman was wearing was definitely the same as the one Violet usually wore. She glanced over to where she'd seen Violet a few moments before and sure enough her table was empty so it had to be her. Alex watched them as they hurriedly left. Clearly they didn't want to be seen. The man however was definitely someone she'd seen at Henry's funeral. In fact, she was sure he'd given a short speech about how wonderful Henry had been so he was obviously a good friend of Henry's. Maybe it had been completely innocent and Violet was simply having dinner with an old friend. Maybe she didn't want people jumping to the wrong conclusion and thinking they were on a date. Although Max's reaction to her suggesting Violet was on a date was more than a little suspicious.

She turned her attention back to Oliver who was glaring at her.

'I've just been looking at the menu. I think I'm going to have the prawns to start and then the mussels,' Oliver said.

Her heart sank. Most people she met were really good about her shellfish allergy but some took offence to it, lord knows why. She got the feeling Oliver was going to be the latter.

OK, she was going to give him the benefit of the doubt. Maybe he hadn't read her text message properly. Maybe he'd misunderstood, although she wasn't sure how she could have made it any clearer.

'I'm not sure if you got my message but I have a shellfish allergy.'

'That feels like your problem, not mine. How does your shellfish allergy affect me?'

'Well it doesn't, but probably around fifteen to twenty minutes after those prawns arrive at the table, I'll be spending the rest of the night puking up in the toilets. It's not much of a first date.'

'You've got a huge sense of entitlement, telling me what I can and can't eat.'

Her eyebrows shot up. 'I'm not telling you what you can eat, I'm just politely requesting that it doesn't contain shellfish or we're not going to have much chance to get to know each other when I'm running to the toilet every two minutes to throw up.'

Although she already knew everything she needed to know about this man if he was going to get this angry over her shellfish allergy.

'You know, people like you are exactly what's wrong with the world,' Oliver snarled. 'You come up with these pathetic allergies and you expect everyone to pander to you. The world doesn't work like that, sweetheart. The world is a tough place and you need to man up.'

'Why did you come here tonight if my allergy was going to be such a problem for you?'

'Because I wanted to tell you that you're an entitled bitch and if I want to eat a prawn, I'll eat a goddamn prawn.'

Alex had a sudden flashback to the night Liam had drunkenly come home from sleeping with another woman.

'*I've just shagged Michelle from the pub,*' Liam had gloated. '*And I ate prawns and they were bloody lovely.*'

She was surprised by how much that still hurt, the realisation that her marriage was over. She had stood by Liam because she'd promised to be there for him in sickness and in health, because the man she had loved was still in there somewhere, but she didn't owe this man anything.

She was just about to stand up and leave when Max clamped a hand on Oliver's shoulder. 'You need to leave, right now.'

'How dare you? My money is just as good as anyone else's.' He stood up to face Max and either he recognised him from his encounter with Cleo or realised he was only three-quarters of Max's massive height but he took a step back.

Max took a step forward. 'Get out or I will throw you out. Literally.'

Oliver didn't need to be told again. He grabbed his coat and stormed out.

'Are you OK?' Max said.

Alex nodded. 'Thank you. I'm sorry I lost you a customer.'

'I wouldn't want to serve him anyway, what a vile man. Stay there, I've already arranged a lift home.'

'Oh I'm fine, I can walk.'

Max shook his head. 'No, just in case he's still out there. Would you like something to eat while you wait? On the house.'

'Oh no, I'm fine. I can get something to eat at home.'

'How about Maria's famous mince pie and ice cream?'

'Oh yes please.' Her stomach rumbled appreciatively.

Max nodded and returned a few moments later with a bowl with a delicious-looking mince pie and a dollop of brandy ice cream on the top. Maria's mince pies were widely recognised as the best in Lovegrove Bay. Alex had no idea what she did to them, but she knew Maria made them from scratch and there were quite a lot of apples and cranberries used as well as the normal sultanas, oranges and brandy or rum. The pastry was the perfect texture that had that snap that shortcrust pastry had, but also melted in the mouth.

She took one heavenly bite and then Max called over. 'Your ride is here.'

She sighed, wondering if she could take this bowl of wonder to go, although the ice cream probably wouldn't travel well in a takeaway box. She turned round to see which taxi driver had been lumbered with driving her two minutes up the hill when she saw Quinn walking towards her.

'Hey,' Quinn said, as he arrived at her table.

'Did Max call you?'

'Yes, of course.'

She scowled at Max and he shrugged before returning to the kitchen.

'I'm sorry your date wasn't successful,' Quinn said, sitting down.

'It was the worst possible first date, in the history of first dates ever,' she grumbled. 'He basically came here to tell me I was entitled for asking him not to eat shellfish and then got really angry about it.'

'He sounds like a complete dick. Why would you eat something if you know it's going to make someone violently ill? I made the decision long ago that I was never going to eat shellfish ever again because I never want you to get sick from simply being around me. And you know what, I've survived that harrowing ordeal.'

She smiled. 'Why is it so hard to find someone as lovely as you?'

She took another bite of the mince pie and then held out a loaded spoon for Quinn. He leaned forward and took the bite.

'Mmm, that's really good.' He licked his lips and sat back. 'You could just date me. At least then you'll know what you're getting and there's no risk of Zara getting shipped off to boarding school or any shellfish-related incidents.'

'You're very sweet, but you're only offering that because I was with Liam and you feel obligated to look after me.'

He frowned as if he wanted to say more. She watched him as she finished off her pie. What would it be like to date him? He'd be sweet, attentive, generous, loyal, just as he was now. He'd probably be amazing in bed, he looked the sort of man who knew exactly what to do to make a woman happy in that department. But he didn't love her. He just wanted to take care of her and, as much as dating him would tick so many of her boxes, not least all those fantasies she had about him over the years, she needed love more than anything.

'I don't think I'm cut out for this dating malarkey anyway. I'm searching for the holy grail and if Dave and Oliver are the standards of men out there, I'll never find it.'

Quinn frowned. 'I don't think the holy grail is a man who doesn't yell at you because you have an allergy, that's just basic respect. You need to aim higher than that.'

'I think I'm aiming too high, that's the problem.' The holy grail was him, Alex knew that, but he was never going to be hers.

She wondered whether to tell Quinn that she'd seen his mum here with a man. However, as Violet had made such an effort not to be seen, she probably didn't want Quinn to know either.

She dropped her spoon in the empty bowl. 'Come on, let's go home.'

Quinn stood and placed a ten-pound note on the table.

'The dessert was free,' Alex said.

'Consider it a tip for looking after you.'

He took her hand and led her out to his car. He opened the door for her and she smiled at how gentlemanly he was.

'You look lovely by the way,' he commented. 'That dress is gorgeous on you.'

'Thank you. I thought I'd make a bit of effort. Looks like it was wasted.'

'Definitely not wasted.'

They got in and Quinn drove up the hill to her house.

'Thank you for coming to get me,' said Alex. 'Did you want to come in for a coffee? Immy's out at yoga and Zara is staying at her friend's for the night.'

'Sure.'

They got out and he followed her into her kitchen.

'So I take it you didn't get your kiss?' Quinn asked.

'Eww, no, thankfully. Knowing how angry he was about my shellfish allergy, I wouldn't be surprised if he ate a crab sandwich before he left home. I have one more date tomorrow with Pip but after that I'm done. I'm doomed never to have a kiss ever again.'

'I don't think you can judge men or the dating world based on two bad dates. There's got to be some good men out there. But if you really want a kiss, we can kiss.'

Alex's heart leapt as she stared at him in shock. He was so blasé about it, like he was offering to change her tyres not give her the kiss of her dreams. It clearly meant nothing to him when to her it would be everything.

'You… want to kiss me?'

'I'm just saying, you're my friend, my best friend, we hug all the time and a kiss isn't really any different to that. If you're looking for a no-strings-attached kiss, we can have that.'

There *would* be strings attached, Alex thought. There was no way she could kiss him and not feel anything or not want something more.

'I'm not sure that's a good idea,' she said slowly. 'I don't want things to be weird between us. Zara needs you. I need you. I don't want you to stop coming round because it's awkward or you're avoiding me.'

'That will never happen. You two are the most important people in my world. Nothing will ever change that.'

She stared at him trying to think of every reason under the sun not to do this when her heart and body were screaming at her to grab this opportunity with both hands. It was something she had dreamed about for years.

'OK,' she said, her heart thundering against her chest.

She couldn't help noticing his face lighting up. 'Really?'

'It's just a kiss,' she shrugged, trying to appear nonchalant when she felt anything but.

He stepped towards her and she felt like she was trembling with excitement. Was this really going to happen after all these years?

He stood in front of her and they stared at each

other. Was it her imagination or was his breathing accelerated?

'What kind of kiss is this going to be?' she asked. 'A little kiss on the lips, will there be tongues or is it the kind of kiss that will blow my socks off?'

He grinned. 'I've never been asked that question before.'

'I feel like I need to prepare myself mentally.'

'Is this what you would ask on a date? Because if it is we might need to work on your dating technique.'

'No of course not, but this is you and we're not on a date,' she said. 'You don't like me in that way so I need to know what to expect so I'm not disappointed.'

'Why would you be disappointed?'

'Well, if I'm expecting my socks to be blown off and you give me a two-second peck on the lips, that will be disappointing.'

'Well, imagine this is a date. I took you to Alberto's, we had a lovely dinner with no shellfish, we had Maria's amazing mince pies. The conversation flowed brilliantly, it was like we've known each other for years. I've brought you home, you've invited me in for coffee, which as a gentleman means strictly coffee, and now we are going to have our first kiss. I'll want to impress you with what an amazing kisser I am, but also be respectful of what you want. So I'll probably start off slow and if you seem like you're enjoying it, I might continue, up the ante on the passion.'

'And what happens then?'

'I'll… blow your socks off.'

She smiled. 'OK.'

He inched closer, his head leaning down towards her.

'Will you grab my bum?' she asked.

He paused. 'Do you want me to?'

She bit her lip. Was that too much for a friendly kiss? Oh sod it, if this was going to happen, she might as well go all in.

'If the mood takes you, sure. And if you want to touch… umm, any other body parts, then go for it.'

'OK,' he said, clearly unsure.

'I mean, you don't have to, but just go with the flow.'

'Right… Can I kiss you now?'

She tentatively moved her hands to his chest. A hint of a smile twitched at the corner of his mouth, but it wasn't as if she could stand there with her hands by her sides while she enjoyed the kiss of her dreams. If this was only going to happen once then she wanted to embrace it fully.

She nodded. 'OK, I'm ready, no more interruptions. Commence operation Blow My Socks Off.'

'You make me smile so damn much, Alex Campbell.'

'Well let's hope you can make me smile too.'

He smirked and shook his head, then he cupped her face and kissed her.

CHAPTER 6

❄

Desire and need slammed into Alex's stomach as soon as their lips touched. She couldn't believe she was kissing Quinn after all this time, and she couldn't help letting out a little squeak of excitement. She slid her hands round the back of his neck, stroking the hair there, and he made a noise of appreciation. She hadn't thought he might enjoy this as much as she would and that gave her a delicious thrill. He was kissing her so slowly, so gently, but she was already so turned on from a simple kiss. Every nerve, every cell in her body was suddenly bursting into life. He moved his hands to her back, stroking up and down her spine, and she couldn't help imagine what that would feel like if she wasn't wearing the dress. Christ, the thought of his hands on her naked body was enough to make her go hot with need.

He slid his hands down to her bum and she couldn't help giggling for a moment against his lips. Quinn Campbell's hands were on her bum.

He pulled back slightly and she grabbed his shirt and pulled him back towards her, kissing him again. He pulled her tighter against him and she felt how turned on he was. She gasped against his lips.

'Sorry, just ignore it,' Quinn muttered.

She leaned up and kissed him hard. Knowing she could have such an effect on him was such a turn-on. It made her feel so beautiful and confident. She moved her hand down his stomach to the front of his jeans, caressing him through the denim, and he growled against her lips.

The kiss suddenly changed to something desperate and frantic and she wasn't sure who was leading that change, but it was very clear from the way his hands were all over her body how much he wanted her.

He suddenly lifted her onto the dining table as the kiss continued and she wondered if he was going to make love to her right here and now. She was surprised by how much she wanted that. He moved his mouth to her throat and then trailed his kisses down towards her breasts, pushing the top of her dress down slightly to give him better access. The feel of his lips there made her stomach tighten with need, that feeling spreading out to the rest of her body.

He gently pushed her legs open and his hand touched the inside of her knee.

'Say stop and I'll stop.'

'Not a chance.'

He smiled and kissed her as he slid his hand up the inside of her thigh. She moaned against his lips as he touched the edge of her knickers and stroked the side of them where they met the inside of her leg, tormenting her with how close he was to where she needed him. Then he moved his fingers to her waistband, hooked a finger through it and slowly pulled her knickers down her legs. She lifted her bum to help him and as he got them past her feet he just tossed them on the floor. He moved his hand back up her thigh and this time there was no preamble, he touched exactly where she needed him.

She cried out against his lips, fisting her hand in his shirt.

'Oh my god, Quinn.'

His touch was exquisite, somehow knowing exactly where she needed to be touched. That feeling grew and tightened in the pit of her stomach as she clung to him and she soared over the edge, feeling like she was flying as she shouted out his name.

He pulled back slightly as she tried to catch her breath, his eyes intense as he watched her.

'Are your socks blown off?'

She burst out laughing. 'Yes.'

He kissed her briefly on the lips. 'Do you want more?'

She nodded. 'I want all of you.'

He kissed her again and then pulled back, swearing under his breath. 'I don't have a condom.'

She frantically thought whether there were any in the house. It was possible Immy had some somewhere but she wouldn't know where.

'I don't either but I'm on the pill and I had a health check a while ago and I've not been with anyone else since.'

'I had a health check a few months ago, I'm clean.'

She nodded and he kissed her again, shifting her legs further apart. He moved his hand to the button of his jeans.

Suddenly the front door slammed closed. 'Mum!'

They broke apart. Quinn quickly grabbed Alex's dress which was rucked up around her hips and pulled it back down. He grabbed her knickers off the floor and shoved them in his pocket as she scrambled down from the table. He moved quickly to the other side of the room, helping himself to a glass of water.

A second later Zara arrived in the kitchen and was fortunately not at all fazed by Quinn being there.

'Why are you wearing a dress?' Zara said.

Alex quickly tried to find some words. 'I had dinner with a friend, only it ended early, she wasn't feeling well.'

'Same. Chloe wasn't well either so her mum dropped me back. You might have overdone the blusher, your cheeks are very red.'

Alex felt her cheeks and sure enough they were hot to touch. She glanced across at Quinn but he seemed completely unruffled.

Just then, Immy walked in through the back door. 'Hellooo, I brought pizza, then you can tell me all about... Hi Zara, I wasn't expecting you here.'

'Chloe was sick so I came home. What pizza did you get?'

'The Farmhouse.'

'Oh yum,' Zara said, taking the box off her aunt and sitting down at the table.

Immy noticed Quinn. 'Oh hey Quinn, there's probably enough for you too.'

'I'm fine, I have to go, I just popped in to help Alex with something. I'll see you all tomorrow.'

He glanced at Alex and hesitated a moment as if working out what, if anything, he could say in front of Immy and Zara, although they were both now good-naturedly arguing over who got the biggest piece of pizza.

'Umm… call me later and we can discuss this a bit more,' he said.

Alex nodded and with that Quinn walked out, leaving her completely stunned, sexually frustrated, tingling with nerves and feeling a little bit draughty around her nether region.

CHAPTER 7

❄

Quinn sat staring at the flames in the fireplace of his cottage. Everything around him was filled with joy and sparkle, the room eagerly awaiting its jolly red resident who would be arriving in a few days, but he felt anything but joy.

On the one hand he'd just had the best kiss of his entire life with the woman he loved. But on the other he knew he'd taken that kiss way too far and possibly ruined everything.

She'd wanted a kiss and he'd practically savaged her like some kind of wild animal. Although she had seemed to be enjoying it at the time, she was obviously regretting it now she'd had a chance to reflect on it. She hadn't called or texted.

That kind of thing really should have happened after he'd started a conversation about their feelings, not just gone in all guns blazing.

He grabbed a crisp and practically butchered the

thing in his hands as he broke off tiny chunks before tipping the crumbs back into the bowl.

Did she have feelings for him? That kiss had escalated so quickly. Some of that had to have come from her or was it just that it had been so long since she'd been with a man?

What if this ruined their friendship? He couldn't lose her.

He'd go and talk to her.

He grabbed his coat, shoved his feet into his boots and walked out the house. He got as far as the edge of the gardens before he stopped. What was he doing? If she wanted to talk to him she would have phoned or texted him. He would have to wait to talk to her tomorrow and hope it wasn't too late.

❄

Alex couldn't settle.

Zara had eaten the pizza and taken herself off to bed, although what that really meant was that she would read for half an hour or so, before eventually falling asleep.

Immy was watching their favourite nature programme on the TV. The episode was about blue whales and though Alex loved whales she couldn't concentrate on any of it.

What had happened tonight? She had never imagined that Quinn would offer to kiss her, but when he did she'd assumed it was an offer from a friend. She'd had no idea he'd enjoy it so much he'd be turned on by it, or want to make love to her. Oh god, the thought of that made her stomach clench with desire. She wanted that so badly. But why had he reacted in that way? Did he have feelings for her too or was it just a heat-of-the-moment thing? She knew he hadn't had a girlfriend for a while so maybe it was just a horny thing and nothing more.

Would it be weird between them now? It had been way more than just a friendly kiss. He'd had his hand between her legs, he'd made her come so hard she'd practically seen stars. Was there any coming back from this? Could they really be friends again after that? Or would that unfinished kiss always lie between them, like a firework waiting to explode?

What she wanted more than anything was to march round to his house and finish that kiss, properly. But was that a terrible idea? But if she wanted it and he wanted it, was there really any harm in it? They were both single and he'd promised her the kiss wouldn't come between them, he'd said it wouldn't affect their friendship or his relationship with Zara. So could she have one night with him to put all these feelings to bed once and for all?

'What's up with you tonight?' Immy asked. 'You're so jittery. Did something happen on that date you haven't told me about, other than the cockwomble shouting at you over your allergy?'

'No, the date was over very quickly.'

'Then what is it?'

'Nothing, I…' Alex sighed. 'It was just something that Quinn said.'

'What did he say?'

'It doesn't matter, well it does but… I need to talk to him.'

'Now? It's nearly ten o'clock.'

'Do you mind looking after Zara for a bit? I mean, you don't need to wait up for me, just be there if she needs anything.'

Which was very unlikely. Once Zara was asleep, she didn't move until morning.

'Of course. Are you OK?'

'Yes… I will be.'

Alex got up and pulled on her shoes.

'Are you going in your pyjamas?' Immy asked, popping a honey roasted nut in her mouth.

Alex looked down at herself. Maybe she should put her pretty dress back on, Quinn had seemed to like that. But then Immy would know something was going on and right now Alex didn't want anyone to know. This was something special, just between her and Quinn.

She shrugged. 'He's seen me in a lot worse. And no one else will see them under my coat. I'll see you later.'

Immy nodded with a frown and then waved her off before returning her attention to the whales.

Alex grabbed her coat and stepped outside into the freezing night before she could change her mind. Snow was falling again and this time it was even beginning to settle slightly. There might even be an inch of it on the pavements and roads the next day. It made everything seem brighter, more magical as it sparkled in the moonlight and the golden glow from the streetlights.

What was she thinking? What was she hoping to achieve from going and seeing Quinn tonight? A night of hot passion? No, that wasn't a good idea. She smiled. It was a bloody brilliant idea. She shook her head. No, she mainly just wanted to know if she and Quinn were going to be OK. That was more important than anything. And then, if he was still willing, maybe she'd get to finish that kiss. If their friendship could survive that incredible kiss earlier that day, then it could probably survive the full monty too.

She walked into Christmas Gardens and straight-away saw there were footprints in the snow coming from Quinn's cottage heading in the direction she'd just come from, but at the fence they seemed to stop and turn back to the cottage. Had he been coming to see her and changed his mind?

She walked up to the bright red front door and knocked. A few seconds later Quinn answered the door.

'Alex? What are you doing out there at this time of night?'

'I needed to see you.'

He took her hand and pulled her inside, closing the door behind her. There was the smell of Christmas in the air, something she knew the elves sprayed around the house ready for when Santa arrived. It smelled of cinnamon and chestnuts roasting and fruity spicy smells. It was delicious. But not half as delicious as the man standing in front of her, in a white t-shirt that showed every glorious muscle on his body.

'I was going to come and see you too, literally left the house twice and then changed my mind. I wanted to call you but I didn't know if it was a good time with Immy and Zara there. And I hadn't heard from you so wondered if you needed some space. I'm so so sorry about earlier,' Quinn said, raking his hands through his hair.

'Why? I'm not.'

'Because you asked for a kiss, not to be mauled like a wild animal devouring its prey.'

'Oh yes, I'm really upset by the best orgasm I've ever had in my life. Absolutely gutted by it.'

'Wait, what?'

Alex stepped closer. 'I loved every single moment of our kiss earlier and I don't regret it, not for a second. Do you?'

'I... I've been feeling horribly guilty that I took it too far.'

'Well you can stop worrying, you didn't do anything I didn't want you to do. In fact, one could argue you didn't go far enough.'

His eyebrows shot up in surprise but he had obviously wanted her earlier, very obviously, so she knew she wasn't flogging a dead horse here.

'Quinn, are we OK?'

'Of course.'

'No matter what happens we'll still be friends, right?'

'Always.'

Her heart was pounding against her chest as she slid her hands round his neck. 'Then I'd very much like to finish that kiss.'

He stared at her, not making a move although she was pretty sure she could feel his heart roaring away too.

'I think…' He swallowed. 'We should talk about this.'

She took a step back. 'I don't. If we talk about it, we'll both come up with a million reasons why this is a bad idea.'

'I don't want to talk you out of this, I want this more than anything, but don't you think we should talk about why it happened earlier? And how you feel about it happening again in the future. I thought I'd ruined any chance of something serious with you by taking it too far with our first kiss, but you're here and you want more and I want more too, but I want a hell of a lot more than just one night.'

She let out a soft gasp. Quinn was offering her more, a relationship. She felt simultaneously sick and giddy at the thought. She hadn't seen that coming. Fear slammed into her so hard it nearly took her breath away and with it came a sudden realisation. This fear she had never really acknowledged was the reason why she had never tried to move on after Liam's death. She had been in love before and it had hurt every day when Liam had chosen the bottle over them. It had hurt watching their lovely, happy marriage be destroyed and there being nothing she could do to stop it. It had hurt when he was unfaithful and when he was rude and nasty to her because the Liam she loved would never have done any of those things. It had been like living with a stranger and she wasn't sure she wanted to go through that again. And while she knew that Quinn would be very unlikely to become an alcoholic – probably even less likely now that he'd seen the damage that Liam had caused – she still couldn't face the thought of losing him in any way, of letting herself fall completely and utterly in love with him and for it to come to an end.

'I'm not brave enough for that.'

He cupped her face. 'You're one of the bravest women I know.'

Alex shook her head. 'I can't take that step with you. If we agree there's going to be more kisses, more sex in the future, dates, holding hands, being together, then I will very quickly fall head over heels in love with you.' As if she wasn't already there. 'And what will happen then?'

'I don't know, marriage, babies, happy ever after,' Quinn said.

'No, I don't want that, especially not with you. It would hurt too much to lose you.'

'Why would you lose me?'

'Liam promised me a happy ever after. Then he found that alcohol made him far happier than I ever could. He chose whisky over me and his daughter.'

'I'm not Liam.'

'I know, but you can't promise me forever either.'

He let out a sigh. 'So you want just one night of great, no-strings-attached sex?'

'I just thought if we had one night it would get rid of all this… sexual tension from that kiss and we could go back to being friends again.'

'You think making love to you will cure me of you?'

'I don't know, I wasn't expecting any of this,' she said hesitantly. 'I wasn't expecting you to offer to kiss me, I wasn't expecting it to be the best damn kiss I've ever had, I wasn't expecting that, afterwards, all I'd be able to think about was your hands and mouth on my body and how much I wanted, no needed, you to do that again, and the very last thing I was expecting was for you to enjoy it so much that you'd want something serious with me. I didn't realise you had feelings for me too.'

'*Too*? That wasn't just a kiss that turned a bit passionate? That was… something for you as well? How long have you had feelings for me?'

'A while, a few years.'

His eyes widened. 'Years? Why didn't you say anything?'

'Because when I tried to kiss you before, you stopped me. I wasn't going to make a fool of myself again. I had no idea you felt anything for me.'

'I stopped you because you were crying and emotional. It didn't seem right to take advantage of that. You were grieving my brother, that was not the right time to kiss you.'

'But I wasn't grieving him. I grieved the loss of him and our marriage months before he died, probably even a year before. I was crying because I felt so guilty, because every time I saw Violet or Henry they would sob buckets over their son. Every time they would look at Zara they would cry that their son would never see her grow up. And I just felt like the worst person in the world because every time I saw you I would fall for you a little bit more. My heart had already moved on and I felt like scum for that. While Violet, Henry and you were still grieving, I had the hots for my husband's brother.'

Quinn stared at her with wide eyes.

'I'm sorry. I don't know what you must think of me,' Alex said.

'I think you're the most incredible woman I've ever met and I've thought that almost from the first time we met. So I had to live with the guilt of betraying my brother too and of falling for my brother's wife at his funeral.'

They stared at each other. He reached for her hand and she let him take it, her heart soaring as he stroked her hand with his thumb. She wanted to take this step so much but she just couldn't do it.

'But don't you see that's why we can't do a proper relationship,' she said. 'You are everything to me. It would destroy me if I lost you too.'

'I know how bad it was living with Liam, I saw him at his worst,' he said sombrely. 'I get that you're scared but I will never ever hurt you in that way. I will always choose you and Zara, always. Love is scary but some-times you just have to take a risk because what's the alternative? Spend the rest of your life alone because you're too scared to let yourself love again? Or date or marry someone you have no feelings for so the risk of pain is less?'

'Maybe I'm just not ready.'

'It's been four years, as you reminded me today. But at least you know now why I was so upset about you dating again. I wanted you for myself.'

Alex's heart was banging so loud she was sure he must be able to hear it. This was what she'd wanted for years, not just the kiss but him, all in. She'd dreamed about it. And now it was being offered she was too scared to take it.

She took a step back. 'I'm sorry. I shouldn't have come. I don't want to hurt you.'

'You're not going to hurt me. You've just told me that you have feelings for me, I'm over the bloody moon. Look, I have waited years for you because I thought you needed time to get over my brother, and in some ways that is true, just not in the way I thought. So I can wait as long as you need for those scars to heal. But I can't do something casual with you. It will never be casual with you.'

They stared at each other, regret and sadness warring in his eyes. She felt the same. What was she doing, why was she saying no to this? But her heart had been damaged so badly by Liam and she wasn't ready to hand it over to someone else.

'I'll walk you back,' Quinn said.

Oh god, this was it, it was over. She swallowed down the pain in her heart. 'That's not necessary.'

'It absolutely is.'

He grabbed his coat and opened the door. She stepped outside into the cold and he followed her, closing the door behind him. He took her hand and they walked the short distance back to her house in absolute silence. They reached her front door and she couldn't help feeling like she'd ruined everything and, to make matters worse, she'd hurt him, despite him saying she hadn't.

'You should go on this date with Pip tomorrow,' Quinn said.

She stared at him. 'What, why?'

'Because I can't give you what you want. Maybe someone else can.'

'But I don't want anyone else but you.'

'You don't want me either, unless it's for no-strings-attached sex and I can't give you that. Maybe you need to date other men to help you decide what you really want. I think what we would have together would be beautiful and special and rare and if you want that, I'll be waiting.'

Alex opened her mouth to protest but he bent his head and kissed her, sweetly and gently so her whole heart melted.

He pulled back and kissed her on the forehead. 'Goodnight, beautiful.'

With that he walked away and she felt her heart breaking at her complete stupidity. She walked back inside her house.

Immy was standing in the kitchen making herself a hot chocolate.

'Hey, do you want one?' Immy asked, without looking up.

'Yes please. Is Zara OK?' Alex said, feeling numb.

'Yes, fast asleep.' Immy turned around to look at her and her face fell. 'What's happened?'

Alex flopped down into a chair at the dining table and told Immy everything that had happened that day: all the way from how Quinn had reacted to her wanting to date, to the kiss and the stupid conversation she'd just had with him.

Immy slid into the seat opposite her staring at her in horror.

'So let me get this straight. You've had the hottest kiss of your life with the man you've been in love with for pretty much four years, he's told you he has feelings for you and wants a proper relationship with you and you don't want that?'

'I do but it's scary and I'm not ready for that yet.'

Immy took a long drink of her hot chocolate as she thought. 'Honey, what Liam did to you has left some horrible scars. He betrayed your love and trust every single day when he chose the bottle over you. Even though he loved you, married you, had a child with you, he showed you that love was worthless every time he opened his mouth and was vile to you,' Immy said bitterly.

She took another sip of her drink. 'It will take some time to build up that trust to believe in forever with someone again. I get that you're cautious. But this is Quinn. The man would walk through fire for you. He has shown up every single day for you and Zara ever since Liam's funeral. He has held you when you've cried. He is here every morning to take Zara to school. And clearly he's not just doing that for sex as he's just turned down a night of passion with you. He wants forever.'

'I know, I'm an idiot,' Alex wailed. 'He is a wonderful man but it's like I've built a wall around me and I can't get past it. I'm too scared to take that step.'

'Those scars are going to take time to heal, I get that, but that really isn't something you can do alone.'

'What do you mean?'

'You could wait ten years and the first time you have a proper relationship with someone, you'd still be scared,' Immy explained. 'The other person, whether that's Quinn or someone else, is the person who will heal those scars, by proving every day they aren't going to hurt you, that you can trust them. What's that old Ernest Hemingway quote? "The best way to find out if you can trust someone is to trust them."'

'You're right, I can only get rid of my fears of being in a relationship by actually being in one,' Alex admitted. 'But being with Quinn won't be a normal relationship where feelings build up slowly, it'll be something serious and big and life-changing from the word go. The stakes are too high. I don't want to lose him.'

Immy nodded. 'Is part of this fear your worry about how he will react once he finds out what happened the night Liam died?'

'That's part of it too. He will hate me.'

'He won't, he will understand. But if you get involved

with him then the sooner you tell him the better and then you can finally put that skeleton to bed.'

Alex sighed. Immy was right, about all of it. But it still didn't make it easier to act on it.

'Quinn thinks I need to go on this date with Pip tomorrow.'

'The nice one you've been chatting to?'

Alex nodded.

'I think you should too.'

'You just told me I should trust Quinn and go for it, or words to that effect. You even quoted Hemingway.'

'But I think you're right, it will be something big if you go out with Quinn. How could it not be? You've practically been dating for the last four years anyway, without the kissing and the sex. He's round here every day, you work alongside each other, you go on days out and holidays as a family. You two hug. He comes round here three or four nights a week to hang out with you and Zara. And you're in love with him. If you went out with him now, you'd probably be engaged by Christmas. And maybe you're not ready for something so life-changing. Maybe you need something a bit more low-key first. If nothing else dating Pip tomorrow might give you some perspective of what you really want. Maybe what you need right now is a nice date, with some flirting, not a marriage proposal.'

'Quinn didn't propose.'

'No, but he said he wanted something serious.'

'I'm not using Pip to get myself ready for Quinn, that's not fair.'

'I'm not suggesting you do,' Immy replied. 'You might like Pip and decide to give things a go.'

'I don't want that either. I only want to be with Quinn.'

'Then be with Quinn.'

'Is this some dumbass reverse psychology?' Alex said.

'No, I'm too tired for that. You told Quinn you wanted something casual, but you can't have that with Quinn. So you either decide to go big with Quinn, have something casual with someone else or have nobody for the rest of your life.'

'Harsh.'

'But true.'

Alex shook her head. Her head was such a mess right now and she hated that Liam had had such an effect on her that all these years later she couldn't even fall in love like a normal person. He had broken her but could his brother really be the one to put her back together again?

CHAPTER 8

❄

Alex was busily wrapping presents for Zara's teacher and teaching assistant the next day. Heavy snow was forecast for the rest of the week and Alex wondered if the school would just close early for the holidays, in which case the presents would have to go today. Problem was she was making a terrible mess of it. She was a wreck. She hadn't slept a wink of sleep all night, part of her remembering the most incredible kiss of her life and part of her squirming over turning Quinn down. He had offered her everything she wanted and she was an idiot for walking away from that. She didn't know how things were going to be between them today. How could they continue being friends after that kiss and that conversation? Would he even come today or would he avoid her? In a way she kind of hoped for the latter; meeting him was going to be awkward as hell.

She heard a knocking on the kitchen door and knew it would be him. She looked up as he let himself in and her heart slammed against her chest. Her desire and need for him after that explosive kiss were still there and seemingly were for him too from the way he was looking at her. Would a one-night stand have changed this sexual tension that crackled in the air between them or would it have made it a million times worse?

'Hi,' he said, softly.

'I wasn't sure you'd come.'

'I will always be here for Zara. But I won't be around the studio today.'

'You promised it wouldn't change anything between us.'

'And it won't. I just need some time to process this and work out how to be around you without wanting to pin you to the nearest hard surface and make love to you.'

Her eyes widened in shock. 'You know I want that too.'

'I know, which makes it all the more difficult.'

She stared at him, desperate to kiss him again. But with Quinn it was all or nothing and she wasn't sure she could do all.

'I'm going to cancel my date with Pip.'

'No, I don't want you to do that.'

'You want me to go out with another man?' she asked.

He pushed his hand through his hair. 'If and when we start dating, I want to know you're all in, no doubts, no regrets.'

She sighed. She wasn't sure she could ever give him

that. 'These fears are not just going to go away overnight.'

He moved closer, stroking her face. 'I know, we can take it as slow as you need. We don't have to rush into anything.'

'I'm just not ready for something big and life-changing.'

And she wasn't ready to tell him the truth about the night Liam died and then lose him forever.

He took a step back from her and she knew she had hurt him.

Just then Zara came running down the stairs. Quinn stared at her as they heard Zara putting on her coat and boots in the hallway and, a few moments later, Zara arrived in the kitchen. She hadn't waited for her gory threat today, and Alex had a good one. She'd have to save it for tomorrow.

'Hey Rocket,' Quinn said.

'Hey.' Zara gave him a hug. 'Are you heading into town again to collect some metal?' she said, grabbing an apple from the fruit bowl and taking a bite.

'Yes, so I'll walk with you if you want.'

Zara nodded. 'You know, it might be more efficient if you were to pick up all the metal you needed once a week.'

Alex watched Quinn suppress a smile. 'But I never know how much I'll need. Sometimes an idea will come to me and I end up using a lot more than I planned.'

Zara seemed to accept this answer, coming over to give Alex a hug goodbye. 'Don't forget I'm at Harley's tonight after school,' Zara said, as if she was the mum in this relationship. 'I won't be back till late.'

Ordinarily, Alex wouldn't let her daughter stay out late on a school night but all they seemed to be doing these last few days of school was watching films and making various Christmas decorations and cakes.

'I hadn't forgotten,' Alex said, giving her daughter a kiss on the forehead. 'Take the presents for your teachers.'

Zara pulled back, grabbed the presents and put them in her school bag then joined Quinn at the door. Zara gave her a wave and then stepped outside. There had been a light dusting of snow overnight; sadly not enough to make a snowman or have a snowball fight, but enough to make her daughter look around in wonder.

Quinn gave her a little wave too but didn't say anything else as he stepped outside. The door closed behind them and Alex sank down at the table with her head in her hands.

❄

Quinn was walking down Cherry Lane, the main high street, a while later, trying to get his thoughts in order. How could he and Alex go back to being just friends after that earth-shattering kiss, especially knowing they both had feelings for each other? And what could he do to get her to take that step with him? If she didn't have feelings for him it would be so much easier to walk away but knowing she had quite possibly been in love with him for four years made it so much harder.

He looked around at the beautifully decorated shops, some displaying their wares among fairy lights, baubles and Christmas ornaments, others having a kind of theme going on with whole scenes in the windows. At the end of Cherry Lane was an ice skating rink and people were gliding gracefully around it. He planned to take Alex and Zara skating in a few days. He'd promised Alex nothing would change their friendship and he had to make sure he didn't break that promise.

He thought about getting a doughnut from Donut Park to cheer himself up. He didn't really have a sweet tooth but their crème brûlée doughnuts were amazing. Although shopping at Donut Park was highly contentious in Lovegrove Bay. With its little independent shops and cafés, a big global chain like Donut Park had never been wanted. For some, the US spelling was the thing they were most offended by. And while he was always happy to support local shops rather than commercial chains, he had walked past there one day and had been tempted in by the crème brûlée doughnuts and despite the glares he got for shopping there, the doughnut more than made up for it. Today felt like the kind of day one of their doughnuts was needed, even if he had to face the wrath of the locals to get one.

Quinn passed a café and thought about popping in to have some lunch before he got a doughnut. He walked up to the window to look at the menu and couldn't help noticing two people, a man and a woman, sitting on the other side of the window, seemingly trying to hide from him behind their menu. He peered closer. The sunlight was on the window so it was difficult to see but he was pretty sure that the woman was his mum. Although without seeing her face he couldn't confirm it. He tapped the window to try to get her attention and the woman buried her face even deeper inside the menu, the man opposite her doing the same, their faces buried so deep in the pages they couldn't possibly be able to read it. He was just about to go in and see for himself when he heard a voice calling out to him.

'Quinn!'

He turned round to see Immy beckoning him from the entrance to her sweet shop on the opposite side of the street. Giving the window one last confused look, he went over to Immy wondering if he was going to get some kind of lecture from her. Alex was bound to have told Immy what happened, they told each other everything.

He'd never really had that kind of relationship with Liam. He'd adored his little brother and they used to play well together as children but with a gap of four years between them the gap seemed bigger somehow when they hit their teenage years. Quinn had been interested in girls and Liam had still been playing on his game console. As they'd grown up, it had felt like they were very different people. Quinn always wondered whether, if he'd taken more of an interest in Liam's life, made more of an effort, he could have helped him more when he needed it.

As he approached he realised Immy was looking annoyed. He'd always liked Immy and he knew how much Alex loved her and relied on her. When the four of them – him, Alex, Immy and Zara – went out together, he'd always got on well with her but they'd never spent any alone time together for him to get to know her really well. She seemed nice. Although his cousin, Xander, who owned the chocolate shop opposite Immy's, always said she was the bane of his life, though Quinn was never sure why.

'Hey,' Quinn said. 'You alright?'

Immy held the shop door open for him and he stepped inside and then, to his surprise, she locked the door and turned the open sign to closed.

'We need to talk,' Immy said.

'Right…'

'What's going on between you and Alex?'

Quinn wasn't going to tell her anything she didn't know, so he'd wait to find out how much she did know first before saying anything incriminating.

'Well I'm sure you know.' He folded his arms across his chest to try and signify that this was none of her business. Clearly she was not a master of reading body language, because she carried on regardless.

'I know you both are crazy for each other, I know you kissed – well it was a lot more than a kiss – and I know she offered you a night of passion last night which you turned down.'

OK, so she did know everything.

127

'I'd like to know why you turned her down.' Immy said.

Surely turning Alex down showed more respect for Alex, why would Immy be annoyed with that? Sleeping with her and moving on felt like a dick move.

'Honestly, I've been asking myself the same question,' Quinn said. 'But I can't do just one night with her and then go back to being friends again. What then? I'm just meant to watch her go off with someone else, once she'd got me out of her system?'

'You are everything to her. She has wanted to be with you for years. I guarantee if you spend the night with her, she'd be back again the next night and the night after that.'

'How is that any better? I sleep with her three or four times then that's it, it's over?'

Immy rolled her eyes. 'Or maybe she comes back to you every night.'

He stared at her in confusion before the penny dropped. 'Have a year of one-night stands?'

'Or whatever it takes. She's not said the words to me but I'm pretty sure she's in love with you and you're in love with her. But she is terrified of history repeating itself. I don't think anyone, least of all her, thinks you would go the same way that Liam went – I've never even seen you drink, let alone get drunk – but she was happy with Liam and overnight she lost him. What she feels for you is huge, maybe even more than what she felt for Liam. She's scared of falling even further in love with you, marrying you and then losing you too. She is over the moon that you have feelings for her, she never saw that coming at all, you're the man of her dreams. But you've told her you can only do something serious, probably because you think a commitment from you is what she's looking for, and it's freaking her out.'

'I told her this morning that we could take it as slow as she wants. I know she needs time, I don't want to rush her into something.'

'So why not tone it down?' Immy suggested. 'A lot.'

'Offer her something casual instead?'

Immy nodded. 'Yes, exactly.'

Quinn thought about it for a moment. 'Exclusively casual.'

'I don't think you have anything to worry about there. She doesn't want anyone else but you. She doesn't even want to go out on this date with Pip tonight now.'

Quinn groaned. 'I told her to go on it, I told her not to cancel.'

'I did too.'

He frowned. 'Yet you're here fighting my corner.'

'I want this to work more than anything. I think you'll be the best thing that ever happens to her and maybe she needs a little nudge in the *wrong* direction for her to realise it.'

Just then there was a knock on the door and Quinn looked round to see his cousin Xander standing there at the shop door, looking angry.

'Oh for god's sake, what does *he* want?' Immy said but Quinn was surprised to see her cheeks flush as if… she was attracted to him. He'd thought they hated each

129

other, which always made things awkward on Christmas Day when they were both at his mum's for the Big Christmas Day Lunch.

Immy moved over to the door and opened it a crack. 'Yes?' she snapped.

'What's going on in there?' Xander said.

'None of your business,' Immy said. She went to slam the door but Xander stuck his foot in the doorway and pushed it open. Moving into the shop he glared at Quinn.

'Quinn.'

Quinn had no idea what was going on here and why Xander was so mad. He'd always got on with very well with his cousins.

He frowned in confusion. 'Xander.'

Xander turned his attention back to Immy. They glared at each other and Quinn wasn't sure if they wanted to kill each other or rip each other's clothes off and make love to each other right here on the floor of the sweet shop.

'You have no right to care what I do and who I do it with,' Immy hissed to Xander, clearly forgetting Quinn was even in the room with them. Was something going on between them? Maybe there was a fine line between love and hate. Had they stumbled across it?

'I might not have any right, but I still care,' Xander said, quietly, stepping closer to her.

Quinn watched Immy's breath catch in her throat, her eyes dipping to Xander's lips.

'Umm… should I go?' Quinn said.

'Yes!' they both said together.

Quinn didn't need telling twice. He quickly left and a few seconds later Xander locked the door behind him.

Well that was something Quinn hadn't seen coming. Now he just had to sort out his own love life.

CHAPTER 9

❄

Alex hadn't seen Quinn all day. She knew he was avoiding her and she hated that. She'd had to plaster on a brave smile with all the customers and inside she couldn't escape the horrible feeling of dread that she had lost her best friend.

Her phone beeped with a notification and she quickly grabbed it, hoping it was a message from Quinn but it was another message from St Nick instead. The Lovegrove Bay community Facebook page had been awash with much excitement all morning as more baubles had been found and yet no one had any idea who was doing it. She felt a delicious thrill that she was the only one privy to this direct line to St Nick. She needed something to cheer herself up so she opened the message.

Dear Alex,

That's a lot of questions but a good detective always pushes to know more. I love cosy mysteries like Midsomer Murders, Death in Paradise, Beyond Paradise, the list is endless. Something dramatic without being sinister or gory and something that has good humour is right up my street. I often watch them with my other half and, while I love solving the clues and finding out who the murderer is before it's revealed, I love watching her get so much enjoyment out of solving the crimes even more. Sometimes I'll even deliberately get the answer wrong because she gets so happy when she beats me to the answer and seeing her happy is the best thing in the world. I guess that's what love is, always putting someone else's happiness above your own.

Alex couldn't help smiling about that. This was clearly a man very much in love and she adored that. It gave her hope in the world. She carried on reading.

I'm neither a milkman, postman or a hairdresser but you're right that I work somewhere that sees a lot of footfall and that gives me the opportunity to talk to people and get to know them. You're also right that I am a man.

So are you ready for your second clue? I work directly for Santa. While that isn't my paid job, I do help the big man a lot in December.

Snowy hugs,

St Nick

. . .

133

'He's an elf,' Alex said, out loud. The following night all the elves would be helping to decorate Quinn's cottage into something beautiful and festive, along with her and Quinn, so St Nick would be there. This was very exciting as there were around fifty elves who all had various jobs decorating the house and gardens but half of them were women. This clue narrowed it down massively. Also, out of the men, she now knew she was looking for one who was either happily married or in a relationship. She knew a few of the elves were older and widowed or young and not in a relationship, so she could narrow it down even more. Later she would write a list of all the male elves and then she could cross off anyone who was single. This was a massive clue and much better than the previous day's clue of not being a painter.

She couldn't wait to show Quinn this latest message. Then her heart sank. What if their friendship was ruined by the kiss and her inability to trust him enough to want a serious relationship? As tonight was Wednesday they were due to watch the latest episode of *Midsomer Murders* together but instead she was supposed to be going on a date with Pip. What she really wanted was to curl up on the sofa with Quinn and, as Immy was out and Zara was at Harley's, maybe they could share a few more kisses as they watched their favourite programme together. Would he want that, even if they weren't properly together?

She switched off her studio lights and locked the

door. She walked past Quinn's studio which had been closed all day.

How must he be feeling right now? She had walked away from a serious relationship with him, that had to hurt. And despite his magnanimous attitude to her dating Pip tonight, that had to hurt as well.

Suddenly she knew what she had to do. Immy had given her a choice of three the night before – go all in with Quinn, date other people or be alone for the rest of her life – and now she knew which one she had to choose. While she didn't feel ready for a serious relationship with Quinn, and she wasn't sure what it would take for her to be ready, the thought of being with anyone else but him, even for a date or a kiss, made her stomach turn. She didn't want anyone else but Quinn and it felt disloyal to go on dates with other people.

She pulled her phone out of her bag and quickly dialled Pip's number, cringing at what she had to do.

Pip answered on the third ring. 'Hey Alex, I'm looking forward to meeting you tonight.'

'Oh Pip, I'm so sorry, I'm going to have to cancel. And please don't take this personally, I've loved chatting with you over the last few days, you seem so lovely and kind. This is one hundred percent a me problem not you.'

There was silence from Pip as she stepped outside into the cold night. Snow was falling thick and fast and no one was around. She decided honesty was the best policy.

'I have been in love with the same man for four years with never any thought that he could possibly feel the same way and last night we kissed and he very much has feelings for me. But he wants something serious and I was hurt very badly in the past and I got freaked out about having a relationship with him and basically ran away. He said if I'm looking for something casual I should go out on dates with other people but I can't do it, I can't be with anyone else but him. It feels like a betrayal and I can't hurt him like that, even if I can't be with him. I'm so sorry.'

There was more silence from Pip.

'I bet you're thinking you've dodged a bullet by avoiding my absolute mess of a life.'

'Well at least I know you didn't take one look at me and then come up with this as an excuse,' Pip said.

'It really isn't you, you've been so nice. I was looking forward to meeting you until last night happened. I'm really very sorry.'

'There really is no need. To be honest, I'm still crazy in love with my ex so it wasn't really fair for me to go on a date with you either. I thought if I dated other people I might eventually get over her, but that wasn't realistic.'

'That's what I thought: if I dated other people, I might fall out of love with him but that was never going to happen.'

'Alex, you want my advice?' Pip asked.

'Sure.'

'A love like that, the kind that takes hold of you and never lets go, you need to grab onto it with both hands. The past is in the past and there is nothing you can do to change it, but your future, that's wide open, that can be whatever you want it to be. You don't want to get to ten years from now and look back at this moment and regret it or wish it had been different.'

'You're so right, but it's easier said than done. I just need to find a way to be brave.'

He sighed. 'If you figure it out, you can tell me what the secret is.'

Alex smiled. 'Thank you for being so understanding and lovely. I'm sorry it didn't work out.'

'No worries at all. Merry Christmas.'

'And to you.'

They said their goodbyes and hung up.

Alex knew that she had to go and see Quinn. Even if nothing could happen between them, he needed to know there would never be anyone else for her. She couldn't bear the thought of him sitting at home now hating the idea of her being on a date with someone else.

She quickly walked down the hill towards Christmas Gardens, going as fast as she could through the snowy conditions. She rounded a corner and saw his cottage sitting among the snow looking every inch something from a Christmas card as light spilled from the windows and wisps of smoke curled from the chimney.

She hurried across the grass and banged on the door. After a few moments, Quinn answered the door.

He blinked in surprise to see her.

'Alex, what are you doing here?'

Before she could say a word, he took her hand and

pulled her inside, closing the door. She could see the log fire burning merrily in the fireplace and shivered slightly as her body adjusted to the warmth.

'What are you doing here?' Quinn said, rubbing her shoulders. 'It's freezing outside. Aren't you supposed to be going on a date with Pip soon?'

'I cancelled.'

'But he was the nice one.'

'He was,' Alex agreed. 'He was lovely and kind and funny. But he wasn't you. And I know I'm not ready for something big and serious with you but there will never be anyone else but you. I'd rather sit in my house alone every night, than be with anyone else but you. Although I'd much rather be sitting *with* you, watching *Midsomer Murders* together, maybe you'd even let me hold your hand.'

His face softened and he cupped her face, stroking her cold cheeks with his thumbs. 'I would like that very much.'

Then he dipped his head and kissed her. She gasped against his lips as she hadn't been prepared for that and then she kissed him back.

Every worry and doubt went out the window as he kissed her, there were no other thoughts about the future or getting hurt, there was no worry about how she would tell him what happened the night Liam died, there was just the two of them, kissing each other as if they were the air they needed to breathe, everything else just faded away. How could a kiss make her feel so much? It wasn't that she hadn't been kissed for years, it was more than that, it was him. They just fitted together so perfectly, she knew this man so well, he was her best friend and she loved him so much.

Quinn slipped her coat from her shoulders and it fell to the floor. Without taking his mouth from hers, he bent down and scooped her up in his arms as if she weighed nothing when she knew that wasn't the case. He carried her into the lounge and laid her down in front of the fire.

He pulled back slightly to look at her. 'Can I make love to you?'

'Yes, definitely yes,' Alex said, without any hesitation. She didn't know what this meant, whether it was a one-off or if there would be more. She didn't care. She needed him so much right now.

He kissed her again, undressing her so she was completely naked. But there were no nerves about being naked with a man for the first time in years, this was Quinn, she trusted him completely. His eyes roamed over her body which made her smile.

'Christ you're so beautiful.'

He bent his head and kissed her again. This kiss, she was never ever going to get enough of it.

He pulled back to look at her again. 'Now in the spirit of picking up where we left off, where did we leave it yesterday before we were interrupted?'

'Well we'd kissed, socks were blown off,' Alex said, stripping him out of his t-shirt, before starting work on his jeans. He helped her by pushing them down and wiggling out of them. 'I don't think there was anything else of note.'

He arched an eyebrow. 'So I didn't give you, what was the words you used, the best orgasm you've ever had?'

'That feels like something I would definitely remember, so maybe start there.'

'OK, I can see I need to try harder.'

He scooted down to her legs and kissed on the inside of her knee, then started trailing his hot mouth up her leg. Her breath hitched as he got closer to where she needed him, then he kissed her right there. She arched up off the floor, that feeling slamming into her so hard and so fast, her body instantly responding to him as if they'd been made just for each other. That feeling spread so quickly like fire on paper, burning everything it touched, and within moments she was shouting out his name, clinging onto his shoulders, her orgasm leaving her completely breathless.

He pushed down his shorts and climbed back up her, catching her gasps on his lips, and she wrapped her arms around him as her body trembled against him.

He pulled back slightly, adoration for her shining from his eyes. She stroked his face. And for a second those fears of falling even further in love and having a relationship with this wonderful man started creeping in. They both knew that this, whatever it was, was something significant. It wasn't possible to keep her heart separated from this.

'Are you OK? We don't have to go any further than this if you're not comfortable with it?' Quinn said.

'No, I want this, I've dreamed about this for years. I'm just scared of getting hurt.'

He kissed the frown that had formed between her eyes. 'Don't think about this too much. It's just two friends making love, it doesn't have to mean anything.'

She stared at him in surprise. 'You're my best friend, of course this means something.'

He kissed her. 'It only means something if you want it to. It can be completely no strings attached.'

Her heart leapt. 'You really want one night of sex and then we'll just go back to being friends again?'

'I never said anything about one night. We can have no-strings-attached sex as often as you want.'

'But… you said you didn't want anything casual with me.'

'I want you in any way you want to be with me. I want to hold your hand while we watch *Midsomer Murders*. I want to be with you every day because I missed you so damned much today. Of course I want forever with you but I can wait as long as you need to be ready for that. And if you want no-strings-attached sex in the meantime, I'm more than happy to oblige.'

She had no words. This was so much to get her head round. She'd woken up yesterday morning and everything was normal, now she'd kissed Quinn, found out he had feelings for her and was offering her as much no-strings-attached sex as she wanted. Her brain was telling her this was a terrible idea, she could never have meaningless sex with Quinn, it would always mean something and someone was going to get hurt. But her heart was telling her to take the risk with the relationship he was offering her, not just sex, it was everything she'd wanted for years.

'We don't have to do this. You can walk away if that's what you want,' Quinn said gently.

'After two earth-shattering orgasms, I can't walk away. I already want more, I want to do this every night with you.'

'And we can, just without any strings.'

She chewed her lip, knowing that wasn't true.

'Look, I'm sorry about the orgasms,' Quinn said, a smirk on his lips saying he wasn't. 'I'll try and make the sex as rubbish as possible, no more orgasms.'

Alex nodded. 'That would be great, rubbish sex would be really helpful.'

'I'll try my best.'

She wrapped her legs around him. 'Do your worst.'

He smiled and moved carefully inside her and nothing had felt so perfectly right as this before, it was like they were two halves of a whole finally reconnecting. He stared at her in wonder, the smile gone from his face. Something shifted between them and her heart felt suddenly so full of him that she thought it would burst from her chest. He started moving slowly against her, his eyes never leaving hers for a moment, and it was too much all at once. Her heart wanted to scream out how much she loved him and tell him how she wanted this forever but she couldn't do it. But she couldn't look away either, this was too important for that.

'Alex,' Quinn breathed, his voice choked.

She wrapped her arms around him, holding him close. This was everything she wanted and needed it to be and everything she'd been wanting to avoid.

He kissed her hard as he started moving against her faster. His hand snaked up to her breast and the feel of his touch made her breath catch in her throat. She ran her hand over his bare, muscly shoulders, stroking down his back and back up to touch his hair, and he groaned against her lips. That feeling in her stomach that had started to fade was already building again, tingles turning into fireworks that were exploding through her body. She clung to him and he pulled back to look at her with such love in his eyes and she knew she would never love another man as much as she loved him. It was that realisation that sent her soaring, shouting out his name and trembling in his arms.

❄

Alex was lying on Quinn's sofa as he lay half on top of her, kissing her like his life depended on it. There was a part of her that knew she needed to get up and run away from this because with every kiss, every touch she was falling for him even more. But the part of her that was in complete heaven lying here in his arms far outweighed the other part.

Sex had never been like that with Liam. She felt a

little guilty comparing the two because sex with Liam had always been lovely but with Quinn it had been so much more. She didn't know why but it had been without doubt the best sex she'd ever had.

He pulled back to look at her and she stroked his face. 'I need to go soon, I don't want Zara to get back home and find I'm not there.'

He nodded. 'I'll drive you back.'

'There's no need, it's only a two-minute walk up the hill.'

'There is no way I'm letting you go home alone.'

He got up and started getting dressed and she had the pleasure of watching his gloriously naked body.

'How was the sex?' Quinn asked, arching an eyebrow at her as if he knew it was the blow-your-socks-off kind.

'Rubbish.' She got up and slipped her arms round his neck and he wrapped his arms round her waist.

'Is that so?'

'Yeah, which is a good thing, I couldn't possibly fall in love with someone who makes love like a floundering fish.'

He smirked. 'A fish?'

'Yeah, when it's ended up on dry land and it's flapping around, it was like that.'

'That does sound bad.'

'Yes it was, but after I've Christmasified your house tomorrow and all the elves have gone, you can have another go at improving your technique if you like. Practice makes perfect after all.'

'I think that sounds like a very good idea. I'm probably going to need lots of practice if I'm that bad.'

She nodded. 'I'm quite happy to help you, that's what friends do.'

'You're very kind.'

'I know, it's very selfless of me. Just so you know, I won't be enjoying it.'

She was already feeling excited about what the night would hold.

'I appreciate your sacrifice.' He kissed her again and she felt herself melt against him.

She pulled back to look at him and couldn't help smiling happily at him.

'Are we OK?' Quinn asked, stroking her face.

'Of course.' She tried to push down her fears, she was too happy right now to want to face them.

'Do you want to talk to me about what you're feeling?'

She sighed. She didn't want to talk about this at all. She wanted to continue pretending it was rubbish or at least that it was something casual. She didn't want to think about her fears for the future or that if they continued down this path she would have to tell him the truth about the night Liam died. She wanted to bury her head in the sand and forget all of that.

She looked down so she wouldn't have to look him in the eye. 'I think we both know that was a lot more significant than we were expecting,' she said, quietly.

He tilted her head back up to face him. 'Yeah, for me

too. I knew it would be amazing, because it's you, but…
I wasn't expecting that.'

She decided to try and claw back some control. 'You
weren't expecting floundering fish sex?'

He smiled. 'Exactly. Look, I know you're scared by it,
but it doesn't have to change anything. This is something casual, friends with benefits, nothing more.'

She looked at him. The way they had made love, the
way he had kissed her and held her after like she was
something precious and adored, nothing about this was
casual, but at least labelling it as such felt like it gave her
some protection.

'You sure?'

'Of course,' he replied. 'I promise I'm not going to
ask you to marry me or anything like that.'

She leaned up and kissed him and he stroked down
her bare back, holding her so gently and lovingly, he'd
practically gone back on his words already.

She pulled back and started putting on her clothes
that had been cast aside in the throes of passion. For the
first time, she noticed all the work the elves had done
Christmasifying the house over the last few days, at least
from the inside. She was part of the outside crew so she
hadn't been part of this. The tree was beautifully decorated, looking like it belonged in a high-end department
store or posh restaurant. There was nothing gaudy or
tacky about this tree, there were no toilet-roll Santas or
handprint angels, or footprint reindeers with googly
eyes like she had on her tree. And while this was stunning, she much preferred her own tree; it had character.

There were red Christmas throws everywhere, large exquisitely wrapped presents under the tree, a holly and pine cone garland above the fireplace and just the right amount of lights around the room to make it twinkly and cosy. She knew the last thing they would add was a large throne for the big man himself to sit on.

'We need to make it to your bedroom next time,' she told him. 'I don't feel right about making love somewhere where hundreds of innocent children will be sitting telling Santa their hopes and dreams.'

Quinn pulled a face. 'Yeah, I know what you mean. I'll wash all these rugs and throws before Santa gets here. My house isn't really my own in December, I'm sorry about that.'

'You don't need to apologise. It's not like we can christen every room in my house with gay abandon either.'

'Well if I do spend the night with you at yours, we'll just make sure we're quiet so Zara doesn't hear.'

'Oh, it's OK for you to stay over but not for me to have a parade of random men there?' Alex teased, referring to his little rant the day before when he found out she was dating. So much had happened since then.

'I hope there won't be any random men at all,' Quinn said.

She smiled. She knew that technically he didn't have any right to stop her seeing other men as they were supposed to be casual, with no strings attached, but she also knew she could never sleep with another man now. He had ruined her for other men.

She slipped her arms round his neck again. 'Fortunately for you, I wouldn't have enough time to teach multiple men how not to be bad at sex. Yours is such a bad case, it will take many months of work, so I'm going to have to work with you exclusively.'

'And I'm willing to put the work in, whatever it takes,' Quinn said, although she knew he was talking about a lot more than sex. 'Come on, let me take you home.'

She pulled on her boots and her coat and stepped into the night. It was magical outside, every surface covered in a sparkly blanket. It was completely quiet, as if the world was just theirs for one night.

'I'll just grab my car keys,' Quinn said.

'Shall we walk? It's beautiful out here.'

'Sure, OK.'

He closed the door and locked it behind him, falling in at her side as they walked through Christmas Gardens. It felt like the most natural thing in the world to slip her hand into his. Without missing a beat, he entwined his fingers with hers.

There was no sound except the crunching of the snow under their feet. The golden streetlights caused the snow to twinkle in the darkness. Flakes were still dancing through the air but they weren't falling as fast as they had been when she'd arrived. All the roofs as far as she could see were covered in sparkly snow, looking almost blue under the moonlight. It looked like the whole of Lovegrove Bay had been Christmasified by the elves, not just Quinn's house. It looked beautiful.

'Oh, I had another message from St Nick,' Alex said. 'And he's a big fan of *Midsomer Murders* too. But also his second clue points to him being one of the elves.'

'Wow? That reduces the pool of possible suspects quite significantly.'

'I know, I'm so excited. Also, he's married or has a girlfriend.'

Quinn seemed confused by that. 'Really?'

'Yes, he said he enjoyed watching *Midsomer Murders* with his other half.'

'Ah right, yes.'

'We'll have to make a list of all the male elves and try to whittle it down from there.'

'Good idea.'

They fell into silence as they walked through the quiet, snowy streets and she knew he was deep in thought.

'Are you OK?' Alex asked.

'Yes, I was just thinking I wish, more than anything, I had been in your life when Liam fell off the wagon. I don't think I could have done anything to help him as I couldn't help him before, but I could have helped you. I hate that you went through that alone. If I'd known, I'd have got you and Zara out of there.'

Alex stopped and reached up to stroke his face. 'And I would have loved you for trying but I couldn't leave him, no matter how vile he became. I think you swooping in and saving me would have pushed him over the edge and it felt like he was hanging on by his fingertips anyway. I tried so hard to help him, getting him into counselling, getting him into rehab, but he had to choose to want to get better and he never did.'

Snowflakes were melting on his eyelashes as he looked at her. 'You were trying to help him but no one was there to help you. I would never have let him treat you that way. And that damage has had lasting consequences. That's why you never moved on before.'

'Yeah, I think so. I didn't realise it before and now I feel like there's a mental block, stopping me from trusting someone with my heart. Liam loved me so much and look how that turned out.'

Quinn didn't say anything for a while. But what could he say? He couldn't turn back the clock.

They approached her house, the one Alex had shared with Liam, the one where she'd watched her marriage fall apart. Maybe she needed a change of scenery; they could sell the house and move somewhere new. Would that help her move on? Or was she the thing that needed to change? She probably needed to fix herself rather than the things around her.

'What will it take to get you to trust me?' Quinn asked, quietly.

'Time. There is nothing you can say or do to take away that pain but one day I will be brave enough to take that step with you.'

'And I'll be here waiting, until you do,' he assured her.

And when she did she would have to be brave enough to tell him the truth about the night Liam died. If not before. She was a coward and she hated herself for not coming clean about it before. Not telling him for all this time made it worse.

They reached her back door.

'I'd ask you in, but after the last few hours I'm pretty sure how that would go.'

Quinn grinned. 'Yeah probably, so I'll just say goodnight and I'll see you tomorrow morning.'

She nodded but she didn't make a move to go in and he didn't make a move to leave either.

He leaned forward and cupped her face and kissed her and she smiled against his lips.

'You need to stop trying to make me fall in love with you.'

He smiled and stepped back. 'Never. Goodnight, Alex.'

He started walking away and she couldn't help smiling. She was in so much trouble.

CHAPTER 10

❄

Quinn walked into Sweet Escapes the next morning to see if they had any more custard Danishes for Alex or perhaps something else. She had a sweet tooth and he liked being able to do this for her from time to time. Plus he figured she'd probably worked up a bit of an appetite from the night before

His cousin Max was serving behind the counter when he approached and Quinn placed his order for a box of strawberry and white chocolate muffins as they didn't have any of the Danishes. The place was unusually quiet. A lot of people would grab stuff on their way to school or work so he was surprised to see he was the only customer. Although it had snowed heavily overnight so perhaps the weather was putting some people off.

'Cleo found a bauble this morning,' Max said, as he boxed up Quinn's order.

'She did?' Quinn said.

'Yeah, it had her famous Christmas tree cupcake on it. She's so excited. And it just makes me want to find the guy who's doing this and give him a big hug.'

'I'm sure St Nick would really appreciate that,' he said, dryly.

Max grinned. 'By the way, is Alex OK after the other night?' he asked.

Quinn frowned in confusion. How could Max possibly know what had happened between them?

'After that idiot was shouting at her because of her allergy,' Max said, clearly wondering why he was having to explain it when Quinn had been the one to come and pick her up.

'Oh yeah, she's fine,' Quinn said.

'Dating is a minefield, there don't seem to be any normal men out there, apart from me and you. Which begs the question, why are you letting her go out with these weirdos?'

'Let her? Since when am I in charge of who she dates? She has to decide that for herself.'

'I meant, you've been in love with her for what, three, four years now. You should be the one to date her not these losers.'

Quinn sighed. He'd never told anyone about his feelings for Alex, least of all his family in case they thought he was being disloyal to his brother. But he guessed he must have been kind of obvious about it.

'That has to be her choice too,' he said. 'And right now, after everything she went through with Liam, she's not ready for another relationship.'

Max frowned. 'Was he up to his old ways with her too? I kind of thought he had sorted his life out when I heard at the funeral that he'd got married.'

'I thought that too and for a while that was true, they were happy. But then he fell off the wagon and she bore the brunt of it for eighteen months before he died.'

'Oh crap, I didn't know,' Max said, his eyes wide. 'I mean, I suspected something like that had happened with the way he died but I didn't realise she'd lived with that for a while.'

'I know, me neither. She never left him because she wanted to help him and now she wears the scars like barbed wire round her heart.'

Max shook his head. 'Then she definitely doesn't need to be dating idiots.'

'Fortunately, I don't think she'll be dating anyone for a while.'

Cleo walked up then, placing a tray of freshly made mince pies into the display cabinet. 'Are you talking about Alex? Max told me what happened the other night at Alberto's, poor love. But she can't give up on love because of two bad dates.'

'I think it's a bit more than that,' Quinn said, wishing he hadn't been drawn on talking about Alex's private business.

'She could double date with me,' Cleo said. 'Then we can help each other weed out the bad eggs.'

'You're dating?' Max said. 'You said you never wanted to date another man ever again.'

'Well that was because my last boyfriend was a

cheating scumbag. But while I don't really want to go down the relationship route right now, I could date to support Alex and to give me a chance to see the calibre of men who are out there.'

'Well, I could be your plus one,' Max said. 'And we can both go along and help Alex. That way, I can eject any weirdos and you don't have to date any of them yourself.'

Quinn suppressed a smirk. If it was obvious that he'd been transparent about his feelings towards Alex, then it was equally obvious that Max had been in love with Cleo for a while. Well, obvious to everyone except Cleo.

'I guess that could work,' Cleo shrugged.

Although that didn't work for Quinn. He knew that what he had with Alex was a very casual arrangement and she'd been very clear there were no strings, but the thought of her lying in his bed after they'd made love and then getting up to date someone else made him feel sick. Fortunately, she had sort of promised him their no-strings-attached arrangement was exclusive, which he knew was a contradiction in terms.

But that wasn't something he could discuss with Max and Cleo.

'I don't think we should push Alex into dating,' Quinn tried. 'She has to be ready for that.'

'I think she needs some help to get back on the horse,' Cleo insisted.

Quinn sighed, knowing he was fighting a losing battle.

'You know, I'm something of a matchmaker,' Cleo

went on. 'I have a knack for finding the right people for each other. Two couples I've set up on blind dates are now happily married. I bet I could find the perfect person for her. Leave it with me and I'll see what I can do.'

Two happily married couples didn't seem like the extensive track record Cleo was making it out to be, so Quinn wasn't exactly worried about some big romantic success story, but it was a little frustrating that he couldn't just tell them that he and Alex were sort of seeing each other – although technically he couldn't even call it that.

He paid for his order and then walked the short distance to Alex's house. There was quite a thick layer of snow on the ground this morning and although it wasn't coming down heavily like it had been the night before, it was still falling gently, adding to the snow that had already fallen.

He could see her in the kitchen as he approached. He knocked softly on the door and let himself in. Her smile at seeing him lit up her whole face and that made him feel warm inside.

He was desperate to kiss her again but he wasn't sure if that was allowed.

'Morning,' he said, moving closer.

'Hi.' Her hands moved to reach for him but then fell back by her sides as if she didn't know the rules either, even though she was the one making them.

'Where's Zara?' Quinn asked.

'In the shower.'

'And Immy?'

'Walking Jacob.'

That was all he needed to know. He stepped up, cupped her face and kissed her and felt her smile against his lips as she slid her hands round his neck. He was never ever going to get enough of this woman. He just wished he could shout about their relationship from the rooftops. And that he could call it a relationship in the first place.

He pulled back to look at her, leaning his forehead against hers, and she smiled up at him.

'Is this allowed in our arrangement?' he asked.

'It's very much allowed.'

'Good, I don't think I could go all day and not kiss you.' He gestured to the box he'd left on the table. 'I brought you these. Before you get excited, no apple Danishes today, so these are the strawberry and white chocolate muffins that Zara loves.'

'Oh, she will love you for that and eating one won't exactly be a hardship for me either.'

'Max and Cleo were worried about you after the other night. Max is worried about you dating idiots and Cleo wants to set you up on a blind date. I, umm... told them you weren't ready to date yet but Cleo was most insistent.'

'Oh, I'll make up some excuse, you don't need to worry.'

Quinn wanted to say that it would be far easier if they were just honest with people that they were seeing each other but it was so new and fragile, he didn't want to put any pressure on her.

Just then there was a thunder of feet as Zara came running down the stairs. He took a few steps away from Alex.

'We have a snow day,' Zara almost shouted, bursting into the kitchen. 'The school is closed.'

'You do?' Alex said, checking her phone. 'Oh wow, you're right.'

'I heard it on the radio. I've never had a snow day before,' Zara said, bubbling with excitement. 'What do we do?'

Quinn smiled. God he loved this kid. 'What do we do? We make snowmen, we have snowball fights, we go sledging and we drink lots of hot chocolate covered in whipped cream and sprinkles.'

Zara's eyes lit up. 'I don't have to do schoolwork?'

He was about to say no but she wasn't his to make those kind of decisions for. Alex might want her to practise her times tables or write a story about a snow witch or something.

'Nope, that's the beauty of a snow day, school's closed so no schoolwork,' Alex said. 'This kind of snow happens so rarely that we have to make the most of it. I'll have to go to work for a few hours around lunchtime, but we can have fun this morning and this afternoon.'

Quinn knew that this time of year was their busiest period and Alex wouldn't want to miss out on crucial sales, but lunchtime was the time of day when most people would come so they had plenty of time to have some fun this morning before the lunchtime rush.

'Yes!' Zara did a little victory dance.

'Go and get changed into something warm and then we'll head out,' Alex said.

Zara bombed out of the room and thundered back upstairs.

To Quinn's surprise Alex wrapped her arms round his neck and she kissed him briefly.

'You don't have to give up your morning at work for us,' she said. 'I know how popular your little monsters are at this time of year, I don't want you to miss out on any sales.'

'Are you kidding? I'm not going to miss out on Zara's first snow day. How often do we get snow like this that we can actually play in? I wouldn't miss it for the world.'

She smiled. 'Thank you. She will love that she gets to share this with you.'

Just then he saw movement out the window and he looked up to see Immy trudging through the snow with a very wet and grumpy-looking Jacob, the snow sticking to his fur in little balls.

Quinn quickly took a step back away from Alex just as Immy came through the back door.

'Wow, it's really deep in some parts. I lost Jacob a few times,' Immy said, stamping her feet on the mat.

'Zara has a snow day,' Alex said.

'I thought she might, the roads are quite bad and so many of the teachers come from out of the area.'

Zara came running back into the kitchen and spotted Immy. 'I've got a snow day!'

'I heard, lucky you. Oh I'm quite jealous, I wish I could join you for some snow fun instead of going to boring work.'

'Well, we can make Christmas cookies this afternoon and we'll be sure to save you some,' Alex said.

'Yes!' Zara punched the air, clearly about to have her best day ever.

'Well that's something to look forward to,' Immy said, giving her niece a kiss on the forehead. She started prepping Jacob's breakfast.

'Go and get your coat and hat on,' Alex said, and Zara ran out of the kitchen at top speed.

'How was your date with Pip last night?' Immy asked.

'I cancelled, I went to see Quinn for a chat.'

Immy stopped what she was doing and looked between the two of them. She must have seen what was written all over their faces. 'Good chat then?'

Alex actually blushed, which he found adorable.

'It was a *very* good chat,' Alex said.

Quinn laughed, he couldn't help it. Alex might as well have hired a plane to write it in the sky.

'Well, finally,' Immy said. 'I've been waiting for you two to *chat* for years.'

The fact that Alex had all but told her sister gave him hope that this was more than the casual arrangement she had agreed with him.

'And where were you last night, you weren't here when I got back?' Alex asked.

'Well I, umm… had a chat with Xander.'

Quinn hadn't expected that.

Alex's eyes widened in shock. 'Another chat?'

'Wait, this was the second chat with Xander?' Quinn asked.

'Second, third and fourth,' Immy giggled, turning away so she wouldn't see their reaction. 'Although I'm pretty sure the fourth one was the last chat. He has Etta to think of. It's complicated. Well not for me, but for him apparently. Anyway, I had fun so that's all that matters. If he doesn't want more fun that's his problem not mine.'

Quinn exchanged glances with Alex. He could tell Immy was trying her best to be nonchalant about it but she was clearly a bit hurt by the brush-off. Xander had made it very clear to anyone who asked, especially his family, that he wasn't looking for another mum for Etta and that he would raise her alone. He had completely withdrawn into himself ever since his wife died, but it looked like Immy had made him peer out of his shell, at least a little. Maybe Quinn needed to have a word with his cousin. Or maybe he needed to keep his nose out of other people's business.

Zara ran back into the kitchen. 'I'm ready.'

'Then let snow day commence,' Alex said.

❄

Alex watched Quinn sledging down the hill with Zara, holding her on his lap like she was something precious, and she knew she had fallen for him a little bit more. Probably the most important thing she was looking for in a man was that he would love Zara as much as he loved her. That hadn't really been a factor before when she'd started dating because she'd known she wasn't really looking for a serious relationship. Yes, she'd been put off by Dave when he'd made it obvious that he didn't like children, because even dating someone casually would be hard if they didn't want anything to do with her daughter. But this – not just tolerating her daughter or being friendly, but loving her like she was his own – was everything.

Cheering from Harley, Zara's best friend and Chloe, Harley's mum, snapped Alex out of her reverie. She needed to make sure she wasn't caught looking at Quinn with loving eyes if she wanted to keep what they had a secret.

'Go on Zara,' Harley shouted as Zara and Quinn hurtled down the hill towards them.

They reached the bottom of the hill, laughing and shrieking together. OK, the shrieking was definitely more Zara than Quinn but they were both clearly having an amazing time.

'That was so much fun, I went way faster with Quinn than I did with you,' Zara said.

Alex thought about whether to have a scientific discussion about why that was the case but, although Zara was a lot smarter than most of the kids in her class (according to her teacher anyway), she wasn't sure if she was ready for a lesson on mass, gravitational pull, friction and aerodynamics. And she had promised her daughter there would be no schoolwork that day.

'That's because he's a better sledger than I am,' Alex said.

'You should go with Quinn, then you'd go super fast,' Zara jumped up and down with excitement.

'I'm not sure I'd fit on the sleigh with Quinn,' Alex said.

'You sit on his lap like I do.'

'I'm probably too big for that.'

'You can sit on my lap,' Quinn said, arching an eyebrow at her.

'Go on. Do it,' Zara urged. 'And I can record the moment you fall off on your phone.'

'What makes you think I'll fall off?' Alex said.

'I think you will. I'll stay here with Harley,' Zara said. The way she said that made Alex think she had an ulterior motive to this idea. Harley nodded eagerly.

Chloe nodded too. 'Go on, I'll watch them.'

Feeling like she couldn't say no, Alex nodded and she and Quinn started trudging up the hill.

'They want to throw snowballs at us,' Quinn said, when they were out of hearing distance.

'Oh, is that right?'

'We can load up with our own snowballs and throw them at them as we fly past.'

'Good idea.'

They walked up the hill a bit, dragging the sledge behind them.

'I was surprised that you told Immy about us earlier,' Quinn said.

'Yeah. I wasn't really intending on telling anyone, but Immy knows me better than I know myself. She would have found out very quickly. I'm a terrible liar and I hate lying to her.'

Quinn was silent for a moment and she wondered what he was thinking.

'Why do you not want to tell anyone?' he said finally.

She shrugged. 'Because how would I describe it? We're not dating, we're not in a relationship but we are so much more than friends with benefits, so much more.'

'But it's no one's business except ours how we define it. You don't need to go into details. We just tell people that we're seeing each other.'

'But telling people leads to an expectation, especially with us, they know how close we are. *"When are you moving in together, when are you getting married, when are you having children?"* And I'm not ready for any of those things. I had that, I had all of that, and my husband threw it away. And my heart says I can trust you, you won't hurt me in that way, but I never thought Liam would hurt me either. I just need time to get my head round this.'

'I understand.'

'You do? I don't want to hurt you. It's not that I'm ashamed of you or anything like that. I also worry how

Violet will react and there's no point upsetting her with this yet.'

'No, that's true.'

'And there's Zara to think of too,' she reminded him. 'I'm not sure how I tell her that we're together. You're her uncle, I wonder if she'll find that weird.'

'Or maybe she'll love it.'

Alex smiled. Zara probably would actually but she still didn't want to have that conversation with her daughter yet. Not when she couldn't even describe what she and Quinn had to herself, let alone to other people.

They reached the crest of the hill and kept walking until they were out of sight from Zara and anyone else down there.

She reached up and slid her arms around Quinn's shoulders. 'Are you OK with this?'

'Yes of course, I'm happy with whatever part of you you want to give me. I don't like hiding it and sneaking around as if we're doing something wrong, but I do understand why you want to keep it quiet.'

Alex nodded. 'This is all so new between us and I don't want it damaged by other people when we're still trying to figure it out ourselves. But I want you to know how important this is to me. You mean the world to me and this is something special.'

'For me too. I'm sorry, I didn't mean to pressure you into something more.'

'It's OK, I understand the need to shout it from the rooftops, believe me. No one is more happy about this than me. I've been wanting this for years. Just give me time.'

'I will.'

She reached up to kiss him and everything about the kiss told her this was the man she was meant to be with but the more she fell in love with him, the scarier it became.

She pulled back. 'Let's get the snowballs ready for our attack.'

They spent a few moments gathering the snowballs, then Quinn sat down in the sleigh.

'Come on, sit in my lap.'

Alex smiled, as she sat down. 'Don't get any ideas.'

'I get lots of ideas about you. Some of them I'm going to try out on you tonight.'

She felt a shiver of delight run through her at that thought.

'I just hope it won't be as bad as last time.' She felt his smile as he kissed her neck. 'Right, where can we put the snowballs? I can carry some in my lap.'

'We can load a few down the sides too.'

They spent a few moments loading as many as they could around the edge of the sleigh and in her lap on top of her coat.

'Right, are you ready?' Quinn asked.

'Yes, just hold onto me. I don't want a video of me falling out at high speed making its way round social media.'

'I'll always hold you.'

He pushed off and the sledge moved forward a little

before it teetered over the edge and then took off down the hill. Quinn wrapped his arms around her, holding her close against his chest, and the sledge very quickly picked up speed.

'Christ, that is fast,' Alex said as the hills and trees whizzed past.

'Er, yeah it is,' Quinn said, uncertainty in his voice, which is not exactly what anyone wants to hear when they are on a vehicle speeding a hundred miles an hour with no way to steer it or stop it.

Within seconds they reached the bottom of the hill where Alex spotted Zara and Harley waiting with arms full of snowballs. She grabbed one of her snowballs and threw it wildly, but it went nowhere near them. However, one of their snowballs hit her square in the face and then they were past them, still hurtling at what felt like hundreds of miles an hour towards the frozen lake.

'Shit,' Quinn said. 'We have to bail.'

'What? You want me to throw myself out of the speeding vehicle?'

'On three.'

'What?!'

But the lake was getting closer and they weren't slowing down even the slightest.

'Three,' yelled Quinn, and with that he launched them both out of the sledge where they tumbled and rolled through the snow together. She finally came to a stop with Quinn on top of her. His eyes filled with concern, his arms cradling her body and head.

'Are you OK?'

'Of course I am, I'm with you.'

A smile brightened his face. 'I so want to kiss you right now.'

'And I really want you to.'

However, any thoughts of kissing went straight out the window as a snowball exploded against the side of Quinn's face. Somebody clearly had a really good aim.

Quinn blinked in surprise and then shot up, roaring like a monster. The two girls scattered, squealing with laughter as they ran away and Quinn chased after them.

'That looked like fun,' Chloe said, her eyebrows waggling mischievously.

'What, the near-death experience?' Alex said.

'No, the bit after that. I didn't know you and Quinn were together.'

'We're not.'

Chloe gave her a look that said she didn't believe her for a second.

'We're not,' Alex insisted, knowing she was a terrible liar and Chloe would most likely see right through it.

'Then you should be. That man is in love with you and I'm pretty sure you're in love with him too. I've always thought you two were perfect for each other. I'm not quite sure what's holding you back.'

Alex was beginning to wonder that herself.

❄

Dear St Nick,

Sorry I didn't reply to your message last night, I had a bit of a busy and unexpected night.

I love that you love Midsomer too and that's something you and your other half share. Does she know you're St Nick, what does she think about you doing such a kind thing for the people of Lovegrove Bay? And if she doesn't know, how are you painting all these baubles without her seeing you?

I know from your clue yesterday that you're one of the elves helping to decorate Santa's cottage tonight and I'm excited that I get to work alongside you, even though I might not know which elf you are. I dare you to come and talk to me tonight. Not to identify yourself, just say a few words and maybe I can whittle down my choices even more.

Warmest wishes,

Alex

CHAPTER 11

❄

Alex arrived back at her house after the lunchtime rush ready to have some more fun in the snow with Zara. Quinn had been dealing with a customer when she left the Wonky Tree Studios so she'd waved and left him to it. She wasn't expecting him to give up his whole day to play with her daughter. This time of year was the busiest for all the artists.

Violet had happily taken Zara for a few hours and they were going to make some Christmas cookies and, by the smell of it as she opened the kitchen door, they'd done exactly that.

The kitchen was spotless, probably more so than when Alex had left, apart from a small area on the kitchen table where they were decorating… heart-shaped cookies.

Zara looked up with a big smile on her face and icing on her fingers.

'We've made Christmas heart cookies, to give as gifts to the ones we love.'

That sounded like they might be confusing their holidays, although to be fair Christmas was about giving gifts to the ones you love too, as well as Valentine's Day.

'That sounds lovely.' Alex glanced at Violet.

'Oh, I couldn't find the Christmas cookie cutters, so this seemed like the best option,' Violet shrugged. 'And they are decorated with Christmas accessories.'

The heart cookies were beautifully decorated with sparkly snowflakes, holly leaves, berries, baubles and little iced snowmen, plus lashings of sparkly sprinkles.

'They look beautiful,' Alex said, picking up a tiny sugar snowflake and popping it in her mouth. 'You've worked so hard.'

'We made loads,' Zara told her. 'I'm going to give one to you, Immy, Quinn and Nanny because I love you all. I wanted to give one to Jacob but Nanny said that was probably not a good idea.'

Alex looked down at the dog and Jacob licked his lips in anticipation.

'No, probably not. Sorry Jacob.'

'I made you a special one to give to Quinn.'

'Oh, I...' Alex found herself blushing and floundering for words. In Zara's innocent view of the world, of course Alex loved Quinn in the same way that Zara did. She clearly didn't mean the head-over-heels kind which was closer to the truth.

'When we were discussing who we were giving them

to, I was trying to explain that there are different kinds of love,' Violet explained, looking flustered herself.

'That's true,' Alex said, not sure if she was ready for this kind of conversation with her daughter.

Just then Quinn arrived in the kitchen.

'I know that,' Zara said, as if trying to explain to the uneducated. 'Mum and Quinn love me because we're family, but Mum and Quinn love each other with heart eyes like the heart eye emoji. I can see it. So I made you a heart biscuit with extra hearts on to give to Quinn and I made the same for him to give to you because you love each other.'

There was silence in the room as Zara opened the tin and brought out two heart-shaped biscuits covered in tiny red hearts. She offered them out to Alex and Quinn.

'What's going on?' Quinn asked, in confusion.

'Zara made heart biscuits to give as gifts to the ones we love. She thinks we love each with heart eyes not just because we're family so she made us special heart biscuits to give to each other,' Alex quickly surmised.

'You have to give it to each other and tell them you love them,' Zara said.

Alex expected more of an awkward silence but Quinn simply shrugged, took the biscuit and handed it to Alex.

'I love you.'

Alex found herself smiling from ear to ear. It was silly. It didn't mean anything but she couldn't stop the big silly grin on her face at hearing those words.

She took the cookie from him and then took the second heart cookie from Zara and handed it to him. 'I love you.'

He now had the same soppy grin on his face.

'See, that wasn't that hard, was it,' Zara said, before returning her attention back to the cookie she was busily decorating.

Alex and Quinn continued to stare at each other with matching grins on their faces before she remembered that her otherwise distracted daughter was not the only person in the room with them. She took a step back and looked at Violet for her reaction to all this only to find she had a big grin on her face too.

❄

Dear Alex,

My other half doesn't know I'm St Nick, well not yet anyway. We don't actually live together so I can paint when I'm at my house, but a lot of the baubles were painted prior to December and that's why there are so many baubles being delivered every day, otherwise I'd never have time to paint them all.

I'm looking forward to seeing you tonight at Santa's cottage. I will try to say a few words to you, if it seems appropriate.

Your clue for today is that I'll also be wearing an elf hat tonight.

Snowy hugs,
St Nick

❄

The decorating of Santa's house was probably the biggest night of the year in the Lovegrove Bay calendar and also the most secret. Which of course meant most of the town would know. Only the elves were supposed to know the date, well that was the theory. As most of the elves were parents of young children, those children needed babysitting while their parents sneaked out to do elf duties. The elves' plans had to be cancelled or rearranged to fit in with being an elf so, by the time the big night rolled around, almost everyone knew. Apart from the children. The magic of the house being decorated overnight was such a special thing for the kids of the town that the adults at least took that part very seriously. There were never any pictures thrown up on social media of the decorating process just in case it was seen by innocent eyes. Any children who lived near or around Christmas Gardens were often squirrelled away to relatives' houses for the night so they wouldn't inadvertently look out of their windows and ruin the magic.

Alex loved doing it, she always looked forward to this night but with the limited sleep she'd got the night before lying in bed thinking about Quinn, and the busy day today playing in the snow, she was exhausted. Still, she did have an extra reason to look forward to tonight as she'd be spending it with Quinn again, or at least she would after all the elves had gone home. She couldn't wait to be with him again.

She was also looking forward to seeing St Nick, even if she still didn't know who it was. She would be on high alert when any of the male elves spoke to her and especially any wearing an elf hat. She knew a few of the elves liked to dress up in character, although most people didn't.

She saw Quinn ahead chatting to someone but stopped dead when she saw he was wearing an elf hat.

Her heart leapt. Was Quinn really St Nick? She thought back to her messages with St Nick. Quinn loved *Midsomer Murders* and all the cosy mysteries, just like St Nick did, and they would often watch them together. Quinn wasn't a painter and he worked in a place with a lot of footfall. Even Flick had thought it was Quinn a few days before. Why had Alex dismissed that when she started getting the messages?

But as she glanced around she realised that pretty much every person there was also wearing an elf hat.

She couldn't help smiling. St Nick had tricked her. Although now the idea had been planted, she would be looking at Quinn a little bit more closely. She tried to be practical about it. She'd never seen Quinn painting but he was always very good whenever they played Pictionary with Zara and Immy, although his drawings were never as detailed as the baubles were. St Nick had called his wife or girlfriend – probably his girlfriend as they didn't live together – his other half. But when St Nick sent that message, she and Quinn weren't together.

They weren't technically together now, but they had certainly been less together then than they were now. The term 'other half' was normally reserved for someone you'd been dating a while or were married to, not just a friend. A lot of things pointed to him being St Nick but there wasn't anything conclusive right now.

She walked closer. He was talking to someone about the fake glittery snowy roof they were going to attach to his roof. It went on in large custom-made panels but overlapped in such a way that it looked like one big snowy roof. They would have to clear the real snow off to put the fake stuff on, which felt counterintuitive but the real snow probably wouldn't last long. In fact the whole of Christmas Gardens was supposed to be covered in fake snow as part of the decorating. Alex wondered if they still intended to do that or maybe come back later considering how beautiful the real stuff looked right now.

It was as if Quinn sensed she was there as he suddenly turned round and a big smile spread across his face, probably matching the one on her own.

Someone came up to him to talk to him, gesturing at the roof and he turned to face them which was probably a good thing. People would start to notice, just like Chloe had when they were stupidly staring at each other while they were sledging earlier that day.

She noticed there was a group of women excitedly talking about something and as she stepped closer she realised that one of them had one of St Nick's coveted baubles.

'I just found it over there, under the tree,' Suzie said, as the other ladies admired it.

Alex stepped a bit closer, not wanting to appear nosy but desperate to see what was painted on this one. She could see it was a little potting shed, surrounded by flowers, a pair of wellies and a spade. It was lovely.

'What will you do with it?' Frankie said.

'I'll give it to my hubby, he loves his little allotment, probably more than he loves me.'

The women laughed.

'Don't you mind that he spends all his time there?' Aggie asked.

'Mind? When he's there I get some peace and quiet.'

All the women laughed again and Alex moved away.

So many of the townspeople had received a bauble, she wondered how St Nick had the time to make them all. He did say that a lot of them had been painted prior to December but it was still a massive undertaking. And surely someone would have noticed St Nick hiding the baubles around town by now, but no one had. How was he managing to do it so secretly?

She sighed because, although the clues were helping, she was still no closer to working it out. Especially if he was throwing her red herrings like the elf hat.

She looked around as preparations were made to start decorating the house and gardens. There were some decorations that were reused year after year, like the lights on the fences and around the windows and eaves of the house and some of the Christmas trees, but other than that there was a different theme each year.

Last year it was a space theme and there'd been lots of googly-eyed cute aliens positioned around the gardens. Quinn had even donated some of his cute cutlery monsters.

This year the theme was 'enchanted forest' and lots of lanterns had been made in the shape of forest animals and, because it was enchanted, there were also fairies and unicorns. These were currently being unpacked out of a large van and it was Alex's job for the night to lay them out around the house and gardens in such a way that it looked like a forest scene, not just dumped out of the van. Another van was unloading Christmas trees and other forest-type trees to help with the scene so she decided to start helping to unload those and positioning them around the house and throughout the garden. It was a lot easier to create the enchanted forest scene once the forest itself was in place.

She went to the back of the van and climbed in. Some of the trees were quite big and she wasn't sure she could move them by herself. Although they were fake so might be a lot lighter than they looked. She was just trying to decide which trees to move first when Quinn hopped up into the van.

'Do you need a hand?' he asked.

'Aren't you on roof duty?'

'Yes, but they are going to clear the snow off the roof first, so I'm not needed for a bit. I can help you unload.'

'I'm not sure how heavy they are, they are only plastic after all.' She lifted one of the bigger ones. 'Oh, they're not too bad. Maybe you can help me lift them down off the van and then I can put them in the right positions.'

'I can do that.'

They worked side by side for a while, unloading the van until there was only one tree left. Alex hopped up into the van to get it and Quinn joined her. He handed her a key.

'The upstairs is locked.'

The upstairs of Quinn's or rather Santa's house was like a self-contained flat – bedrooms, bathroom, kitchen, lounge – so Quinn could continue to live there separate to the Christmassy goings-on downstairs. The upstairs door was always locked during the day so no wayward child would find their way into Quinn's part of the house. Tonight there were a lot of elves going in and out of the house, helping themselves to refreshments that had been laid out in the house, using the toilet and adding last-minute decorations to the downstairs. While they knew all the elves and no one was likely to traipse around the private part of his house uninvited, Alex knew Quinn had locked it just in case.

'When you're finished and people are starting to head home, just go upstairs, let yourself in and make yourself at home. I'll be up as soon as I can to join you.'

Alex felt a little shiver of excitement at the thought of what the night held. While she understood why Quinn didn't like the sneaking around, it did add an extra thrill to their relationship.

She nodded and pocketed the key.

'Oh, I have this for you,' Quinn said, pulling out an elf hat. She laughed as he positioned it on her head.

'Where did this come from?'

'I don't know, one of the elves was handing them out.'

'Which one?' she said, probably a bit too urgently.

He looked surprised by her tone. 'I… don't know. Actually there were several people giving them out, I think, someone just gave me one and told me I had to wear it. Why?'

'St Nick sent me a message to say he would be wearing an elf hat tonight.'

Quinn laughed. 'A good mystery just wouldn't be the same without a few red herrings.'

'Ordinarily I'd agree, but I only have four more days left to figure it out. On Christmas Eve, if I haven't found St Nick, he will disappear forever.'

'You'll solve the mystery, I have no doubt, you're brilliant at stuff like that.'

'When I first saw you wearing the hat, I did wonder whether it was you. Some of the clues even point to you too.'

'Is that right?' He didn't seem remotely fazed by her potentially discovering his secret.

'I can neither confirm nor deny those rumours.'

'That's not a no.'

'It's not a yes either,' he grinned and she knew he was teasing her.

One of the elves came to the back of the van. 'Quinn, we're ready for you now.'

'OK, I'll be there in a second.'

He quickly unloaded the last tree for her, gave her a wave and headed back towards the house.

She spent a few hours moving around trees and animal lanterns, with the help of some other elves, to create the perfect forest scene. With the fake and real snow and all the other lights and decorations it looked beautiful.

People were starting to call goodbye and head home, although some were still finishing off. Alex headed towards the house, catching Quinn's eye as he finished off the last bit of the roof. He nodded, subtly, then flashed his hands to show he'd be about five minutes. She walked into the house where a few other elves were just tidying up before leaving. She waited for the downstairs to be empty before she quickly sneaked up the stairs, let herself into Quinn's flat and looked around. There were a few simple Christmas decorations in here, a tree and some lights. It looked nice, but nothing like the over-the-top Christmas grotto downstairs.

She washed her face, cleaned her teeth, got undressed so she was completely naked and then slipped into his bed, waiting for him, wondering whether to lie in an alluring pose.

She waited ten minutes and then waited some more.

The next thing she was aware of was Quinn slipping into the bed next to her, taking her in his arms and holding her close.

'Oh, god, sorry,' Alex mumbled. 'I fell asleep.'

'I could tell, but it's OK, it means I get to do this instead which is just as good.'

Alex felt her eyes closing again as she snuggled into his chest. 'Just give me five minutes and I'll be ready to go for a night of passion.'

She heard him chuckle softly and kiss her head, then she knew no more.

CHAPTER 12

Alex woke up in the early hours of the morning. It was pitch black outside but the snow was making everything seem so much brighter.

She was lying on Quinn's bare chest with his arms wrapped around her. A quick look under the sheets showed her he was completely naked too and there was something wonderfully intimate about that. She looked up at him while he slept. She was so in love with this man and she knew she was playing a dangerous game here because spending time with him like this meant she was falling in love with him that little bit more. This was everything she'd ever wanted and she was too afraid to take it for fear of losing it all over again. Somehow, not putting a label on it felt safer but she knew that it wasn't.

She knew she couldn't live the rest of her life in fear and worrying about the what-ifs but that didn't make it any easier. And somehow losing Quinn would hurt more than losing Liam and she felt horribly disloyal acknowledging that but she knew that was the truth. Maybe it was because, by the end, she had resented Liam and the life she led with him so much that it was harder to look objectively at the life they'd had together before his best friend died. Or maybe it was because her feelings for Quinn were so much stronger than those she'd had for Liam.

She thought back to the day before when she and Quinn had told each other they loved each other. It had been such a simple, silly thing, love declared by an over-decorated cookie, but it had meant the world to her. She hadn't had a chance to talk to him about it and whether it was true; she didn't know if she wanted to because what if he said he didn't really love her? She'd also have to tell him whether her declaration was true and it would be very confusing to have to explain that she was utterly head over heels in love with him yet didn't want a relationship with him. She didn't even understand that herself.

Also there was the fear of finally telling Quinn the truth about the night Liam died. She couldn't go much further into this... relationship or whatever she was trying to call it without telling him. She made a snap decision: she would tell him what happened as soon as he woke up, then at least if he decided he hated her and didn't want any more to do with her, she could get out of this relatively unscathed. Who was she trying to kid? While she knew she'd be distraught if it all ended now, she'd be completely heartbroken if she never got to see Quinn again.

His eyes suddenly fluttered open and he smiled when he saw she was awake.

'Hey beautiful,' he said, stroking her hair.

Her heart soared with happiness.

'Hi. Sorry for falling asleep.'

'It's totally fine. I couldn't get away for a while. Besides, holding you in my arms was undoubtedly the best way to fall asleep.'

She smiled at that. 'I slept really well too, you must be good for me.'

'I like to think so.'

'You know you mean the world to me.'

He smiled. 'If you feel for me half of what I feel for you then I'd be happy.'

'It's probably more than that, a lot more.'

'It's impossible to feel more than what I feel.'

She laughed. 'Are we competing to see who feels the most for each other?'

'Ah, it's a competition I would win,' Quinn said, stroking her face. 'If you asked me to marry you, I'd be marching you down the aisle the very next day. If I asked you to marry me, I suspect I'd be seeing an Alex-shaped hole in that door.'

She stared at him in shock. 'You… You want to marry me?'

'Look, I'm not pressuring you in any way, I will wait however long it takes for you to get there. But I'm already there. I meant what I said yesterday. I never envisaged saying those words to you for the first time over a cookie with your daughter and my mum in attendance but I'm in love with you and have been for years.'

Alex stared at him, tears welling in her eyes.

'Hey, don't cry. I'd never want to do anything to upset you. Please just forget I said anything.'

She shook her head. She never wanted to forget hearing those words. Quinn loved her. Tears spilled down her cheeks. And now she could lose it all.

He stroked them away, eyes filled with concern. 'I'm so sorry.'

'Don't be,' her voice was choked. She wanted to say it back, to tell him she'd been in love with him almost since the first time they'd met, but the words were stuck in her throat.

So she did the only thing she could do, she leaned up and kissed him. He cupped the back of her head and kissed her back. She poured every ounce of love she had for this man into this kiss and she could feel the love he had for her too.

She pulled back before the kiss could turn into something else. 'I need to tell you something.' Oh god, now she'd blurted it out there was no going back. She sat up. 'And I think you're going to hate me.'

'Well, that's impossible.'

She took a deep breath. 'It's about Liam.'

'OK.' He sat up too, leaning against the headboard as she kneeled up next to him.

'And the night he died.'

'He was drunk, got in the car and lost control and drove into a tree. What more do I need to know?'

'It was my fault,' Alex all but whispered.

He frowned. 'How could it possibly be your fault?'

'You have to understand I had lived with the worst version of him for eighteen months. I was at breaking point.'

'I know how hard it must have been for you.'

'I knew I had to leave him not just for my own sanity but for Zara. She was getting older and wiser to what was happening and I didn't want her to grow up in that environment. But I was always scared that leaving him would push him over the edge. Then one day he picked Zara up from nursery. I had no idea he was going to do that, I was due to pick her up at three but he got there before me, I don't know why. I never left her alone with him because I just didn't trust him to look after her properly when he was always drunk. When I got home shortly after he'd picked her up, he was playing with her and it was quite obvious he was out of his head drunk. He'd picked our daughter up and driven home with her when he was drunk.'

Quinn took a sharp intake of breath.

'When I think about what could have happened.' She shook her head angrily. 'And that was the final straw. I snapped. I told him I was leaving and taking Zara with me. I said I would push for full custody and anyone looking at the state of him would give it to me. I told him he'd never see his daughter again. I was just so angry and I wanted to hurt him like he'd hurt me for the last eighteen months. We had a massive row and he got in his car and drove off. I immediately phoned the police to warn them that he was drink driving and they found his car half an hour later embedded in a tree. He never made it. And to this day, I've lived with the guilt that he died because of me, because I told him I was taking his daughter from him. She was his entire world. I'll never know if he simply lost control of the car or if it was deliberate but he would never have got in that car if it wasn't for me.'

She wiped the tears away and Quinn stared at her. He frowned but he didn't say anything. Oh god, it was over. More tears spilled over onto her face.

'Do you want me to go?'

He blinked in surprise. 'Why would I want you to go?'

'Because you must hate me, your brother is dead because of me.'

'No, honey, you can't think like that. Alcoholism is a sickness, and he had so many opportunities to get the help he needed and he didn't want it. Some people just can't be saved. None of this is your fault. My brother behaved abysmally. You had to do what you had to do to protect you and your daughter. And so what if things got a little heated? It was his decision to collect his daughter from nursery when he was drunk, his decision to get back in the car and drive off. And it wasn't the first time he'd driven while drunk. If he'd survived that accident, there would have been other times that had nothing to do with you. I can't believe you've been living with this guilt all this time and you never told me.'

'I never told you because I thought you'd hate me for it.'

He smiled sadly and cupped her face. 'I could never ever hate you. And regardless of what happened, you were not responsible for my brother's death. Only he was responsible for that.'

He pulled her onto his lap, wrapping the blanket around her and stroking her face. 'I love you with everything I have and there is nothing you could ever say or do, there is nothing that you did in the past, that can ever change that.'

'Really?'

'Yes, absolutely.'

'Do you think Violet will feel the same?'

'Well, I don't think she loves you in the same way I do – I'd be a bit worried if she did – but she knows what Liam was like. She won't blame you for this. No one could ever blame you for this, knowing what you had to put up with.'

Alex let out a huge sigh of relief. She'd finally got it off her chest after all this time and it was OK, she could finally let go of all this guilt she'd been clinging to for all these years. He pulled her close against his chest, stroking her back, and she felt all that stress melt away.

After a while she drew back and kissed him briefly on the lips. 'Thank you.'

'You have nothing to thank me for.'

'Thank you for loving me.'

'Oh, you make that very easy. You are the most wonderful, incredible person I've ever met.'

She smiled and kissed him, feeling so much relief that he was still here and he loved her, no matter what. She stroked his face and very quickly the kiss turned into something more. He slipped his hand between her legs and she moaned against his lips at his perfect touch, that feeling tightening and escalating out of control before she could catch her breath. She shouted out all manner of weird noises, gripping onto his shoulders as he took her over the edge.

She sat up and shifted so she was straddling him and took him deep inside of her. He let out a groan of pleasure and kissed her hard. He moved his hands down to her hips, holding her tight against him as they moved against each other. Already that feeling was building again inside of her until her whole body felt tight and coiled ready to explode.

He pulled back so he could kiss her throat, her chest, her breasts and she felt so completely adored by this man. She lifted his chin so she could kiss him again, knowing she'd never ever get enough of kissing him.

She pulled back slightly, leaning her forehead against his, her breath heavy against his lips.

He stroked her face. 'You are tremendous, Alexandra Campbell, and I love you so much.'

And it was those words that sent her soaring over the edge, her orgasm thundering through her like a freight train, shouting out his name as he moaned hers.

After, as he held her close, her body trembling in his

arms, he stared into her eyes and whispered that he loved her again and she kissed him, knowing that she wanted forever with this man, if only she was brave enough to tell him that.

❄

Alex all but floated home a while later, holding hands with Quinn as they walked along the snowy streets. He was in love with her. She had never felt so utterly happy as she did right now. It was everything she'd ever wanted. But when she thought ahead to marriage, more children, a happy ever after, that was when she started feeling scared about losing it all. The hurt she felt when she all but lost Liam overnight, the angst of living with his addiction for eighteen months, the anger, the shouting, the nastiness, the pain of the betrayal she'd felt when he'd chosen to spend time with the bottle instead of her and his daughter. She had lost her perfectly happy little marriage slowly and agonisingly every day and she couldn't bear going through that again.

This way was so much safer. Live for now, not think about the future.

Although she knew that was selfish and while it might be easier for her to live like this with no commitment, it probably wasn't easier for Quinn who was patiently waiting and hoping for her to give him more.

And she wanted to give him that. She didn't want to keep stringing him along and hurting him without giving him something.

She looked up at him, and he smiled down at her as tiny snowflakes swirled around them. God, her heart felt so full of him.

'I love you,' she blurted out before she could stop herself.

He stopped and turned to face her. 'What?'

There was no going back now even if she wanted to, which she didn't. She wanted to give him this.

'I know it's weird to hear me say that when I insist we're in a no-strings-attached, silly friends-with-benefits arrangement, but I do love you. So much. I've always loved you.'

A big smile stretched across his face and he cupped her face and kissed her. He pulled back, leaning his forehead against hers.

'Well, you have no idea how happy this makes me.'

She looked down, frowning slightly, hoping he wasn't going to get carried away.

He put a finger under her chin and lifted her head to look at him.

'This changes nothing, I promise,' he said, gently. 'We're still friends with benefits. It's just that one of those benefits is that we love each other. I promise, I'm not going to be giving you an engagement ring come Christmas Day. I'll wait as long as you need to be sure you can trust me.'

'I do trust you, I'm just…'

'Scared. I get it, I really do.'

'You do?'

'What you went through with Liam was horrible and

heartbreaking. I know it will take a while to get over that. And I have time.'

'Thank you.'

They walked on for a short while until they came to her house and propped up outside her gate was a small white box. Alex gasped when she realised what it was.

'St Nick has left a bauble.'

She picked up the box carefully and peered inside. There was St Nick's trademark white porcelain bauble, this one painted with a stunning bouquet of peonies.

'Oh, it's beautiful. I love it.'

'St Nick must have known they're your favourite flower,' Quinn said.

'You think he left it for me?' Alex said, in surprise.

'Maybe,' Quinn said. 'I mean, it is right outside your house.'

'Yes, but I can't keep it.'

'Why the hell not? It says on the gift label, keep, re-hide or gift to someone else. Why can't you keep it?'

'Because everyone who has found one so far has gifted it to someone else. It would be selfish of me to keep it.'

'That's not the case at all. Some people have gifted them, some have kept them. I'm sure St Nick wants the bauble to end up with someone who will find joy in that particular design, that's why he says to gift or re-hide it if that bauble isn't specific to the person who finds it. But this one is specific to you, it's *your* favourite flower.'

Alex wasn't convinced, although she really wanted to hang this on her tree. It was gorgeous.

'Maybe someone else has found it and gifted it to you,' Quinn went on. 'That would be insulting to the person who gifted it to you if you were to give it away. And it was outside your door. If St Nick or the person who gifted it meant it for someone else, it would probably have been left somewhere a bit more public or communal. I think this was meant for you.'

Her heart leapt at that thought. 'Well I certainly don't want to offend anyone by giving it away.'

'Come on, let's find a place for it on your tree. And if you feel guilty about it, you don't need to tell anyone, it'll be our little secret.'

She followed him back inside. The house was silent as it should be in the early hours of the morning – Immy had promised Zara an all-night movie marathon but Alex knew Immy would have had her in bed way before midnight. Although the school had already announced they would be closed the next day too, which was supposed to be Zara's last day at school, so it didn't really matter if they'd stayed up later.

They walked into the lounge where the tree glowed in the darkness, the Christmas lights twinkling.

'Where will you put it?' Quinn asked.

Alex took the bauble carefully out of the box and looked at the tree. 'I think right here next to Zara's roller skates would be the best place.'

She hung it on one of the branches where it caught the light of the fairy lights perfectly. It looked wonderful.

'I love the idea of gifting these Christmas baubles

secretly, and it's certainly captured the hearts of the people of Lovegrove Bay, but there is one problem.'

'What's that?' Quinn asked.

'His anonymity means I can't ever thank him. No one can.'

'Oh, I think he knows how grateful people are, it's a small town, I'm sure he is seeing all the reactions to it. Besides, someone like St Nick, doing something like this, he's not doing this for thanks, he's doing it to spread a little Christmas joy.'

Alex nodded. 'This thing he's doing is so lovely and I don't think he realises how touching and significant it is for the people who receive them. You saw how delighted Zara was with her roller skates bauble the other day, St Nick never got to see that. Unless it is you then you did see it. But so many people have messaged me after seeing that Facebook post saying how happy they were to receive them, some of them have real significance because the baubles remind them of lost loved ones. I just want to give whoever it is a big hug and say thank you. I really hope by Christmas Eve I will have found out who it is and maybe I'll even give him a bauble of his own. Something he really wants or loves to say thank you for all of this.'

'That does sound nice. Any clues from the Facebook posts and comments?'

'Not a single one. No one has ever seen him. How can that be?'

'He obviously doesn't want to be found, apart from by you.'

'Well, if he keeps throwing me red herrings like he did with the elf hat, I'm not going to find him either.'

'I thought it was pretty funny.'

'I did too, but it doesn't help.'

'Maybe he wants the magic to last until Christmas Eve, then all will be revealed.'

Alex looked at him through narrowed eyes; maybe it really was him after all.

CHAPTER 13

'Morning,' Quinn said, letting himself into Alex's kitchen the next day or rather later on that same morning.

Her face lit up at seeing him and he loved her reaction. His heart felt so full of her. This was the woman he was going to marry one day and, yes, that day may be many years in the future but the fact he got to be with her now, albeit secretly, was good enough for him.

She surreptitiously looked over her shoulder to see if Zara was around before wrapping her arms around him and giving him a kiss. 'Morning,' she said, the biggest smile on her face.

'I love you,' Quinn whispered. He was never going to get tired of saying those words to her or hearing them from her too. He never thought this would happen so it was like having all his Christmases come at once.

'I love you too, so much. Come for dinner tomorrow night, I want Zara to get used to seeing you more often, not just popping in before school or at work. I want her to be OK with this before we launch it on her.'

That made him feel happy too. If Alex wanted to tell Zara that must mean she wanted more than this friends-with-benefits arrangement.

'Of course, I'd be happy to,' he said.

'Happy to do what?' Zara said, appearing in the kitchen with her nose in a book.

Quinn quickly stepped back away from Alex, cursing that he hadn't heard her coming.

'Umm, Quinn is coming for dinner tomorrow.'

Zara nodded, her attention focussed on the book. 'OK.'

'Hey Rocket, I have some news. Santa's house was decorated overnight,' Quinn said.

The book was lowered, her eyes wide with excitement. 'For real?'

'Yes. It looks pretty cool.'

'Did you see it happen?'

'Didn't see or hear anything. Went to bed around eleven, woke up this morning and it's completely transformed. The elves must have done it through the night.'

'That's amazing. I bet they did it with magic.'

'I imagine so.'

'And I've just heard that Santa is arriving this evening, at five o'clock,' Alex said, as if his arrival hadn't been planned with military precision for the last six months or more.

'That's amazing. Can we go and see it this morning?' Zara said, excitedly.

'Yes, of course,' Alex said.

'I'll go and get dressed,' Zara said, for once abandoning her book. 'And you two can carry on kissing.'

She left the room and they stared at each other in shock.

'I guess she's OK with it,' Alex said.

'I guess so.'

※

Word had clearly got around as what looked like hundreds of young children were wandering round Christmas Gardens and the house in awe as they looked at all the decorations and lights. Alex hadn't had a chance to have a proper look at all the decorations last night and the overall effect, but in the daylight and with the fake and real snow sparkling in the winter sunshine, it looked spectacular. Christmas trees were placed around the gardens in a kind of forest trail with little animals and magical folk dotted along the path, and all of the trees were beautifully decorated with lights or garlands or baubles. The house itself looked wonderful, with two large beautifully decorated Christmas trees that were easily twelve foot high or more standing sentry either side of the door. The door was surrounded by a huge bauble garland archway and there were several oversized wrapped presents dotted around. Each window was festooned with a bauble wreath and lights and there were illuminated icicles and snowflakes hanging from the eaves. The whole house was capped off with the incredible roof which looked like the snow was a foot or more deep as it sparkled in the daylight.

Zara was looking at it all with wide eyes and her mouth open. 'It's beautiful.'

'It really is,' Immy said. 'The elves have done a wonderful job.'

The house door was open and people were wandering around inside. Santa wasn't officially due to arrive until tonight, but in the meantime the children were delighted to have a little sneak peek into his home. Alex knew that Quinn's upstairs flat would be locked so there was no chance of anyone rooting around in his home and touching his stuff.

'Is it weird that people are in your home?' Zara said to Quinn.

'Not really. It's Santa's home, he just lets me stay there for the rest of the year as he doesn't need it until December. So I can't complain about it when he does come back. And I get to stay upstairs while Santa moves in downstairs so it's not like I have no place to stay.'

'You can always stay with us,' Zara said, simply.

'What?' Quinn said.

'Harley's mum's boyfriend has just moved in with them and, when I asked why, Harley said it's because they love each other. You two love each other so you should move in.'

'It's… not quite so simple as that,' Quinn said, awkwardly, while Alex had no words at all. Immy snorted with suppressed laughter.

'Harley says it's like having a second dad,' Zara went

200

on. 'Only better because her real dad is mean to her mum and Harley doesn't like it. She says Jake is nice and plays with her and sometimes brings her toys and gives her hugs. And I said my dad was mean to my mum too but now he isn't here and you could be my dad, because you're nicer.'

Alex let out a little gasp. 'What do you mean, your dad was mean to me?'

She had tried to shield Zara from Liam's nastiness as much as she could, but she couldn't exactly shut Zara in her room whenever he was in a nasty mood because that would have meant her being in her room for the last eighteen months of Liam's life. She had tried to tell herself that Zara, at three and four years old, was too young to understand, but clearly not.

Zara nodded. 'He made you cry. I remember that. He made you cry a lot. Quinn never makes you cry.'

Alex bit her lip. She had no recollection of crying in front of her daughter. She always tried to walk away from Liam when he got too nasty, and obviously took Zara with her, but she'd always tried to keep the tears at bay in front of Zara. It broke her heart that Zara had negative memories of her dad. Before his friend died Liam had been a wonderful father. She resolved to try and find some videos of him and Zara in happier times. But she had no idea how to address this.

Immy gave Alex a consoling stroke on the back. Alex knew she would never jump to Liam's defence; her sister had despised the man ever since she'd found out what Alex had lived with for the last eighteen months of his life. Alex looked at her sister. She was pissed that not only had Liam made her cry but that Zara had seen it.

Quinn cleared his throat. 'Your dad was a good man, but he got sick and that sickness made him do and say mean and nasty things. The man he was before he got sick would have hated that he made your mum cry – he loved you both very much.'

Alex smiled with love for him, he always knew the perfect thing to say. Immy was clearly biting her lip to disagree that Liam was a good man but her sister knew that Alex never wanted to speak ill of Liam in front of Zara, regardless of his appalling behaviour.

Zara was quiet for a while. 'I don't really remember him.'

'We can talk about him any time you want to,' Alex said. 'And I have lots of photos and videos of the three of us together, we can look at them too.'

'And I have many stories of what we got up to when we were kids,' Quinn said. 'You just need to ask and I'll bore you with them for hours. Nanny will have plenty of funny stories about him too.'

'OK, maybe I'd like to look at some videos of him some time.'

'Just say the word,' Alex said, even though she knew watching those videos would hurt because they had been happy and Liam had thrown all that away so easily.

'But I'd still like a new dad,' Zara went on. 'I haven't had one for a long time. And if you two love each other why can't Quinn move in like Jake did?'

'Quinn is very special to us,' Alex said carefully. 'And

there will be a time in the future when he will move in with us. Or we'll move in with him but—'

'In Santa's house?' Zara almost screamed with excitement.

'Well we might, we haven't talked about it,' Alex said, feeling like they were going off topic quite spectacularly.

'Why haven't we talked about it?'

'It has to be the right time,' Quinn said.

'No it doesn't, we can talk about it anytime, we could talk about it now,' Zara said. 'Can we move into Santa's house, Mum, can we?'

'Why don't we go and have a closer look at the forest trail and the house,' Immy said, helpfully. She held out a hand for Zara and, surprisingly, she took it. They walked, or in Zara's case bounced, towards the house, leaving Quinn and Alex alone.

'And there was I thinking that if Zara knew about us it might be easier than trying to sneak around,' Alex said. 'But there was nothing easy about that.'

Quinn was looking serious. 'She's bound to compare herself to other families, especially as most of her friends all have dads and she doesn't.'

'True. She's never said anything to me before about wanting a new dad. I wonder if that's because she always got what she needed in that regard from you.'

'I've done what I can but her upbringing is all down to you, and probably Immy,' Quinn said. 'You've done the job of a mum and a dad. She's brilliant, sensible, funny, clever and all of that is down to you.'

'Oh, I don't think I can take any credit for that, she's

brilliant all on her own.' Alex paused, biting her lip. 'I'm sorry she said those things about Liam, I know that must be hard to hear.'

'That he was mean? I saw that with my own eyes. I'm sad that she saw it though.'

'Yeah, me too,' Alex sighed. 'I never knew she saw me crying. I've never said anything negative about Liam to her as I always hoped she remembered the good times not the bad. Thank you for saying what you did.'

'It's true, he was a good man, when he didn't drink. He was my best friend growing up and I miss that. I'd like to see those videos too, to remind me of the man he really was. Because right now I'm angry that his own daughter grew up thinking he was mean, he should never have put her through that.'

'I know and part of me now regrets staying as long as I did.'

Quinn shook his head. 'You stayed to help him and that took a lot of courage, and it was a lot more than what his family did for him.'

She chewed her lip while she thought about how to address the elephant in the room but Quinn got there first.

'Don't worry,' he said. 'I won't be packing my bags and moving in any time soon. Also, I'm not quite sure how we would keep the magic of Christmas alive if you and Zara moved into Santa's house with me.'

'No, that's true. Although I'm sure she would love being one of the elves and being in on the secret when she's a little older.'

'Well, you are both welcome to move in with me at any time, whenever you're ready,' he told her. 'I reckon we can make the Santa thing work, even if it means we all move back in with Immy at the start of December.'

She looked at him. 'You're so blasé about this.'

'About Santa? I'm sure we can come up with some workaround if she's living there.'

'About us.'

'Oh. I wouldn't say blasé.'

'The way you talk, you're so confident about our future as if you know we'll be living together, married, happily ever after one day.'

'I have no doubts about that,' he said. 'We love each other, we'll get there. And I think you know that too. You told Zara that I would be moving in with you at some point, you didn't say might, or maybe or deny all knowledge of it. You know we were meant to be together. And it doesn't matter if it takes a few years for you to be comfortable with that.'

'What if I never get there?' she asked. 'What if I'm never ready to move in with you or get married or have babies?'

His face softened. 'I would love to have children with you. One day.'

Alex's heart leapt at the thought. She wanted that life with him more than anything. She smiled. 'I want that too.'

He grinned. 'Then we'll get there. When you're ready. Now let's go and look at the decorations and the house before Zara picks out which bedroom she's going to have.'

❄

'I have a plan,' Alex said, walking into Quinn's studio later that morning, just as he was getting ready to head out for the day. She knew he had to drive up to Exeter today to collect some metal for his monsters. He made the journey at least once a month and he'd be gone for most of the day.

'What kind of plan?'

'I've collated where all the baubles were found, based on all the comments on my Facebook post, and you might be surprised to know that, while a lot were placed near the relevant person's house, the majority of them were found in Christmas Gardens.'

Quinn raised an eyebrow. 'Really? The majority? I feel like a lot were found in the high street, the beach and other busy communal areas too.'

'Thirty-four percent were found on Christmas Gardens.'

'How is that the majority?'

'Well, twenty-six percent were found in individual locations, left outside or near someone's house. Twenty-seven percent were found near or around the main high street and thirteen percent were found near or on the beach.'

'That doesn't feel like an overwhelming majority then.'

Alex narrowed her eyes at him. 'It's enough that Christmas Gardens is now a place of interest.'

'It doesn't mean that St Nick lives near it. Just that he's picked a busy place to leave the baubles, somewhere he knows the baubles will be found very easily.'

She narrowed her eyes at him again. 'I never said he lived there, just that it was a place of interest.'

'Right, OK.'

'I'm going to do a stakeout tomorrow night after we go ice skating. Zara would love that, especially if there's doughnuts.'

Quinn shrugged. 'OK. I'm happy to do a stakeout with you. Although it might be a dull night. St Nick might be anywhere.'

'Well, at least I could rule you out if there are baubles placed somewhere else that night and you're in the car with me.'

He smiled. 'You really think it's me?'

'I'm not sure. There is some indication that it is you. But I'm a bit thrown by St Nick mentioning his other half, though. We weren't together at that point and that's the kind of thing you say about a wife or girlfriend.'

'So maybe it's not me.'

'And maybe it is.'

'You could just ask me, if you're that frustrated by not knowing. I'd never lie to you, about anything.'

Alex frowned. She suddenly didn't want this to be over, she was enjoying the thrill of the chase. Like finding out the truth about Santa, she didn't want to ruin the magic, not yet anyway and she certainly didn't want to find out like this with no fanfare. If it was him, she wanted to find out on her own not have it presented to her as a fait accompli.

'No, I need to find stronger evidence before I accuse you. Just like in Cluedo, you *suggest* that it might be Miss Scarlett with the dagger in the conservatory, you don't *accuse* until you have all your ducks in a row.'

'You need more ducks.'

'Yes, and I'm going to find them.'

'OK, I have to go.' Quinn moved forward to give her a kiss. 'I'll see you tonight for the parade. And maybe after I could come back and hang out with you all.'

'Zara has her Brownies Christmas party sleepover after – she has a better social life than I do and I have a top secret meeting,' she laughed.

'What's the top secret meeting?' Quinn asked, pulling his coat on.

'I have no idea. Cleo wanted to meet and she said it was top secret, so I probably shouldn't have told you that! Forget I said anything.'

He laughed. 'I'll try.'

'But you could come round after my meeting, spend the night. I don't have to pick Zara up until nine the next day.'

'Now that sounds like a perfect plan.'

'We'll have to be quiet though, Immy is in the room right next door.'

'I can do quiet. Can you?'

She laughed. 'I can try.'

He smiled, gave her another kiss and walked out.

✳

Dear St Nick,

Very clever throwing me a red herring last night with the elf hats and, yes, I suppose I did find it funny that every single person was wearing one. Although as that clue was less than helpful I think you owe me two clues today.

Did you manage to speak to me? I spoke to so many men last night, some for a few minutes, some no more than a hello, so I'm not sure I can whittle it down with that either.

So I'll ask you a few questions to try to narrow it down some more.

How old are you, or at least can you give me an age range?

What colour eyes do you have?

What colour hair?

Warmest wishes,

Alex

✳

Alex was just finishing off a paper sculpture bauble with an ice skating theme when she saw movement at the door. She looked up and smiled when she saw Violet.

'Hello, my dear,' Violet said, giving her a kiss on the cheek. 'I was just meeting a friend for coffee upstairs and thought I'd pop in and say hello.'

'Well, I'm very glad you did.'

'Where's Zara today?'

'She's at her friend Harley's house. Her mum works from home so she can be there while the girls play.'

'That's nice.'

Alex noticed that Violet suddenly seemed nervous.

'So, how's the dating going?' Violet asked.

'Oh, umm…' She really wanted to tell Violet about her and Quinn, but she wasn't sure how she would react. Violet was trying to be supportive about her dating even though she was worried what it meant for her future relationship with Zara. At least Alex's relationship with Quinn wouldn't jeopardise that. But Alex had been married to one of her sons and was now having a semi-serious relationship with her other son. She wasn't sure Violet would be OK with that. She decided she would wait for Quinn to be with her before she broke the news. She also wanted Quinn with her for when they told her about the night Liam died but maybe that could come later.

She thought carefully how to answer the question about her love life so she wasn't directly lying to Violet. 'I had two very bad dates and decided I didn't want to date any more random men.'

'Oh, that's a shame. Cleo said you weren't dating anyone right now but I wasn't sure that was true.'

'You and Cleo were talking about me?'

'She's worried about you,' Violet said. 'She told me she's going to matchmake you with someone.'

'Yeah, I really don't want that.'

'I tried to tell her that but she insisted she had the perfect man for you.'

'I'll talk to her.' As Alex was seeing Cleo that night, she would very firmly put some boundaries in place.

There was silence then as Violet awkwardly fiddled with the strap on her bag. 'I wanted to ask your advice actually. Hypothetical advice obviously.'

'Umm, of course.'

'So say you meet someone, it goes well, really well actually. At what point would you tell Zara? And how? Hypothetically.'

'Well, I would probably just invite the man around a lot so Zara would get used to seeing the man around the house – this is obviously once I knew that I was serious about the man. Then once I knew she was comfortable with him, I'd probably tell her then.'

'Hmm, right. I suppose exposure is key,' Violet said, more to herself than to Alex. 'Do it slowly. Maybe Christmas Day.'

'Sorry?'

Violet blushed and Alex realised this wasn't a conversation about Zara at all.

'Violet, are you seeing someone?'

Violet dismissed it with a scoff. 'Of course not.' Then she sighed. 'Yes, yes I am but I haven't told anyone yet, least of all Quinn. Max sort of knows. I turned up on a date at Alberto's the other night and he was working, but he knows better than to start telling people my private business.'

'I thought I saw you there,' Alex said.

'There was me thinking I'd got away with it.'

'Well, I couldn't be sure as you had your whole face

covered with a scarf, but even that looked a bit suspicious. I thought the place was about to be robbed,' Alex teased. 'Why don't you want to tell anyone?'

'I was married to Henry for fifty-six years, I figured falling in love with someone else only two years after he died, some people might think it's disrespectful to Henry, that I'm moving on too soon.'

'I don't think anyone would think that,' Alex said, though she knew there were some people in the village who absolutely would. There were some people who thrived on gossip, the more malicious the better. 'Besides, if anyone does think that, it's absolutely none of their business.'

Though it was a lot easier dishing out that advice than taking it. She was the one who wanted to keep her and Quinn's relationship a secret, at least for now.

'It's a little more complicated than you think,' Violet went on. 'I'm dating Michael, Henry's best friend.'

'Ah.'

Alex knew exactly what it felt like to be in a forbidden relationship too, or at least some people would see what she had with Quinn that way. She knew some people wouldn't be comfortable with her dating Liam's brother either.

'I don't really care what the people of the town will think or say,' Violet said. 'I've been round the block enough times for that sort of thing to roll straight off my back but I worry mostly what Quinn will think. He loved his dad very much and he might think I'm trying to replace Henry. It was never my intention to date anyone, this thing with Michael just sort of happened and… he makes me very very happy. I'm in love and I never ever thought I'd utter those words again.'

Alex nodded. 'I think Quinn will understand a lot more than you think. Plus he loves you, he only wants you to be happy again. He might be surprised but he won't be angry. Why not invite Michael to Christmas Day lunch, just as a friend, and see what the reaction is? If you feel it's right, you can always tell Quinn then.'

'Yeah, that's a good idea. There'll be lots of people there, as always. Most people won't even notice there's an extra person, or wonder why he's there.'

'Exactly.'

'Talking of who's coming and who isn't, is Immy going to be there?' Violet asked.

'Of course, she wouldn't miss it.'

'Xander is coming too. I think there might be something going on between them.'

Alex certainly wasn't going to confirm that, she'd take Immy's secrets to the grave.

Violet looked at her. 'Hmm, your silence speaks volumes.'

'Silence can mean many things. I thought they hated each other,' Alex said, trying to divert Violet from her train of thought.

'I went to go to Immy's sweet shop the other day, and the door was locked and I peered through to see if she was in there and saw her and Xander at the back of the shop kissing, then he grabbed her hand and dragged her into the storeroom.'

Alex blinked in surprise. She wondered if that was the day Immy had ended up spending the night with Xander or whether that was a completely separate occasion. She cleared her throat because there was nothing she could say to divert Violet from that. That was stone hard evidence.

She still kept silent though.

'I think she'd be good for him,' Violet went on. 'He needs someone lovely to bring him back out of his shell. I think we should set them up on a date or something.'

'I think we need to stay out of it and let them forge their own paths.'

Violet sighed. 'I suppose you're right. Well, must go, but if you decide to change your mind about dating, I have the perfect man for you.'

Alex smiled. 'Thank you, but I'm doing just fine right now.'

Violet nodded, gave her a wave and left.

❄

Dear Alex,

My apologies for the elf hat joke. But you can't have a good mystery without a few red herrings. I did wear an elf hat though, like I promised, I just didn't specify that there would be others wearing hats too. I'm not sure that justifies two clues. I did come and speak to you, as promised, too.

My clue today: I'm not a huge fan of sweet things, I prefer

214

something savoury, but the exception to that are the crème brûlée doughnuts from Donut Park. They are little bites of heaven.

I'm not sure I can answer your questions without completely giving away my identity but I will answer one. I'm older than thirty but younger than fifty-five.

Snowy hugs,
St Nick

CHAPTER 14

❄

Quinn let himself into Alex's kitchen later that night as Alex, Immy and Zara were all busily getting layered up with hats, scarves and gloves ready for the parade.

'Hey,' Zara said, noticing him first.

'Hey Rocket, how was your day with Harley?'

'Good, we made the world's biggest snowman. Jake helped.'

'That's great, you'll have to show it to me before it melts,' Quinn said. He could see that the idea of having a new dad was definitely appealing to Zara right now. He hoped he could be that for her one day and he vowed if he ever got that honour he'd make damned sure he would do a better job than his brother ever did.

He glanced over at Alex who was watching him. He so wanted to walk over and kiss her right now. Immy knew about them, Zara sort of knew, but he wasn't sure how Alex would feel about such a public display of affection, so he settled on a little wave.

'Are we all ready? We don't want to miss Santa,' Alex said, ushering everyone out of the door. Immy and Zara went first, chatting away at a hundred miles an hour about Santa, the reindeer and the Brownies Christmas party sleepover. Immy was so good for her.

As Alex ushered Quinn out, she stroked her hand up his back and leaned up and gave him a quick kiss on the cheek. He was looking forward to doing so much more that night.

Zara took his hand as they started walking down the hill and he quickly pushed any dirty thoughts about what he'd like to do to her mum out of his head.

'I've drawn some monsters for you,' his niece told him. 'Maybe you can turn them into real-life monsters.'

'I'd love that. I'm always looking for inspiration for new monsters.'

'I think I'd like to be an artist like you and make monsters when I grow up. That's the coolest job ever.'

'It is a cool job. I love it.' Quinn didn't want to tell her it didn't pay particularly well. It paid enough to cover his bills, just about, but some months paid more than others and he was able to put money in savings for those months that he didn't make enough. But he wasn't going to do anything to dampen her dreams, especially as he knew her career choices would change a hundred times between now and when she turned eighteen. And if she still wanted to make monsters for a living when she was older, he'd do everything he could to help her. If she wanted to be an astronaut he'd do everything in his power to make that happen too.

'Look, there's my snowman.' Zara pointed excitedly to the huge snowman standing in the middle of a large garden belonging to the little pink house on the corner. She dragged him over to have a look. 'Isn't it brilliant?'

'This is really cool,' Quinn said.

'Literally,' Immy laughed.

'It's massive,' Alex said. 'It has to easily be eight foot tall or more.'

Zara was beaming. 'It took us hours to build it and Jake had to get a ladder out so we could put the buttons and carrot on the face.'

'You've done a fantastic job,' Quinn said. 'He's really smooth and he has a great shape. If you're going to be an artist you have to take the time to get these little details right and you've done this perfectly.'

'Like St Nick,' Zara said, as they started walking back down the hill towards Christmas Gardens. 'He takes time to get the little details right, like knowing that purple is my favourite colour.'

'Yes, that's right,' Quinn said.

'And knowing that peonies are Mum's favourite flower.'

'Yes.'

'Not many people would know those things,' Zara said.

'That's true, they wouldn't,' Alex said, looking over at Quinn.

He smiled.

'Maybe it's someone we know,' Immy said.

'We live in a small town, everyone knows everyone,'

Quinn said. 'Zara wears purple a lot so a lot of people would have seen that. Alex often has peonies in a vase in the front window so people would have spotted that too. It's someone who pays attention, I'll give you that, but I wouldn't necessarily be looking that close to home.'

Alex stared at him and he knew he'd said too much.

'But I feel sure we'll catch them on this stakeout. They won't be expecting someone to be watching out for them,' Quinn said.

'They might be in disguise,' Zara said.

'They might be,' Quinn said, an idea forming in his mind.

'We could go in disguise too,' Zara suggested.

He wasn't sure what the point of that would be but he'd happily sit in a car dressed as a clown or whatever disguise Zara wanted, if that made her happy.

They joined the crowds that were lining the streets ready for Santa's big arrival. He was coming from the direction of Mistletoe Farm, just up the hill, so a few people had already gathered along the roads from that direction, to get a clearer view of him and the reindeer, but most people wanted to see him arrive at Christmas Cottage so were surrounding the roads around Christmas Gardens.

As Quinn also lived in the cottage, he had set up the best spot to welcome Santa. They were going to stand in the doorway of the little shed next to the house so they could watch Santa pull right up to the house.

He ushered the women through the gardens and up

the driveway and then unlocked the shed so they could stand in the doorway, out of the way of reindeer hooves but close enough to feel the warmth from their breath.

As the town clock chimed five o'clock, everyone fell silent, listening for the tell-tale sound of the jingle bells on the reindeers' harnesses.

After a minute or two, someone yelled that he was coming and the crowd of people waiting to get a glimpse of the big man started whispering excitedly among themselves. Then Quinn heard it, the soft jingle of the bells which grew louder as Santa got closer. People started cheering, shouting and waving. Then he saw the tops of the reindeers' antlers and Santa's hat, peeping out above the heads of the crowds. He quickly lifted Zara up to sit on his shoulders, hoping she would get a better view from up there.

Santa did one complete circuit of the road around the outside of Christmas Gardens before coming up the driveway and they got their first unhindered view of him and the reindeer.

The sleigh was bright red with gold edges. A huge sack full of beautifully wrapped presents sat in the back behind the big man himself, who was dressed in a deep red velvet suit lined with white fur and accented with gold buttons. There wasn't quite enough snow for it to be dragged along like a real sleigh, so there were wheels secreted inside the sleigh runners – you'd have to look really closely to see them but Quinn knew they were there. But the most impressive thing was the eight real reindeer marching along, heads held high, their velvet antlers glistening in the Christmas lights. They were wearing red and gold leather harnesses that had bells all over. The whole thing looked utterly spectacular.

Santa waved at the crowds as he pulled the reindeer to a stop right outside Christmas Cottage. One of the workers from the farm, dressed as an elf, stepped forward to take control of the reindeer and, with a wave and a big 'Ho, ho, ho,' Santa stepped off the sleigh and walked into the house.

None of the children would be meeting Santa that night because those meetings were smaller, quieter, more intimate moments when Santa took the time to chat to all of the children, so there were scheduled meetings over the next few days for that. But the children were allowed to come up and say hello to the reindeer, who would also be there for the next few days, under the careful eye of the farm workers who owned the reindeer.

Some people were already making their way up the drive to meet the reindeer so Quinn quickly ushered Zara forward to stroke them before the crowds descended.

'They're beautiful,' Zara said reverentially, holding out a hand to stroke one of the creatures' velvety necks.

The farm worker handed Zara a handful of lichen and directed her to hold her hand flat. Her eyes lit up with pure joy as the reindeer whiffled it out of her hand.

More people came up to stroke the reindeer and Quinn took a few steps back to allow other children room to meet these majestic beasts. But he kept an eye on Zara, enjoying how much she was loving meeting them.

Just then Max walked over and clapped him on the back. 'Hey mate, are you free tonight?'

'Yes, for a few hours anyway.'

'Great, can you do me a huge favour?'

'Of course, whatever you need. Although I was going to ask you to do me one, so maybe I'll scratch your back if you scratch mine,' Quinn said.

'Yeah sure, I'm happy to help.'

'You haven't heard what I need from you yet,' Quinn pointed out. 'You might run a mile once you hear.'

'Whatever you need, I'm there,' Max said.

Quinn smiled. 'OK, let's deal with your favour first. How can I help?'

'Can you be Cleo's plus one on Alex's date tonight? I said I'd do it but I have to work.'

He'd obviously misheard, there were a lot of people around.

'On Alex's what?'

'Her date. You and Cleo will be double dating them. You'll be Cleo's date while Alex and this dude are on their date. That way, if the bloke is a weirdo, you'll be there to look after her.'

Quinn's heart dropped. 'Alex is going on a date tonight?'

He thought back to earlier when she'd told him she had a top secret meeting. Was that the date?

'Yes, it's all set up.'

'But Alex doesn't want to date anyone right now.'

'Trust Cleo, she says she has chosen the absolutely perfect man for her.'

'Does Alex know?'

'No, she just thinks she's meeting Cleo.'

'Shouldn't we tell her?'

'And give her a chance to come up with a million reasons why she can't make it? No way. She needs to get back on the horse, or so Cleo says, and she can't let those two bad dates put her off.'

'I don't think that's fair,' Quinn protested. 'She should be the one to choose who and when she dates, not Cleo.'

'It's one drink with a man, and you and Cleo will be there. What's the worst that could happen?'

Quinn wasn't sure, but he didn't have a good feeling about this.

❄

Alex hurried along the road towards Alberto's ready for her top secret meeting with Cleo. She was running a little late and she hated being late but the meet-and-greet with the reindeers had taken a little longer than she'd thought. Harley's mum had taken the girls off to their Brownie Christmas party, Quinn had disappeared off to do a favour for Max and she'd hurried as fast as she could down to the main part of the town.

Quinn had been a bit quiet after they'd met the reindeer and she had no idea why. She'd seen him chatting to Max so their conversation might be why he'd been a bit withdrawn. She would have to talk to him about it later tonight or, if Max was working at Alberto's tonight, she might try and have a word with him.

Although, as she soon realised, that wouldn't be necessary as Quinn was standing outside Alberto's looking very smart in a suit that seemed to cling to every muscle in his arms and legs. He looked gorgeous.

He saw her and waved.

'Hey, what are you doing here?' she asked. 'I thought you were doing a favour for Max?'

'I am but… Look, I should have told you before but I only just found out an hour ago when Max asked me to be here and he swore me to secrecy but I don't think it's fair for you to walk in there unprepared.'

She frowned. 'What's going on?'

'Cleo has organised a blind date for you. I'm here as her plus one so we can double date with the two of you.'

'What?'

'She thinks you need to get back on the horse and that you shouldn't hide yourself away because of those two bad dates. She didn't tell you because she knew you wouldn't want to come.'

'Well, she'd have been right. She should have asked me, instead of springing it on me.'

'To be fair, I think she's only trying to help,' Quinn said. 'She doesn't know that being with Liam has caused you anxiety about dating again and she doesn't know about us.'

Alex sighed. 'Look, I'll just go in there and tell her I'm not interested, you don't need to worry.'

She opened the door. She was annoyed that Cleo was interfering in her life like this but she knew it came from the best intentions. Cleo had seen her willing to go on those other two dates so she must have thought she was ready. She couldn't have known that the only reason Alex had gone on those dates was because she'd known she'd never find something serious. That was before she got involved with Quinn, a relationship that would never be casual and that could only be the kind that was big and life-changing and that was what was scaring her.

She walked inside and Quinn followed her. Cleo immediately spotted her and came over to greet her.

'I'm so glad you're here. I have a surprise for you.'

'I know, Quinn just told me. Cleo, you should have asked me, not sprung this on me as a fait accompli. I'm just not ready to date right now.'

'I promise you, this man is absolutely perfect, I would never have set this up if I didn't know him and know that he's so completely perfect for you. He's tall, dark hair, deep blue eyes, he's big and muscular and looks amazing in a suit.'

'Cleo, I don't care what he looks like. If you've set me up with a guy just because he's attractive then you're barking up the wrong tree.'

'No, no, no. His looks are just a bonus. He is kind, gentle, patient, great with kids. He's funny, intelligent, willing to drop everything to help a friend. He's just a really lovely guy. And my sister dated him briefly around five or six years ago and said he was amazing in bed.'

Alex shook her head. 'I'm sorry Cleo, I'm sure he's great but I just don't want to date anyone right now.'

'But he's here, he's come a really long way. He will be gutted if you came in, took one look at him and did a runner. Look, you don't have to spend the whole night with him, just meet him for one drink, that's all I ask.'

Alex looked at Quinn who shrugged as if to say it was up to her, but she knew he was annoyed with all this. But Cleo was right, she couldn't hurt the man's feelings by leaving before even meeting him. If she was in his shoes and showed up for a date and the man arrived and walked straight back out again, she would be devastated. Doing that would make her no better than those other two losers she'd dated. Regardless of the fact it wasn't going to go anywhere, not least because she was head over heels in love with Quinn, if the man had come all this way to meet her, she at least owed him a drink. But she knew Quinn would be hurt if she agreed to this, and quite rightly so. Even though he would be there to see that nothing romantic was happening, she couldn't ask him to sit there while she was on a date with another man. While she didn't want to hurt the man's feelings, Quinn was more important to her than some random man she'd never met. The only way out of this was to tell Cleo she was seeing Quinn so couldn't date anyone else. The other man would be hurt but at least he'd understand why.

'Cleo, I have something I need to tell you.'

Quinn moved forward, a hand on her back. 'It's just one drink. There's no harm in it.'

'What?'

'I know you, I know you don't want to do this, but you'll feel horribly guilty for weeks after if you refuse to meet him. So let's have a drink with him,' Quinn said.

She nodded reluctantly.

'Yay!' Cleo cheered. 'Look, go and sit down over there and I'll come and make the introductions in a minute.'

Alex walked over to the small circular booth and Quinn followed. 'Why did you say yes to this?' she asked.

'Because you're a good, kind person and I could see you didn't want to leave the man hanging or hurt his feelings.'

'But I don't want to hurt your feelings either by agreeing to date another man. I promised we were exclusive and I meant that.'

'You were going to tell Cleo about us to get out of it and I didn't want that.'

'You didn't?'

'Of course not. I want you to be ready for that, not be forced into it.'

Her heart filled with love for him; he was being so gracious about this.

'Sit down,' Quinn said. 'And try to smile. That scowl is not the kind of first impression you want to make on this perfect man.'

She sat down and Quinn sat diagonally opposite her,

leaving a space for this apparently perfect man to sit opposite her. 'For the record, I don't want to impress him.'

'But I know you don't want to be rude to him either, that's not who you are and none of this is his fault.'

Alex sighed. He was right. And he was being a lot more magnanimous about this than she was.

'I'm not going to kiss him or hold hands with him or anything.'

'I know.'

'I'll shake his hand when he comes over.'

'That's fine.'

'And then I'll pick my nose, that will scare him away. Maybe throw in a loud fart to really put him off.'

The smile spread on his face. 'I bloody love you.'

She smiled. 'I love you too.'

'Just promise me you're not going to fall head over heels in love with this man.'

'That would be impossible because there is not a single man in the world who could make me feel what I feel for you.'

He smiled and looked around. The place was pretty full with people having pre-Christmas drinks and cele-brations.

'I'm looking forward to the day I can take you out on a date where I can hold your hand across the table and tell you how beautiful you are,' Quinn said.

'Soon, I promise. And you're looking devastatingly gorgeous tonight in that suit. I'm not sure how I'm going to concentrate on anything this man is going to say with you sitting next to him. This man has already lost out to you and I've not even met him yet.'

Alex felt guilty saying that but it was true. This poor man had come all this way for a date that was already dead in the water.

Cleo arrived at the table supposedly to do the introductions but there was no sign of any man. She had the biggest smile on her face.

'So this is Quinn, he's thirty-two, loves rugby, kayaking, paddleboarding, quiz nights and murder mysteries. He is a metal-work artist. This is Alex, she's thirty, she has a brilliant, seven-year-old daughter. Alex loves sea swimming, in the summer months anyway, gardening, also in the spring and summer, she loves action films and romance books, but has a special place in her heart for any fantasy romance. She also loves watching murder mysteries so that's something you two have in common. Have a good night.'

Cleo started to move away but Alex stopped her in confusion. 'What's going on?'

Cleo gestured to Quinn. 'This is your hot date. I told you I'd arranged a date with your perfect man and here he is. Have a good night, the meal's on us,' she gestured to Max who was grinning at them both from behind the bar.

Cleo moved away and Alex looked at Quinn. 'We've been set up,' she laughed.

'So it seems.'

'Did you know about this?'

'No idea, Max just asked me to double date with you

about an hour ago. Look, we don't have to stay, we can have a drink and go home.'

'Hell no, I have a hot date with the most perfect man in the world, a free meal and, while I'd never normally sleep with a man on a first date, I'm pretty sure I'm going to break that rule for you tonight.'

He laughed.

Her heart felt so full of him. He really was perfect for her in every way, Cleo couldn't have set her up with a better man and maybe she needed to make that clear.

She reached across the table and took his hand. He looked around nervously for a moment but she was gratified when he entwined his fingers with hers. 'She described you perfectly, gentle, kind, patient, and you've been so patient with me. I think it's time we make it very clear that I'm not on the market for anyone else ever again.'

'You don't have to do that,' Quinn said. 'You don't have to prove anything to me or to anyone. I know where I stand with you and I don't need anything more than that.'

'But maybe I do. I'm tired of hiding it. If I want to hold your hand in public or hug you or kiss you I will. When someone asks if we're together, like they've done many times before over the years because they've seen how close we are, I want to say yes, because we are and not just in a friends-with-benefits way – you've always been so much more than that to me. Cleo saw what we were fighting against for years: that we are meant to be together.'

He frowned slightly. 'OK.'

'Why are you frowning? I thought you would be happy about this. I'm yours and I want the world to know.'

'I just don't want you to regret it.'

'How could I regret being with you? I love you. I know I've been scared of labelling it as a relationship as that's big and scary and life-changing but that's what we're in. We're sleeping together, we've told each we love each other, we're exclusive to each other, we've even talked about our future. Labelling it as no strings attached is just rubbish. There are strings whether we want them or not. And I'm so sorry that I'm messing you around.'

'You're not messing me around. You want to take things slow and I totally understand why. Liam hurt you badly and you want to be careful with your heart and who you give it to.'

'I've already given it to you.'

'OK, but we can take this as slow as you want or need.'

Alex nodded. 'I know. Now as the meal is free, shall we have a look at the menu?'

They started looking through the menu and she didn't let go of his hand as she did. When she glanced over at him she could see he was looking ridiculously happy about it, even circling the back of her hand with his thumb, making her feel weak and needy.

'Are you ready to order?' Max said, as he arrived at their table.

Quinn scowled at him. 'Was this your idea?'

'It was a mutual thing,' Max shrugged, clearly not bothered by the scowl. 'Cleo wanted to set Alex up with someone wonderful and I said there was someone who was perfect for her right under our noses.'

'And you didn't think you could just be honest with us?'

'Nah, neither of you would have come if we had. But from where I'm standing, it doesn't seem to have been a bad idea.' He gestured to their hands.

'Well actually—' Quinn began, clearly about to tell Max that they had been seeing each other for a while.

'We've decided, as you've got us here on a date that we'd treat it like a date,' Alex quickly said.

Max grinned. 'Well, I genuinely hope it works out for you.'

They placed their order and he left.

'Why didn't you tell him we've been seeing each other for a while?' Quinn asked.

'Oh, let them have it as a win. It is a good match. What would you have done if we weren't together and they set us up on this date?'

'I would hope I would have the courage to tell you that I loved you and if you wanted to date a real man who would treat you like a queen, it would make me the happiest man alive.'

She smiled at that. 'And I would have said yes. Then I'd have probably suggested we get out of here to consummate our new relationship.'

He laughed. 'Don't tempt me.'

Max brought over the drinks, giving them a mischievous eyebrow wiggle. Alex wondered whether he'd heard the comment about consummating their relationship. He left them to it and Alex decided to change the subject so she wasn't thinking about running out of here for a night of hot passion.

'What are you most looking forward to about your Christmas celebrations?'

'Oh, lots of things. The rugby club Christmas party should be good. They are doing a big murder mystery night where everyone is getting dressed up and everyone has a character to play. I have to go as a mad scientist. I love stuff like that. It's right up my street. But mostly I'm looking forward to spending more time with you and Zara on Christmas Day. I'd really like to wake up with you in my arms on Christmas morning.'

She smiled at that. 'I'd really like that too. I'm sure that can be arranged. Zara seems rather blasé about it all.'

'Well, that would definitely be something to look forward to.'

❄

The meal had been delicious and the conversation had flowed easily just as it always did. As first dates went, it had certainly been one of Alex's best.

Cleo had sat up at the bar all night, chatting away to Max and giving them excited thumbs up every time they looked over at her.

The plates had all been cleared away and they were just finishing off their drinks. Alex decided it was now or never. She scooted round the booth so she was next to Quinn.

'I'm going to kiss you now.'

He looked alarmed. 'Here? In front of everyone?'

'Don't look so scared.'

'I'm scared for you. If we kiss, the whole town will know within half an hour. There'll probably be a bulletin on Facebook or the neighbourhood forum.'

She laughed. 'I don't think our love lives are that interesting.'

'If you were just dating some random man, people probably wouldn't care less, but you're with me, Liam's brother. Lots of people are going to think that's weird or inappropriate.'

'And lots of people who have been rooting for us to get together for years will be delighted for us.'

He scowled.

'I don't really care what people think, do you?' Alex said.

'I care that you'll be subjected to some not so nice comments.'

'Oh, let them talk. It will only be hot news for the next few days until the next piece of gossip comes along. And it has to come out eventually. We can't keep it secret forever.'

'Yes, but we can soft launch – be seen together for a while, then slowly up the ante, be seen holding hands, then maybe a kiss on the cheek – before we unleash a proper kiss on them.'

'And drag out the reaction and gossip even longer? This way, we get it out of the way in one big hit, the pearl-clutchers can all talk about how terrible it is and hopefully it'll be old news before Christmas.'

Quinn didn't look convinced.

'Look, what's the worst that can happen?' she asked.

'The worst is that our fragile tentative relationship could shatter before it's even begun.'

Alex looked at him in surprise and she stroked his face. She realised that by holding back, her reluctance to properly define their relationship and her desire to keep it a secret had made him doubt what they had and she hated that.

'I don't fear that at all, what we have is special. I love you.'

She leaned up and kissed him and after a second he kissed her back. He stroked her face and she melted against him. She heard an excited yelp come from near the bar which she guessed was Cleo, and could hear other people talking in excited whispers too. Quinn was right, this was going to be big news. But as the kiss continued everything faded away and she was only aware of this man, his scent, his touch, his taste, the feel of his lips against hers. This wonderful man was hers and she wanted everyone to know that – but more importantly she wanted him to know that too.

She pulled back slightly and looked at him. 'Let's go home.'

He nodded and stood up. She slid out of the booth and he helped her on with her coat, his fingers deliberately grazing the back of her neck. She looked back at him, his mouth just inches from hers, and the look he gave her was dark with need. It made her feel weak with just the thought of being with this man again. She was never going to have enough of him.

Just then Cleo came bouncing over. Quinn took a step away from her but Alex firmly took his hand and pulled him back by her side.

'Did you enjoy your meal?' Cleo asked.

'Very much so.'

'It looked like it. But you don't need to hurry off, you can stay for dessert or coffee or—'

'We have somewhere important we need to be,' Quinn said and Alex giggled.

A lady called Tina who was sitting having dinner with another woman tutted loudly and Alex nearly laughed. Why would anyone care what Alex did or who she was with? What harm was she doing to anyone else? The only person who had any right to be upset by Alex moving on was Violet and, judging by her reaction to her and Quinn declaring their love for each other over iced cookies the other day, it seemed she was OK with it too.

Deciding to annoy Tina some more, Alex curled herself around Quinn. 'We've got a lot of lost time to make up for.'

Tina glared at them and Alex ran a hand up Quinn's

chest for good measure. Quinn stared at her incredulously.

A huge smile spread across Cleo's face. 'Well, that sounds like the date went very well.'

'Very well,' Alex said, looking at Quinn like she wanted to eat him.

'How much do we owe you for the meal?' Quinn asked.

'No, no, on the house, as I said. It was our pleasure.'

After another warning look from Quinn, Alex resisted saying that shortly it would be *their* pleasure.

'Thank you, Cleo, tonight has been an eye-opener,' Alex said.

'For me too,' muttered Tina, loud enough for people at several tables to hear. There were a few giggles.

Alex looked around the room and was surprised to see how many people were invested in her and Quinn and she didn't know how to feel about that.

Quinn squeezed her hand and she looked up at him. 'Come on, let's go home.'

She nodded and gave Cleo a wave before allowing Quinn to lead her outside into the coolness of the snow.

'Why are you trying to wind Tina up?' Quinn asked. 'She's the biggest gossip I've ever met.'

'Why is she bothered by this?' Alex shrugged. 'It doesn't affect her or anyone.'

They started walking up the hill towards her house with Quinn holding her hand. 'Some people will find this weird, they'll judge you for sleeping with your husband's brother and judge me for sleeping with my brother's wife.'

'If Liam was alive, sure, I could understand people getting upset by that level of betrayal but, beyond that, surely the only thing anyone should care about is that I'm happy for the first time in years. Besides, where were these people when I was living with a verbally abusive alcoholic? All these people who are so invested in my life now didn't give a crap about me back then. So they can talk and bitch and whisper but you have made me the happiest woman alive and if that upsets them that says more about them than it does about me.'

Quinn stopped walking and turned to face her. He cupped her face and kissed her and she smiled against his lips.

'You make me ridiculously happy too and to hell with what anyone thinks.'

She took his hand and started marching up the hill with some speed. 'Come on, I want to show you my bedroom.'

He laughed, caught up with her and scooped her up into his arms, then ran the last little bit to her house. He put her down as they reached the door.

They tumbled into the kitchen and Immy looked up from where she was working on her laptop.

'Hey lovebirds.'

'Hey, we're, umm… just going to—'

'Listen to music in your bedroom?' Immy laughed.

'Yeah, something like that.'

'Don't worry about me, I've got a big date with an

action movie I want to watch, lots of explosions, gunfire, cool stunt driving, it's very loud. I won't hear a thing. And it's a long one too. Just in case you want to… listen to more music later. And when I go to bed, I'll sleep with my headphones in and David Attenborough talking to me about the forests and the oceans. Just for your information.'

Alex grinned. 'Good to know.'

She took Quinn's hand and led him up the stairs. 'This is my room,' she showed him the door. 'Immy's room,' she gestured to the door right next to it. And then pointed to the one opposite hers. 'Zara's room.'

'Ah yes, I can see we're going to have to work on being really quiet.'

She pulled him inside her room and started work on removing his clothes. 'I'm not sure you can do quiet.'

'I'm not sure you can either. I've heard you scream. So maybe next year, or whenever you're ready, we get a new place together. Somewhere that isn't overtaken by Santa and his elves every December, somewhere that isn't tainted by memories of Liam and somewhere where Zara's room is a significant distance from ours.'

She laughed.

'And somewhere that has a little granny flat for Immy,' Quinn went on.

She smiled with love for him that he would include her sister in their future plans.

'That sounds perfect.'

'Really?'

'Yes, providing the weirdos of the town don't come after me with pitchforks and burning torches.'

'There is a real possibility of that,' he said. 'But I'll protect you.'

'Will you fight to the death for me?'

'Always,' he assured her.

'Fortunately, I don't think it will come to that. A few busybodies getting upset about me having the best sex of my entire life. They can jog on.'

'The best sex of your entire life?'

'Yes, well so far.' She ran a finger down his chest. 'Unless you think you can do better.'

'I'll give it my best shot.'

He picked her up and threw her down on the bed. She laughed as he struck a few really bad model poses before climbing up the bed over her. He kissed her and she couldn't help giggling against his lips. He made her so damn happy; how could anyone be opposed to that?

CHAPTER 15

Alex woke the next morning, wrapped in Quinn's arms. Life really couldn't be more perfect right now.

Quinn kissed her on the forehead and she looked up and smiled at him. 'Why don't you come and join me in the shower and then we can pick up Zara from her Brownie sleepover and go for breakfast somewhere.'

'That sounds perfect.'

He climbed out of bed and she had the pleasure of watching him walk across the room to the ensuite completely and gloriously butt-naked. He disappeared into the bathroom.

She stretched and reached out for her phone. She was surprised to see she had been tagged multiple times on the neighbourhood forum. The forum had started a year or so ago as a place to bring the community together. It was supposed to be a place people could advertise cake sales, or sell bits of furniture or ask for recommendations for plumbers, builders or gardeners.

It was also supposed to be a place for lost dogs or cats. What it had turned into was a cesspit of moaners. If someone hadn't parked their car correctly, you better believe a photo of their bad parking would go up on the forum shaming the person for being irresponsible or selfish. If there was a dog on the beach in the summer, there were multiple photos of the dog and the owner with locals berating people for not knowing the rules. If a neighbour had the audacity to have a barbeque, yep they were hauled over the coals too. Affairs were often outed on the forum too, people's private business – it really wasn't a pleasant place to visit and Alex avoided it as much as she could. It was the first time she'd been tagged in any post there though, what could she have possibly done wrong?

She groaned when she saw the post was from Tina, the woman at Alberto's the night before. She knew what this would be about before she even opened it.

She clicked on it and rolled her eyes when she read it.

Tina Parker-Barrington

I had a meal at Alberto's last night which was ruined by the behaviour of one of the other customers, Alexandra Campbell. When my husband died I knew there would never be any other man for me, out of respect for my dearly departed William, but only a few years after Liam Campbell died, Alexandra has been seen cavorting with three separate men this week, like some kind of floozie. The man has barely had enough time to go cold. But the worst crime of all is that one of those men is none other than Liam's brother, Quinn. I was shocked to see them holding hands throughout their meal, kissing at the table for everyone to see, when that kind of behaviour is best reserved for one's own home, then they rushed off at the end of the meal to do lord knows what. They were so preoccupied with their forthcoming coitus they didn't even have the decency to pay.

But it's the betrayal that stings the most for me. Liam was a good, kind boy who many of us knew from his gardening service he used to do around the town. I talked to him many times when he would come round and trim my bush and he always spoke about how much he loved his wife and daughter. He would be turning in his grave to know that Alexandra is cavorting with his brother behind his back. What kind of woman would do that?

And shame on Quinn Campbell too. I always thought he was a nice boy and I felt so sorry for him losing his younger brother. But then I find out he wanted nothing to do with Liam before he died and spent the whole of Liam's funeral flirting with his wife. Then he swooped in here and started sleeping with her shortly after his brother's death. They should be ashamed of themselves.

Alex started reading through the comments to see what people's reactions were to this rant. The problem was the kind of people who went on the forum and read these posts and took the time to comment on them were the same old moaners who would berate someone for using a plastic bag for shopping instead of a canvas one or for mowing their lawns on a Sunday, the day of rest. So, annoyingly, most of the comments agreed with Tina.

Verity Forbes-Davenport: *It's disgusting!*

Jacqualyn Rumsey: *Both of them are scum, poor Liam.*

Jodie Brown: *They should be ashamed of themselves.*

Kim Trent: *Sleeping with two brothers, sounds a bit incestuous to me.*

Frankie Kennford: *It's not incestuous to sleep with two brothers, it's incestuous to sleep with your own brother. Idiot.*

Mary Mandalay: *I can't imagine how poor Violet will feel about this. Has anyone told her?*

Tina Parker-Barrington: *I have.*

Jacqualyn Rumsey: *I phoned her last night. She didn't say a lot, I imagine she's horrified.*

Rosie McCoy: *Violet is a very good friend of mine, I can tell you now she will be furious about this, Liam was always her favourite child and Quinn dishonouring his memory like this will be very upsetting.*

Bella Millaburn: *And what about poor Zara, she must miss her dad terribly and the one man she thought she could trust does this.*

Verity Forbes-Davenport: *Imagine if this works out and they get married, poor Zara will be raised by her uncle, how weird is that?*

Jodie Brown: *This whole thing is weird.*

. . .

There were a few nice comments too but they were far outweighed by all the bad.

Julie Wright: *If they are happy, what business is it of anyone else's?*

    Suzie Q: *Good for them, Alex deserves to be happy again.*

    Emily Krimble: *I don't find it weird at all. They were both grieving the loss of Liam and have become close as a result of their shared grief. If they are happy and not harming anyone else, why the hell not.*

    Cleo Knight: *To be clear, they didn't run out on their bill, I bought their dinner for them as I set them up on a blind date. I'm not sure if they were just pretending to get on well to make me happy or whether they really did hit it off, but I think they are perfect for each other. If things get serious between them, Quinn would be an amazing dad to Zara. If it turns out to just be one night of passion, that's great, they are both single and who they do or don't sleep with is their own business.*

    Tina Parker-Barrington: *One-night stand = Slut.*

    Cleo Knight: *Oh get a life. There's nothing wrong with sex between two single consenting adults. Maybe you should try it, it might finally put a smile on your face.*

Alex put the phone down, not wanting to read anyone else's opinions on whether she should be sleeping with Quinn or not. There were over a hundred comments although most of those were from Tina and her cronies,

Verity, Jacqualyn and Jodie, all bitching and moaning between themselves and shooting down anyone who tried to defend Alex.

She got up and walked into the bathroom where Quinn was in the shower. She stepped inside the cubicle with him and wrapped her arms around him so her face was against his back. He took her hand and held it against his heart. After a moment he turned round and wrapped her in his arms as the hot water pounded down on top of them. She held him tight. How could this possibly be wrong? She belonged here in his arms. He tilted her chin up and studied her face.

'What's wrong?'

'There's a post about us on the neighbourhood forum.'

'I'm not surprised. Was it from Tina?'

'Yes, and loads of commenters are agreeing with her.'

'What did it say?'

'That basically we should be ashamed of ourselves for betraying Liam, who was a nice kind boy, and I'm a slut for dating three different men this week. A lot of the comments say that we're disgusting and scum.'

A scowl darkened his face. 'I'll deal with this.'

'What are you going to do?'

'I'm going to have a word with her.'

'You can't do that, she'll put a post out saying you're threatening her or something.'

'No threats, just a firm word.'

Alex sighed. 'Liam was so loved in Lovegrove Bay, everyone knew him and everyone was so sympathetic towards him when his best friend died. They were always asking how he was doing. I'd say he wasn't doing well, but I never told anyone that he'd become a massive alcoholic with a terrible temper and was verbally abusive. I kept that part of him hidden from the people of the town because I thought one day he would choose life over alcohol, he would want to get better – if not for me, for his daughter. One day I thought he would finally choose not to drink and, although our relationship was irreversibly damaged, I didn't want the people of the town treating him any different. I thought his recovery would stand on the shoulders of those who wanted to support him and if he didn't have that then recovery would be that much harder. I didn't think anyone would want to help him or employ him if they'd found out he'd been abusive to me and cheated on me. And if they'd have treated him like scum he might have gone scuttling back to the bottle again. But now they hate me for what they see as a betrayal of the man they loved.'

'What do they expect you to do? Wear black and live in mourning for the rest of your life? You're thirty years old.'

'I think it's the fact that I'm seeing you that's the problem. Or, as Tina put it, the worst crime of all. It's not just moving on, it's moving on with Liam's brother that they hate.'

'Well, tough. We're not doing anything wrong. We're not going to stop seeing each other just because a few moaners have got a bee in their bonnet.' Quinn frowned as he studied her. 'Are we?'

'No, of course not. I just wish I could be blasé about it, like I was last night. I wish I could not care what people think, but it does bother me.'

'I'll fix it, I promise, but it will only last a few days before they find something else to be upset about,' he said. 'You just have to ride out the storm until then.'

'I know you're right. It's just frustrating. People even took the time to tell Violet last night, they actually phoned her to tell her, bloody busybodies. I worry how she is going to react to this when she didn't react positively to me dating in the first place. I thought at first she would be OK with it, because she was smiling when Zara forced us to tell each other we loved each other a few days ago, but maybe she was just laughing at the silly situation. Violet's friends say she will be horrified.'

'Well, we'll talk to her too.' He cupped her face and kissed her. 'It'll be OK, I promise.'

Alex nodded though it did nothing to ease the sadness in her heart. Her bubble of happiness had well and truly popped.

❄

With just three days until Christmas excitement levels were almost palpable as they made their way to Christmas Gardens to see Santa later that morning. Zara was bouncing with anticipation as they walked along. Alex smiled that her jumper-and-jeans-loving daughter had wanted to wear a dress today to see him and she looked gorgeous.

Alex suspected this would probably be the last time Zara would want to visit Santa. Her worldly-wise daughter was growing up fast and this year she'd asked way too many questions about Santa that Alex had struggled to answer convincingly. She imagined that this time next year, Zara would know the truth so Alex was going to make the most of this last one. Zara had even invited Quinn along, which he was thrilled with. Immy was bringing Jacob too, to try and get a photo for next year's Christmas cards. Even the dog seemed to have caught onto the excitement as he was pulling Immy along and giving little barks of joy.

They had a fifteen-minute slot for Zara to chat to Santa so the children weren't just rushed in and rushed back out and, because it was all timed and run like a military machine, there wasn't a lot of queuing. After a few minutes of chatting to the elves outside and stroking the reindeer, they were whisked inside the cottage which, impossibly, looked even more festive since the last time Alex had been in there.

Santa was sitting in a big cosy red armchair and there were other chairs next to him for the children to sit on.

'Hello Zara,' Santa said.

'Hello,' Zara said, suddenly quiet. Maybe nerves were taking over.

'Come and take a seat.'

Zara sat next to him and Alex glanced over at Quinn who was videoing their encounter on his phone.

'Are you looking forward to Christmas?' Santa asked.

Zara nodded excitedly. 'Yes, very much.'

'What are you most looking forward to?'

'My roller skating party tomorrow night. That's going to be epic. Having lunch at Nanny's. That's always fun. She makes amazing puddings and there's always lots of chocolate and everyone plays games in the afternoon and even the adults all join in. And presents, I always get books and I love books.'

'Wow, that sounds like a wonderful Christmas.'

'It is.'

'And I believe you have some questions for me?'

'Yes,' she said eagerly. 'How do you get around the whole world in one night?'

'That's an excellent question. Because of the time zones, I actually have over thirty-one hours of night time to deliver all the presents, which is quite a lot. The reindeer are magic and can fly at incredible speeds, and the sleigh is powered by rocket fuel, making it the fastest vehicle in the world.'

Santa was obviously quite pleased with this answer. Zara, however, wasn't taking any prisoners. 'When meteors hit the earth they are travelling so fast they normally burn up in the atmosphere. How do you not burn up when you're travelling so fast?'

Quinn suppressed a snort of laughter.

Immy shook her head. 'That kid is so freaking smart,' she whispered.

Santa's smile faltered for just a second. 'We have a magical bubble around the reindeer and the sleigh that keeps us cool and allows us to breathe at such high altitudes.'

Zara nodded. 'That's pretty cool.'

'It is. Christmas magic is the coolest thing ever.'

Zara nodded.

'Now is there anything in particular you wanted for Christmas?' Santa asked.

'A new dad,' Zara said, without missing a beat.

Alex's heart leapt.

'Oh,' Santa eyed Quinn. 'Umm… what's wrong with the dad that you have?'

'Quinn isn't my real dad, silly.'

'Oh of course, my mistake. I know all the children in the world, but sometimes I have a hard time keeping track of all the adults.' He looked at Quinn and back at Zara, then said something Alex hadn't been expecting. 'You two look alike.'

Zara nodded. 'He's my dad's brother but my dad died many years ago and now I'd like Quinn to be my new dad.'

Alex glanced at Quinn who had the biggest smile on his face as Zara spoke. He was still recording the whole thing on his phone and she hoped this would be something he would look back on with fond memories.

'Well, being a dad is a big responsibility,' Santa said. 'What makes you think Quinn is up for the job?'

'He's nice to me, reads stories to me with silly voices, he plays games with me, he listens when I talk to him, he buys me books and toys sometimes and sometimes he buys me cakes and sweets. He walks me to school every morning but pretends that he has to go into town to pick up some metal but it's because he cares about me and doesn't want me to get hurt, he also tells me he loves me at the school gates and gives me the best hugs.'

Alex swallowed a lump in her throat.

Santa was smiling. 'Now those sound like very good dad qualities.'

'And he makes Mum happy, very happy,' Zara continued. 'I think that's what a dad should do. They need to make mums happy too. That's important. My real dad used to make my mum cry and now she smiles all the time because she is in love with Quinn and when she smiles and laughs that makes me happy too. I think she needs a new husband as well, so she's not sad anymore.'

Santa nodded thoughtfully while Alex blushed furiously. He must be used to hearing personal family stories like this one and knew how to deal with them, without interfering in people's private lives. He was sure to say something like, 'Well, we'll have to see what I can do,' or 'A new dad is a little beyond Santa's control.'

He cleared his throat. 'Quinn, do you want to be Zara's new dad?'

Alex's eyes bulged out of her head. Why would he ask that?

But Quinn didn't even pause before answering. 'Nothing would make me happier, I love her.'

Zara's smile grew on her face. 'And I love you.'

Santa clearly wasn't done. 'And would you like to be Alex's husband?'

How did he know her name?

Quinn nodded. 'That would make me the happiest man in the world. I love her with everything I have.'

Santa turned to Alex. 'And do you love Quinn?'

She swallowed. 'Of course I do. He makes me ridiculously happy.'

Santa turned back to Zara. 'Well, it might not happen straightaway but it looks like you might get your wish after all.'

'Yay, thank you Santa,' Zara said.

'Umm, yes, thanks,' Alex said.

'Did you want to take some photos?' Santa said, innocently, as if he hadn't just promised the world to Zara.

'Yes, thanks,' Alex said. She took a few photos with her phone and then Immy took the opportunity to have a few photos taken with Jacob sitting next to Santa before they were ushered out the back door.

'Well, that was… interesting,' Immy said.

'I'm getting a new dad for Christmas,' Zara said. 'And Mum gets a new husband.'

'Not for Christmas,' Quinn was quick to explain. 'Santa did say it might take a while.'

'Why would it take a while?'

'Because adults don't like to rush into anything,' Immy said. 'They like to take the time to make sure something is the right decision before they do it. If they need to buy a new car, they don't just rush out and buy one that day. They take the time to research which model is the best, they talk to people about their experiences with the car, they might go and test drive a few before they buy one.'

'But how can it be a wrong decision?' Zara said. 'They love each other, they make each other happy. Are they going to test drive other mums and dads before they make a decision?'

'Yeah, that might have been a bad analogy,' Immy muttered.

'No, we won't be doing that,' Alex said. 'But this is very new for us, so we need time to get used to the idea of living together or getting married.'

She felt like she was protesting against books in a library. Her and Quinn's love story was already inevitably set in stone. Zara was right, they loved each other, they made each other happy, they knew each other so well; why was she holding back from taking that step with him? She knew this man was her future so what would it take for her to say, yes, I want to get married to you? What was it she was looking for?

❄

Quinn knocked on Tina's door a short while later as he tried to decide how to play this. He wanted to appeal to her better nature but he wasn't sure she had one of those. He wanted to protect Alex and he'd do whatever it took to do that.

After a few moments she came to the door and Tina's eyes widened when she saw who it was.

'Quinn, hi.'

'Can I come in?'

'Umm… I…'

'I won't be long.'

'Er… sure, come in.'

She moved back to let him in and he stepped inside.

'Please take a seat,' she gestured to her black leather sofa. He sat down and she took the armchair opposite him. 'What can I do for you?'

'You know why I'm here.'

Tina had the good grace to look awkward – which was something, he supposed. If she was defiant about her opinion this would be a lot harder, but as was the case with most keyboard warriors, they were never brave enough to say these things to people's faces.

'Alex was really upset this morning about your post on the neighbourhood forum and quite honestly I was shocked by it. I could understand that kind of hatred towards her if she'd been seen kicking puppies or stealing a kid's toy or mugging an old lady but having a boyfriend hardly feels like the crime of the century.'

'It feels like a betrayal of Liam.'

'Does it? Does it really? He's been dead over four years. He loved her, do you really think he would want her to be alone and miserable for the rest of his life? Or do you think he'd want her to find someone else and be happy again?'

Tina clearly faltered with what to say to that before she folded her arms across her chest and fixed him with a look. 'It's not right that she moves on with Liam's brother. How do you think he would react to that?'

'Actually, I think he would be happy for us. As you probably know we weren't on speaking terms for a few years before his death and I never met Alex until his funeral but Liam and Alex had a conversation about it, one of those silly, what would you do if I die, conversations. He told Alex that he wanted her to find someone else – he said that if we ever met we'd hit it off and that if he could choose anyone for her to marry and be a dad to Zara it would be me.'

Tina stared at him. 'How do I know you're telling the truth?'

'You don't, but I know my conscience is clear. And this thing between me and Alex, it isn't just a silly meaningless fling, we love each other. And I will do everything I can to make her happy. Surely the people of Lovegrove Bay would want that for her after everything she's been through?'

'Well… yes, I suppose.'

'And Zara, I love her like she's my own. She has missed out on so much without Liam in her life, it's time she had someone who is there for her, always.'

'Yes, having a loving father figure in her life is important,' Tina agreed. 'But I still don't think—'

'Can I show you something?' Quinn asked, fishing his phone out of his pocket. He found the video and stood up to show it to Tina. 'This is Zara's visit to see Santa this morning.'

Tina watched as Zara talked about how she wanted a new dad for Christmas and how much he meant to her and Quinn could see he might have actually thawed

Tina's cold heart. He heard Zara mention how Liam made Alex cry and he cursed under his breath. In making his plan to win Tina round he had forgotten about that bit. The video came to an end.

'Alex was so worried about starting a new relationship and it would be awful if she walked away from happiness for her and her daughter because the whole town is attacking her for it.'

'No, that would be wrong, very wrong,' Tina said, quietly.

'So can I have your assurance that this won't happen again?'

'Yes, of course.'

'And some kind of apology to her wouldn't go amiss.'

'Yes, I'm sorry, I'll do that,' Tina said, looking suitably chastised.

He nodded. 'Thank you.'

He turned to leave.

'What did Zara mean, that Liam made Alex cry?' Tina asked.

Quinn cursed. He'd thought he'd got away with that. He didn't want to tell her anything that could ever get back to Zara. And Alex had kept Liam's problem with alcohol under wraps for years so he wasn't about to spill that but maybe the town should know that Liam wasn't as squeaky clean as they believed. Then maybe Alex moving on wouldn't be such an issue.

'Can I count on your discretion?'

'Of course.'

That wasn't likely but he'd take it. 'Liam had an affair.'

He didn't think one night could technically be counted as an affair but the betrayal was still the same.

Tina gasped. 'No!'

'Yes, I'm afraid so. They were very happy together but then his best friend died and he took it very badly. Alex tried everything to get him counselling to no avail but one of the ways he found comfort was in the arms of someone else. This was about eighteen months before he died. Alex knew then that their relationship was over but she stayed because she wanted to support him through his grief. She is a good, kind person, a wonderful wife and mother. She never deserved that.'

'I never knew.'

'No one did, she kept that secret because she didn't want the people of the town to shun him when he needed their support to get over his grief.'

'That's… noble. Most women would want revenge.'

Quinn shook his head. 'She isn't like that, and she knew Liam wasn't himself.'

'That poor girl,' Tina said.

'Yeah. But that's why her happiness is so important to me now, she's been through enough.'

'I'll sort it, you mark my words.'

'Thank you.'

He walked to the door and Tina let him out. As he walked up the road he let out a sigh of relief.

❄

Dear Alex,

You only have a few days left before I disappear forever. Maybe you've started to get a good idea of who I am or maybe you still have no clue, but you probably shouldn't put all your duck eggs in one basket.

The bauble I leave tonight will be another big clue to my identity. It's one of my hobbies, something I love to do, although I'm sure it will find a home with someone else who loves that hobby too.

Snowy hugs,
St Nick

CHAPTER 16

Alex was busily making a few more Christmassy decorations to sell in her shop. Since getting back from their visit to Santa there had been a steady flow of customers all looking for last-minute gifts. Her book page baubles were proving very popular as gifts so she was making more of those. They didn't take too long and she had a bit of a production line going where she was trying to make ten different ones at the same time. Zara was also making a few, and Alex had promised her that if any of hers sold all the money would be hers. Zara's were simple but really effective. Alex looked around the shop. Half of her stock had been emptied over the last few days so she wanted to try and restock as much as possible. She was still open tomorrow and probably until lunch on Christmas Eve, but that was up to her if she wanted to work that late. She might just take the day off to do Christmas activities with Zara.

'Hello!'

Alex looked up to see Violet standing in the doorway and her heart leapt. Quinn and Alex had been intending to pop by to see Violet that evening to talk to her about their relationship. Quinn had gone to talk to Tina so she felt a bit vulnerable possibly having to face her wrath by herself.

Fortunately, Zara was there to break the ice.

'Nanny!' Zara abandoned her craft efforts and ran over to give Violet a hug.

'Hello, my beautiful girl,' Violet said, enveloping Zara in her arms.

'We went to see Santa this morning and I asked him for a new dad and a new husband for Mum,' Zara told her. 'He asked Quinn if he wanted to be my dad and he said yes and that he loved me very much. And he asked him if he wanted to be Mummy's husband and he said yes and now I think they might get married and I'll probably be the bridesmaid. Harley is going to be bridesmaid at her mummy's wedding to Jake so I think I'll probably be bridesmaid too for Mum and Quinn. And then I'll have a new daddy and I'm so excited because I love Quinn too.'

Alex stared at Zara in horror. If Alex had been hoping to approach the topic gently that had gone straight out the window.

'I see,' Violet said, giving nothing away. 'Why don't you go and get us all some mince pie muffins from the café.' She opened her handbag and gave Zara some money. Zara ran out of the room.

'Violet, we were going to tell you, but everything is

so new and—' Alex stalled as Violet put her hand up to stem the tide.

'I'm not mad.'

'You're not?'

'No, and you know I understand better than anyone about keeping relationships a secret, I'm doing that exact same thing myself.'

'I wanted to tell you when you were here the other day but I wasn't sure if it was best coming from Quinn or if we should at least tell you together.'

'It would have been nice to be told rather than finding out from that busybody, Jacqualyn Rumsey, but I long suspected you two had a connection. Quinn moved to Lovegrove Bay so he could be there for you. He moved his studio to here to be close to you. He never told me but that boy has been in love with you for years.'

'I've been in love with him for years too,' Alex said, quietly.

She nodded. 'I think he held off out of respect for Liam and out of respect for you and your grief.'

'Yes, and I held off out of respect for you.'

Violet's eyebrows shot up. 'For me?'

'You'd lost a son. I knew it would be inappropriate for me to move on with Quinn so soon after Liam's death.'

'I was heartbroken that Liam died, of course I was, coupled with guilt that I could have done more to help him with his drink problem. But knowing how he died I always wondered if he had reverted back to his old ways. Then Quinn told me what happened eighteen months before he died, that his best friend died and he'd snapped. I always knew something like that would push him over the edge. But I know how awful he was to be around when he was drunk. If you lived with that for eighteen months I imagine it was somewhat of a relief that he died.'

Alex looked at her in surprise. 'I was never relieved that he died, I never wished for that, but I was relieved it was over. He was rude and nasty to me every day and to wake up knowing that I wouldn't have to deal with his vile moods that day or ever again was a huge relief.'

She hadn't wanted to tell Violet any of this before as she hadn't wanted to ruin her memories of her son. But Violet had lived through it too, before their estrangement, she knew only too well what Liam was capable of.

'I'm so sorry,' Violet said. 'I wish we'd spoken about this before but I was so desperate to have a relationship with Zara after the funeral, I didn't want to pry too much into your life and start asking you questions about Liam's alcoholism. But I would never have thought badly of you for moving on, no matter how soon it was after his death.'

'I grieved the loss of our relationship eighteen months before he died,' Alex said. 'I think that's why my heart fell in love so quickly, I was ready to move on even if I felt so guilty doing so.'

'You have nothing to feel guilty for.'

Alex bit her lip. 'Is it weird that I'm moving on with Quinn? Half the town seems to think it is.'

'Half the town can mind their own bloody business.

And most of them have secrets far worse and more sordid than you could even imagine. It's not weird at all. You spent so much time together after Liam died because Quinn wanted to be there for you and Zara so it's only natural that you two connected on that level. I'm happy for you. Quinn is a good man and he'll look after you with a fierce loyalty. He's never been in love before so I'm so glad he's found that with you. You are a wonderful woman and I think you'll be good for each other.'

Just then Quinn arrived in Alex's studio, clearly having run up the stairs.

'I saw your car in the car park,' he said to his mother and gestured, obviously a little out of breath. He focussed his attention on Alex. 'Is everything OK?'

'Everything is fine,' Violet answered for her. 'I'm very happy for you both. Now let me go and see how Zara is doing with those muffins.' She moved to the door and then turned back. 'But if I have to hear about your engagement from bloody Jacqualyn Rumsey, there will be hell to pay.'

'I promise you'll be the first to know,' Alex said. 'Well, after Zara. In fact she'll probably be the one to tell you she'll be so excited.'

Violet smiled. 'I look forward to it.'

With that she left them alone.

Quinn quickly crossed the room and took her in his arms. 'Was she OK?'

'She was more than OK with it, she's really happy.'

'Really?'

Alex nodded. 'Well, she's not impressed she found out about it from someone other than us but she's happy. She saw it coming a mile off. She says we'll be good for each other.'

'Well, you're certainly good for me.'

She smiled.

'I am relieved she's happy,' Quinn said. 'With Dad and Liam gone, she's only got me and I'd never want to do anything to hurt her. I mean, if she wasn't happy we'd have to try and win her round because there was no way I'm ever giving up on you, but I'm glad we won't see any resistance there.'

'And maybe, if she ever starts dating someone, you can remember this and keep an open mind,' Alex suggested.

He shook his head. 'I don't think that will happen, she loved my dad.'

'You never know when love might strike, sometimes it appears in the unlikeliest of places. Take Xander and Immy for example, who'd have ever seen them two together? I mean, it may never happen for them, love, but even them sleeping together is a bit of a shock, so keep an open mind.'

'I thought I saw Mum with a man the other day actually, but I couldn't be sure it was her as she was hiding her face in the menu in a café. But even just seeing her hair and clothes, I'm pretty sure it was her.'

Alex decided to change the subject. She certainly didn't want to drop poor Violet in it.

'How did it go with Tina?' she asked.

'That went surprisingly well too. You might even get a public apology from her.'

Alex laughed. 'I'll wait with bated breath for that one.'

'Yeah, I'm not sure that will happen either but she did say she was sorry and regrets posting what she did.'

'Well that's something. Can you go round and speak to everyone else in the town too?'

'If that's what it takes to make you happy then I will.'

She smiled with love for him. 'You make me happy, I don't need their validation. Zara and Violet are happy. I don't need anything more than that. Let the people talk if that's how they get their kicks. I know what we have is special and there's nothing that can stand in the way of that.'

❄

Alex watched as Zara helped Quinn around the ice skating rink. They had been skating for about half an hour and Alex had just got off the ice to have a rest. Although she could skate, she felt like she was using muscles in her legs and feet she didn't even know she had. Quinn, however, was skating like Bambi on ice, all shaky legs and feet going in opposite directions. Zara was holding his hand and very patiently trying to teach him how to do it. She looked so ridiculously happy.

God, Alex loved this man so much. He was every-thing she ever wanted in a partner and so much more. He completed her, made her whole again. And suddenly she realised what St Nick meant when he referred to his girlfriend or friend as his other half. Being together just made sense like they were two halves of a whole.

And that had been the sticking point between being able to pinpoint Quinn as St Nick. She couldn't understand why he would refer to her as his other half when they weren't together at that point. But now she understood it. He had always been the other half of her heart.

Just then Quinn and Zara came over to the barrier where she was sitting. Even though Quinn had been struggling, his face was glowing with happiness. He was loving spending this time with Zara as much as Zara was.

'Wow, skating is exhausting,' Quinn said, taking his woolly hat off and running his hand through his hair.

'We've only just started,' Zara said, laughing.

Quinn looked at Alex strangely. 'You look like you're figuring something out.'

'Just putting my ducks in a row.'

He smiled. 'Is that right?'

She slowly pointed to three imaginary ducks in a line in front of her that led between her and Quinn. 'Quack, quack, quack.'

'You're weird,' Zara laughed.

'That's why you love me.'

Quinn smiled. 'Are you ready to make your accusation then, Barnaby?'

'Not quite yet.'

'OK.'

'Come on,' Zara said, 'I want to show you some tricks.'

She tugged his hand and he winked at Alex as he skated away. 'I think a good trick will be me not falling over on my butt.'

Alex watched them together and smiled. Suddenly she was joined in the seats by the mum of one of the kids in Zara's class. Alex didn't really know her but she'd probably nodded hello to her a few times at the school gates.

'Hi, I thought I'd come over and say hello,' said the woman. 'I'm Kayleigh, Jessica's mum.'

'Hello,' Alex said. Jessica wasn't one of Zara's friends so she wasn't sure where this was leading to.

'I just wanted to say, I find this whole thing a bit weird,' Kayleigh gestured between Alex, Quinn and Zara.

Alex blinked in surprise at the audacity. 'Why?'

'Because he's her uncle.'

'Yes, but he's not my uncle, so I'm not sure why it's weird.'

'If it gets serious between you, what will she call him? Uncle Dad?' Kayleigh laughed.

'Well right now she calls him Quinn so if... *when* we get married, I imagine that won't change.'

'You're really going to get married?' Kayleigh pulled a face.

'I'm sorry, I fail to see how this is any of your business.'

'It just feels weird. Even Jessica was asking me about it.'

'Look at them,' Alex said, pointing to Zara and Quinn. 'Look at how ridiculously happy they are together. Surely that's more important than anything else, that Zara is loved and happy. Surely anyone with an ounce of kindness would want that for me too.'

'I just think he can do better than his brother's cast-offs.'

Alex felt her mouth fall open in shock at the pure rudeness.

'It's just so weird, everyone says so,' Kayleigh said.

'Fortunately I couldn't give a rat's ass what anyone else thinks.' Alex smiled as she realised that was true. She didn't care. They could talk and gossip and laugh all they wanted, it wouldn't change a thing. 'I'm in love, he loves me. I am so freaking happy right now. Some sad, lonely people who have nothing better to do with their time than stick their nose in other people's business really aren't going to impact on me. Now excuse me while I join my family.'

She got up and skated over to join Quinn and Zara. She wrapped her arms around Quinn and gave him a kiss in front of everyone. Let them talk. They couldn't ruin this for her, no one could.

❄

Quinn peered out the window of the car into Christmas Gardens. They'd only been there on their stakeout for fifteen minutes and Zara was already bored, lying curled up under a pile of blankets in the back seat of the car, reading a book. Zara had insisted on a proper car stakeout, like you see in the movies and TV shows and although he'd been happy to go along with that, doing it from his house would have been much more comfortable.

There were plenty of Christmas snacks stuffed in the car: mince pies, Christmas-pudding-flavoured fudge, gingerbread men, mini chocolate yule logs, even apple-and-cinnamon cakes decorated with little iced Christmas trees. Alex was still unpacking all the snacks onto the dashboard as if they were going to be here for months, not just an hour or so. Plus she'd made a flask of white hot chocolate which she was currently pouring out into plastic mugs. She then sprayed squirty cream on the tops and sprinkled them with tiny marshmallows before handing the mugs to Quinn and Zara.

Quinn smiled as he took his. She really had thought of everything.

They were parked at the side of the gardens with the house on the far side from where they were, all lit up and twinkling under the abundance of lights. Although slightly unnecessary, Zara was intermittently watching the house and surrounding gardens through a pair of binoculars.

They took a few minutes to drink their hot chocolates, the windows steaming up slightly with their hot breath.

Quinn finished his mug and Alex took it off him and put it, along with hers and Zara's, back in her bag.

'I got another message,' Alex said as she continued to unpack yet more snacks. Quinn knew Alex hadn't told Zara about the messages because she didn't want her daughter to figure out St Nick's true identity from the clues and then blab it all over the town. Alex had promised St Nick anonymity and it looked like she was going to keep that promise. Quinn also knew that Alex didn't necessarily want to ruin the magic of St Nick by telling her who it was.

'What did he say?' Quinn said.

'He said I should be careful about putting all my duck eggs in one basket.'

'That's an odd expression,' Quinn said, trying not to laugh.

'I thought that too.'

'Most people just say don't put all your eggs in one basket, they don't specify which breed of bird.'

'No, exactly,' Alex agreed. 'I feel like it might be another clue.'

'That he likes ducks?' Quinn asked, innocently.

'Maybe. I got some snacks for you too. I know you don't really have a sweet tooth, so I got you some sausage rolls and steak slices from Sweet Escapes, I know you like them.'

He smiled. 'Thank you, that's really thoughtful.'

'And while sweet things are not really your preference, I did get you these crème brûlée doughnuts from Donut Park to try. See if I can convert you to the sweeter side.'

Quinn took them and couldn't help smiling. He had

hoped that tonight's forthcoming stunt meant he might be able to throw Alex off the scent for a little while longer but he'd clearly been too obvious with his clues and his emails. Should he lie and say he didn't like them? Although he promised her he'd never lie, not even about this.

'They're my favourite,' he said.

He could see the realisation dawning across Alex's face and knew his secret was blown. Her whole face lit up with utter joy and she reached out to stroke his face. 'You are the most wonderful, kindest man and I love you so much.'

He had hoped to do a big reveal on Christmas Eve but maybe this way was better. No fanfare, just this quiet moment between them.

'What are we going to do if we see St Nick?' Zara said, interrupting their moment. 'Will we apprehend him?'

'Well, he hasn't actually done anything wrong so I'm not sure he deserves to be arrested,' Quinn said.

Zara giggled. 'I didn't mean that. I meant, will we go up to him and speak to him, let him know he's been caught red-handed?'

'I don't know, I quite like the idea of us knowing but him not knowing that we know,' Quinn said. 'As today is only the twenty-second, St Nick might have several more baubles he wants to give to people before the big day. If we tell him he's been rumbled he might not want to give them and that would spoil it for any intended recipients.'

'That's true,' Alex said.

'You'll know who it is and that's enough. What you choose to do with that information is up to you.'

'What if we don't know who it is?' Zara said.

He'd hoped to get away with that question and just put in her mind about not chasing after St Nick when they saw him.

'I think you'll know. This person knows the people he's targeting, he knows your favourite colour, your mum's favourite flower, people's favourite animals and hobbies. This can't be a mystery person – it's someone who lives here, it has to be.'

'What if he's in disguise?' Zara asked.

This kid was way too smart.

'Why would he be in disguise?'

'In case someone is watching him to try and catch him.'

'How would he know someone was trying to catch him?'

'You might have told him,' Zara said, innocently.

'Why would I have told him?'

'Because you don't want us to find out who it is.'

Quinn knew Zara was super smart, but he hadn't been expecting her to read his actual freaking mind.

'Why would I not want you to know who it is?' he said carefully.

'Because you might be in cahoots with him.'

He laughed. He loved this kid so much.

'It would make sense it was you,' Zara said, peering through her binoculars at him. 'Most of the baubles were found here in Christmas Gardens where you live. You would know what my favourite colour is and what Mum's favourite flowers are. You know a lot of the people who've got baubles.'

'I think those things are merely coincidences.'

Zara huffed and went back to reading her book.

'Are we… actually going to see anything tonight?' Alex whispered. 'Because if not we could go home right now.' She placed her hand on his thigh and arched an eyebrow at him.

'Oh no, we're going to see something, I'm sure of it. I'm not sure what we'll see but we'll see *something*.'

She looked at him in confusion.

Quinn was saved from any further questions by Max's arrival. They hadn't discussed what disguise he should wear, just that he should wear one. Quinn had assumed, as he was supposed to be St Nick, that Max might dress as Santa Claus but instead Max had gone for one of those inflatable T-rex costumes. Maybe the costume shop in town had a limited supply of festive outfits at this time of year.

They all watched in silent disbelief as Max waddled across Christmas Gardens carrying the precious white box between his tiny claws. The costume was definitely not the best to wear in snowy conditions as he was slipping and sliding all over the place. Those tiny, costumed arms were not the best for holding anything, let alone a highly breakable porcelain bauble. Quinn's precious bauble was likely going to end up as a casualty in this charade.

Max teetered to the left so severely they all gasped. He managed to right himself but then lurched violently to the other side. The box wobbled in his tiny claws. He slipped and waddled and staggered then suddenly his two feet shot up in the air and everything seemed to happen in slow motion as the box flew up in the air too. Max landed on his back, but miraculously the box fell on top of him, which hopefully managed to cushion its fall.

Max wiggled and rolled around in a desperate attempt to get back up but to no avail.

'Should we go and help him?' Alex said.

'I'll go, stay here with Zara,' Quinn said.

'Why?' Zara moaned.

'Because dinosaurs are dangerous.'

He quickly got out and ran across the gardens to where Max was lying. 'Are you OK? Are you hurt?'

'No, thankfully the inflatable part of the suit cushioned my fall.'

'I'm not sure the T-rex costume was the best choice,' Quinn said, helping his cousin to his feet with a great deal of effort, since Max's feet kept slipping and sliding underneath him.

'No, with hindsight, probably not, but I thought it might make Zara laugh.'

'It's definitely something she will remember. Here, give me the bauble.'

Max readily handed it over, obviously happy to be free of the responsibility.

'Are you OK to get back?' Quinn asked.

'As soon as I'm out of sight, I'll get out of the costume.'

Quinn suspected the getting-out-of-sight business would take a lot longer than Max was hoping.

Max waddled off and Quinn watched him for a short while to make sure he didn't fall again, then he took the bauble back to the car.

'Was he OK?' Alex said.

'Yes, he was fine.'

'So who was it?' Zara asked.

'I don't know, I didn't ask.'

'You didn't ask?' she said incredulously.

'Well no, the man had clearly gone to a lot of trouble to preserve his anonymity. I didn't want to ruin that by unmasking him or asking the T-rex for some ID. But I can confirm he was a man. Or a very deep-voiced woman.'

'I can't believe you didn't find out,' Zara said.

'It just didn't seem fair, not when he was on his back like a beached whale.'

'And you didn't recognise the voice?' Alex asked, clearly playing along.

Quinn shook his head. 'But I did collect the bauble from him.'

He handed it to Zara.

'It's a rugby ball!' Zara said in delight.

'Ah, that would explain the message,' Alex said, quietly. 'You like rugby, Quinn, you should have this bauble.'

'Ah, umm, no, I mean, I do, but I'd rather someone

else had this bauble.'

'No, you haven't had one yet, you should have it,' Zara insisted.

'Max and Xander like playing rugby too, maybe we can give it to one of them,' Quinn tried.

'And Mr Gillespie next door loves watching rugby, we could give it to him,' Alex said, giving Quinn a look that said she knew she was fighting a losing battle.

Zara shook her head. 'No, I want Quinn to hang his bauble on our tree next to ours. It's a family tree and he's part of our family.'

Fortunately he hadn't painted this bauble for anyone specifically, just as another clue for Alex, but it looked like he'd now inadvertently given himself one of his own baubles.

'OK, we can hang it on your tree,' Quinn said, giving Alex a shrug.

'Shall we go home?' Alex said. 'I've got something I really need to take care of.'

She gave Quinn a look and he quickly started the engine. 'Yes, let's go home.'

He drove deliberately round the full length of Christmas Gardens just to make sure Max wasn't flat on his back somewhere, struggling to get out of his costume, but when there was no sign of him, he drove back up the hill towards Alex's house as Alex hurriedly packed all the snacks away.

They walked back into the house. There was no sign of Immy but Jacob was curled up in his basket fast asleep.

'Go and brush your teeth and get changed for bed, I'll be up in a few minutes to read you a story,' Alex said to Zara.

'Can Quinn read it to me?'

'Yes, of course,' Quinn said.

'Yes!' Zara ran upstairs.

Alex looped her arms round his neck. 'So it was you, all along?'

'Yes, are you mad?' He wrapped his arms around her.

'No, not at all. How could I be mad?'

'Well, I never directly lied to you, but there was a whole lot of deception.'

'In the best possible way. This was such a lovely thing to do. Thank you.' She leaned up and kissed him, pressing herself up against him, and he held her tighter.

She pulled back. 'And maybe I have special ways to thank you tonight.'

'Well I look forward to that.'

'Will you stay?'

'All night?' Quinn queried. 'What about Zara?'

'We'll deal with any questions she might have about that tomorrow.'

'Then yes, of course. But now you've figured it out, a deal is a deal. You get one custom bauble of your choice.'

'Then I'd like one of Jacob, for Immy.'

'I'll have it ready for Christmas Eve.'

'And I meant what I said before,' Alex added. 'I'm going to make you a bauble too, something you really want. Just as soon as I figure out what I can make for you.'

'You don't need to do that. I didn't do it for any kind of reward, just to put a smile on people's faces.'

'I want to.'

'OK.'

'Quinn!' Zara called from upstairs. 'I'm ready for my story.'

'OK! I'm coming.'

He gave Alex a brief kiss and pulled out of her arms.

'Make it a short story,' Alex said as he ran out the room.

'Oh I will.'

CHAPTER 17

❄

Alex was just trying to finish her breakfast when Immy came downstairs still in her pyjamas. She'd finished work for the Christmas holidays now and wouldn't be going back for a week. Quinn had left early, not to avoid awkward questions with Zara but because he needed to go back home to get changed.

'Hey,' Immy said, stretching and yawning sleepily. 'How did the stakeout go last night?'

'Well, we saw someone in disguise delivering a bauble. He was wearing one of those inflatable T-rex costumes. The poor guy was staggering and sliding all over the place and then he fell over and Quinn went to help him out.'

That was all truthful but Alex wouldn't be telling her sister that she'd finally found out it was Quinn all along, not unless Quinn told her she could tell Immy. She'd promised him full anonymity and, while she knew she could trust Immy completely, she didn't want to go back on her promise. She felt a bit bad about having to lie to Immy and Zara but it was only a little lie or a work-around of the truth.

'So did you find out who it was?' Immy asked.

'No, Quinn didn't think it was fair.'

'I can't believe you saw St Nick last night and you're still no closer to finding out his identity. You had the perfect chance to unmask him, *Scooby-Doo* style, and you didn't take it.'

'It didn't really seem fair, the poor guy had fallen over.'

Immy took a sip of her coffee that Alex had made for her. 'I think I know who it is.'

'You do, who?'

'I think it's Quinn.'

Alex's eyes widened in surprise that Immy had figured it out too.

'But he was on the stakeout with us, in the car, when we saw the T-rex.'

'Yes, the perfect alibi.'

'Ohhh! You think he got someone to cover for him, pretend they were St Nick to give Quinn a watertight alibi?'

'Exactly,' Immy said, proudly. Clearly all the cosy mysteries that Alex had forced Immy to watch had rubbed off on her.

'What makes you think it's Quinn?' Alex asked.

'Well, the fact that the majority of the baubles were found in and around Christmas Gardens is a bit suspicious, it gives Quinn plenty of opportunity. The person clearly knows things about us: Zara's love of roller skating, her favourite colour, your favourite flowers. It's definitely someone who knows us. And lastly, while it would make sense that St Nick is delivering these baubles with some kind of scarf and hat covering his face, I don't think he's walking round the town in full disguise. Someone would see him and it would be too noticeable if it was something ridiculous like a unicorn costume or an inflatable T-rex. Also, the T-rex costume is really hard to manoeuvre in at the best of times; I've been in one and it's really difficult – factor in several inches of snow and you've got a recipe for disaster. You said the poor guy was slipping and staggering all over the place. If St Nick was using the T-rex costume on a regular basis, he would know how hard it is to walk in it and either he'd get better at walking around in it or change the costume for something more practical. The person in that costume last night clearly had no idea how to walk safely in it. I would guess it's the first time he wore it. Which means either St Nick knew you were there and knew he would have to amp up the disguise so he wouldn't be recognised or that wasn't St Nick, just someone pretending to be.'

'But he had the bauble,' Alex protested.

'Yes, so if it wasn't St Nick, it was someone in cahoots with him. And if it was the real St Nick, someone, probably Quinn, told him you were going to be there.'

'So if Quinn isn't St Nick, you think he's St Nick's accomplice?' Alex asked.

'Exactly. I have no actual proof. I think in a court of law they would say this was circumstantial at best. But I have my eye on young Quinn Campbell.'

Just then Alex heard footsteps coming down the stairs, this time not filled with excitement and joy, but sounding as if Zara was plodding. She arrived in the kitchen a few moments later.

'Hey, you OK?' Alex asked.

'Just tired,' Zara said, yawning widely.

Clearly the late-night stakeout had taken its toll.

'Are you going to work already?' Zara asked, sitting down at the breakfast table.

'Not yet, but soon. Are you ready to go?'

Zara yawned again. 'Soon.'

'Or, if you don't want to go to work with your mum today, you can stay here and help me wrap the presents,' Immy said.

'Oh can I?' she asked her mum.

'Of course.'

'Yes!' Zara did a little victory punch. 'I'll be in charge of ribbons and bows.'

'That sounds like a plan,' Immy said.

'Great idea,' Alex said. 'Then you can take it easy and be well rested for tonight. You have your roller skating Christmas party, you don't want to miss that.'

'Oh yes,' Zara said. 'I'm really looking forward to that.'

Although she didn't sound like she was looking forward to it, Alex knew she was just tired and would be feeling much more alert and enthusiastic in a few hours' time. Zara wouldn't miss a chance to do roller skating for the world and tonight there was a roller skating disco, Zara's favourite thing.

There was a knock on the back door as Quinn let himself in.

'Hey.' Quinn came over and gave Alex a quick kiss on the cheek. 'I'm just popping in as I'm off to work early today because I'm leaving early this afternoon for my rugby club Christmas party tonight.'

'The murder mystery one?' Zara asked, her eyes lighting up. Anything to do with gore and she was invested.

'Yes, I have to go as an evil mad scientist, so I'll have to spend a few hours this afternoon getting into my costume. I've been watching YouTube tutorials on how to make yourself look old with special effect make-up, so I'm going to have a go at doing that this afternoon to make my skin all saggy and wrinkly.'

'Will you send us photos?' Zara said, excitedly.

'Of course. I've been looking forward to this for months, it will be a lot of fun, but I'm probably most looking forward to seeing everyone's costumes. Everyone normally puts in a lot of effort. I'll take photos of everyone and text them to you.'

Zara had a mobile phone which unlike many of her friends she almost never used. It was off most of the time. She just took it out with her in case she needed to ring Alex for any reason. It made Alex feel happier knowing she had it in an emergency or if Zara needed her. It made Zara roll her eyes every time Alex asked if she had it with her. At least looking out for photos from Quinn's party might actually make Zara want to take it with her tonight.

'You're going to look so funny,' Zara said, resting her head on her arms.

'Right, better go, I'll catch you later.' Quinn gave Alex another quick kiss, ruffled Zara's hair, gave Immy a wave and ran out the door.

Immy gave him a mock suspicious glare as he ran down the path, which made Alex smile. If only she knew.

❄

Alex walked into the Wonky Tree Studios a short while later and went straight up to see Quinn. He looked up from where he was working when she walked in and smiled.

'Hey.' He took her in his arms and gave her a kiss. He suddenly looked wary. 'I have some news. Tina has issued a public apology.'

'She hasn't,' Alex said, in surprise.

'Have a look for yourself.'

Quinn fished his phone out of his pocket, swiped the screen a few times and then handed it over.

Alex could see the post was on the neighbourhood forum, just like the last one. There was a part of her that almost didn't want to read it.

. . .

Tina Parker-Barrington: *I would like to formally apologise to Alexandra Campbell for my previous post. It was not my place to cast judgement on someone else's relationship and I'm not sure why I felt the need to negatively comment on something that makes someone else happy. Alexandra and her daughter have had a tough few years and I wish them both only happiness from here on in.*

'That's nice, and she's taking complete accountability for her actions,' Alex said, looking up from the screen. 'I'm not sure what you said to her to make her do such a U-turn with her feelings, but it worked.'

'Well, that's what I wanted to talk to you about—'

'Hang on, let me finish reading.'

It has also come to my attention that Liam was not as squeaky clean as everyone was led to believe, which goes to show no one can really know what goes on behind closed doors and what people are secretly living with. My heart breaks for what Alex had to go through.

Those in glass houses shouldn't throw stones, or as the bible says, 'Let he who is without sin, cast the first stone.' We should all be mindful of throwing stones at our neighbours when we all have our own faults and weaknesses.

. . .

Alex read it through again and felt her blood run cold. She looked up at Quinn. 'What did you tell her about Liam?'

'I was going to tell you but—'

She took a step away from him. 'What did you do? You've told the most indiscreet person and the biggest gossip in the whole of Lovegrove Bay my deepest secrets. Why the hell would you do that?'

'They're not your secrets, they're Liam's. And why are you still protecting him after all this time?'

'I'm not protecting him, I'm protecting Zara. Do you think I ever want her to find out what her dad was really like before he died, what he did to me? No kid needs to hear that.'

Quinn pushed his hand through his hair. 'Look, I just didn't want anyone to think he was this perfect man, because he was far from that. People loved him and, regardless of this statement from Tina, people will still look at you unfavourably because they feel you are betraying the memory of this wonderful, beloved member of the community. I just felt they needed to know he wasn't so saintly.'

'So you told the whole town that he was an alco-holic? That's my business and you had no right to share that.'

'I only spoke to Tina and I never—'

'Look at these comments,' Alex interrupted. "*What do you mean, Liam wasn't squeaky clean,*" and "*What do you know that we don't?*" and this one "*Come on, Tina, dish the dirt.*" Dish the bloody dirt, like my life is now this exciting form of entertainment. It was bad enough when people were gossiping because I was dating Liam's brother but now they have something extra exciting: I was married to an abusive alcoholic. Why would you do this?'

'I was trying to protect you. But I didn't—'

'Protect me, you've destroyed me,' Alex interrupted.

'I've destroyed him, not you. People will feel sorry for you.'

'I don't want their pity.' She took another step away from him. 'I don't want to even be near you right now.'

'Listen, I never told—'

'Please stop talking, and if you respect me at all, you'll stay away from me for the rest of the day.'

'Alex, wait, I didn't tell her…' Quinn started but she turned and walked away, refusing to listen to what he had to say and, thankfully, he didn't follow her.

She needed time to process this. How could she correlate the man she loved, the man who was so kind he would leave painted baubles around the town for everyone to find, with the man who had betrayed her secrets so easily? She knew he'd done it to try to help her, but he had chosen the worst possible thing to share. She felt sick at the thought that pretty soon the whole town would know Liam was an abusive alcoholic and that meant Zara would hear about it too.

CHAPTER 18

Despite working in the room next door to hers, Alex didn't see Quinn for the rest of the day. Many customers from the town came, grabbing last-minute gifts, but none of them looked at her with pity or judgement, in fact none of them spoke about Liam or her and Quinn at all. Was it possible that Tina would keep her secrets? Or maybe so much time had passed that this wouldn't be a big deal after all.

At three, there was a knock on her door and she saw Quinn standing there. She didn't know what to say to him.

'I'm leaving now as I have to get ready for my Christmas party,' Quinn said.

'OK.'

He walked into the room, which was thankfully empty of customers. 'I never told Tina Liam was an alcoholic. I knew you wouldn't want anyone knowing that. I told her he had an affair. I thought it was the lesser of his crimes but would at least show her he wasn't as squeaky clean as she thought.'

'Oh.' Relief coursed through Alex. She could probably cope with people knowing that. Affairs were always hot gossip at the time they came out in the open, but that was only because the two people involved were still around and people could make comments to them when they saw them. However, the furore always died down pretty quickly. Liam's affair, if you could call a one-night stand that, had been years before. Probably no one would care about that now. And if they did it was unlikely something that would come back to haunt her or Zara several years down the line.

'But you're absolutely right,' Quinn continued. 'I should never have told Tina that, it wasn't my place. I just saw how upset you were by the post and people's comments and I wanted it to stop. I showed Tina the video of Zara asking Santa for a new dad, so that she would see how happy she is about us and how in love we are, in the hope that she couldn't be hateful in the face of love and happiness. She saw Zara say that her dad made you cry and she asked why. I should have told her that it was none of her business or at least politely found a way not to share your private business. I'm sorry.'

She swallowed down the lump in her throat. 'OK.'

Quinn nodded and gestured to the door. 'I'm going to go. I have to make this face look old and saggy.'

'That might take a while.'

'Yeah.'

He gave her a little wave and walked towards the door.

'Come round tonight, after the party, if you want to,' Alex said.

He paused. 'If that's what you really want.'

'Yes. That's if you're not too drunk for make-up sex.'

He laughed and came back to her. He took her in his arms and kissed her forehead. 'I am sorry.'

'I know, it's OK.'

'It is?'

'Yeah.'

'OK, then I'll come round. And I won't be drunk. I'm teetotal now so I won't even be drinking a drop.'

'What?'

'I decided last week when you first told me about Liam and how you were scared of losing me. I know you didn't specifically mean losing me to alcoholism. But I thought it might give you peace of mind, like me giving up shellfish. You never have to worry that I'll be coming home drunk to you or Zara, you'll never have to worry that I will be angry because I've drunk too much to be able to control my emotions. And if that gives you one less thing to worry about, if that helps you trust me that little bit more, then why the hell not.'

She stared at him in shock. 'I don't need you to give up drink for me.'

'But I want to,' he assured her. 'I've never been a big drinker so I won't miss it. It's such a tiny thing for me, but maybe a bigger thing for you.'

Alex shook her head. This man was going to ruin

her. She leaned up and kissed him because she couldn't find the words to describe how that made her feel. Safe. He made her feel so safe.

'I love you,' she whispered against his lips.

'I love you too.'

'Then I'll see you tonight.'

He nodded, gave her another brief kiss and then left the room.

❄

Alex was busily singing along to Christmas songs on the radio as she made a fresh batch of mince pies. Zara had gone to her roller skating party – even though she still seemed a little tired, she didn't want to miss it. Immy was at her yoga group's Christmas dinner so Alex was alone. She was going to wrap some of their presents shortly as tomorrow was Christmas Eve.

Quinn had sent her photos of himself as a mad scientist earlier. He was almost unrecognisable as the make-up he'd expertly done on himself made him look forty or fifty years older. She knew he was really looking forward to the evening and seeing everyone else's costumes.

She put the mince pies in the oven, washed everything up and then went upstairs to start wrapping the presents.

Suddenly she heard a noise downstairs which sounded like someone coming through the back door.

'Hello!' called Quinn.

Her heart leapt. What was he doing here? She knew she'd promised him make-up sex but she didn't think he'd forego his much anticipated party for it.

She quickly ran downstairs to see Quinn in full costume and Zara looking decidedly pale and sorry for herself.

'Oh my god, what's happened?' Alex took her daughter in her arms and looked at Quinn in confusion.

'I don't feel well,' Zara said, tearfully. 'I feel sick and my tummy hurts.'

'Why didn't you call me?' Alex said.

'I did, and Immy, but no one answered.' Zara looked at her in that accusing way that only children could, the kind of look reserved for someone who had utterly betrayed them.

'What? My phone is here.' She grabbed it off the table to find that it was off. She switched it back on but it was utterly unresponsive. 'Oh no, I think the battery is dead.'

'So I had to phone Quinn.'

'I'm so sorry,' Alex said to Quinn. He had been talking about this party for months.

'It's not a problem,' he shrugged.

'Thank you so much for picking her up. You get off – hopefully you won't have missed too much of your party.'

'It's totally fine, don't worry.'

She turned her attention to her daughter. 'Let's get you into bed and I'll get you a hot water bottle and some Calpol.' She waved goodbye to Quinn and ushered her daughter upstairs. 'Have you eaten a lot tonight?'

'No, I had one sausage roll and a tiny cupcake.'

'OK, was there anyone else feeling poorly?'

'No, everyone was having a lot of fun,' Zara said tearfully, as she plodded up the stairs.

So Alex could probably rule out any kind of food poisoning, although that kind of thing normally took a few hours to take effect. She really hoped it wasn't something serious like appendicitis but there were so many bugs going around right now, so hopefully it was just one of them.

She helped Zara get changed into her pyjamas and then got her into bed. There was a soft knock on the door. She opened it and Quinn was there with a hot water bottle and a bottle of Calpol. Her heart felt so full of love for him.

'Here you go, Rocket,' Quinn said gently, passing Zara the hot water bottle.

'Thank you,' Zara said pitifully. 'I'm sorry about your party.'

'It really isn't a problem. You and your mum will always be my number one priority. You two are far more important to me than some silly party.'

Alex swallowed a lump in her throat. She gave Zara some medicine. 'OK, we're going to leave you to rest. Do you want anything?'

Zara shook her head.

'Let us know if you do or if the pain gets worse,' Alex said.

Zara nodded and rolled over to face away from them. Clearly Alex wasn't forgiven just yet.

She ushered Quinn out of the room and back down the stairs.

'Thank you so much,' she said sincerely. 'The fact that you would drop everything to help Zara means so much to me. I know how much you were looking forward to tonight as well.'

'It's a party, it's one night. You two are the rest of my life. Of course that's more important. There was no question about me picking her up.'

God, she loved this man so much. He was right. He was her future, she knew that with all of her heart. And now she knew what she had to do.

'I love you so much.'

'I love you too, that's why I'm here.'

'Please, go back to the party, you won't have missed much if you go now.'

He shook his head. 'No, I'd rather be here and make sure Zara is OK.'

'It's probably just a bug. Her friend had it early in the week and it turned out to only be a twenty-four-hour thing.'

'I'd still rather be here.'

She leaned up and kissed him, although it was slightly weird to kiss him when his face was so wrinkly with all the make-up he was wearing to make him look like an old mad scientist.

Suddenly an idea came to her. 'Will you do something for me?'

'Anything.'

'I know you promised me a custom bauble of Jacob

and I still really want that. But will you do me one more?'

He smiled. 'Of course. What do you want?'

'I want a bauble that just says the word "Yes" on it.'

He looked at her in confusion. 'What's that for?'

'I can have secrets of my own. Besides, it's something for Zara, a little idea I'm playing with.'

'I'll bring it round tomorrow night.'

'Mum,' came a wobbly voice from upstairs.

'Yes, honey?'

'I've just been sick.'

'OK, no worries, get back into bed and I'll be up to sort it out in a second.'

'I've thrown up in my bed.'

'OK, get into my bed then.'

Alex turned back to Quinn. 'Are you sure you want to stay for this? It could get messy.'

He smiled. 'I wouldn't miss it for the world.'

CHAPTER 19

❄

It was Christmas Eve night and Zara had gone to bed. Despite throwing up as if it was an Olympic event the night before, Zara had made a good recovery that day. She had spent most of the morning lying on the sofa and watching Christmas movies but by the afternoon she'd been back to her old self. And Quinn had stayed through it all, helping clean up, sitting with Zara and reading to her. He was exactly what Alex wanted in a life partner. Someone who was there for her no matter what. Quinn had gone home for a few hours once he knew Zara was out the woods and Alex knew he was painting the baubles for her.

Immy was just finishing off her hot chocolate and then she was going to head to bed too.

There was a soft knock on the kitchen door and Alex looked up to see Quinn letting himself in, a box in one hand and an overnight bag in the other. He smiled at Alex then turned his attention to Immy.

'Hey Immy, this was left outside for you,' Quinn said, offering out the box.

Immy frowned and took it from him and then squealed in delight. 'It's Jacob. Oh my god, it's even got his one floppy ear. I love him. Thank you.'

Alex peered over her sister's shoulder. It was so life-like, so detailed, it really was beautiful.

'Oh, you don't need to thank me,' Quinn said.

'I know, I know, it's from St Nick,' Immy replied.

'Yes, but it's not him you need to thank,' Quinn told her. 'Alex was the one who requested I do this specifically.'

Immy looked at Alex and back at Quinn. 'So… you *are* him?'

'Yes.'

'All those baubles, they were all painted by you.'

'Yes.'

She looked at Alex. 'And you knew?'

'As of the night of the stakeout yes, but I promised him I wouldn't tell anyone.'

'My lips are sealed. You asked him to do this?'

'Yes, as a thank you for everything you've done for me.'

'Oh honey, you're my sister and I love you. You never need to thank me for being here for you. I always will.'

Alex smiled and hugged her.

Immy looked at her bauble again with a smile. 'I really do love it, thank you, both of you. Right, I'm off to bed, long day tomorrow. Most annoyingly I have to put up with seeing Xander over my Christmas lunch.'

'Well, we can make sure you're sat furthest away from him,' Alex said, giving her a sympathetic smile.

'That works. Night.'

Immy gave them both a wave and disappeared upstairs.

'I have the other bauble you asked me to make,' Quinn said. 'I'm not sure what you want me to do with it.'

He pulled it out of his bag and Alex could see the word 'Yes' surrounded by holly leaves and berries.

'Just hold onto it for a second,' she instructed him.

She picked up the box she had prepared earlier and took it over to him.

She handed him the box. 'This is the bauble I promised to make for you as a thank you for all of ours. I wanted to portray something you really wanted.'

Quinn smiled and opened the box, taking out the clear bauble she'd made with her book page decorations inside. This one simply showing an engagement ring. His eyes snapped to hers.

'I love you so so much,' she said softly. 'You are everything I want and need. You make me ridiculously happy and I would love to marry you, as soon as possible, so we can start the rest of our lives together.'

He stared at her and when he spoke his voice was choked. 'Are you sure you want this? We don't have to rush. I can wait as long as you need to be ready.'

'I'm ready now. You have proved to me again and again how utterly perfect you are for me, how loyal, kind, reliable, strong, generous and supportive you are. I can't ask for a better partner. Will you marry me?'

He stared at her, clearly floundering for words.

'Now you can open your bauble,' Alex said, gesturing to the one he'd painted.

He looked down at the word 'Yes' on his hand-painted bauble and laughed.

'Yes, of course, a million times yes. I love you. You make me so happy and it would be the greatest honour to have you as my wife.'

She leaned forward to kiss him and he pulled her into his arms, kissing her hard.

'I love you,' he whispered against her lips. 'Let me show you.'

She nodded and he scooped her up in his arms and carried her off to her room. As the clock struck midnight to mark the start of Christmas Day, she knew she had the greatest gift in the world, right here in her arms.

CHAPTER 20

❄

It had been a perfect Christmas Day so far. Alex had woken up this morning wrapped in Quinn's arms and couldn't be happier that she got to do this every day for the rest of her life.

Snow had fallen thick and fast again overnight and they'd woken up to a thick sparkly layer of it covering the grass, trees and roads. It looked magical.

They had opened presents together and then she'd broken the news to Zara and Immy that she and Quinn were engaged and they were both over the moon for them, especially Zara. They were heading to Violet's house for the big Christmas Day lunch and planned to discreetly take Violet aside, maybe once lunch was out the way, and let her know they were engaged.

Alex knocked on Violet's door and listened to all the noise inside. Quinn's aunts, uncles, all his cousins, including Xander, Max and their brothers and various other relatives, would all be in attendance for Violet's

Big Christmas Day Lunch. They always borrowed chairs and tables or brought their own and the dining area seemed to stretch through several rooms and round corners and even went up and down stairs. It was quite easy to spend the whole day there and still not speak to everyone, especially with the way that all the tables were laid out. Violet would spend most of the day in the kitchen dishing up food for everyone and she clearly loved every single moment of it. It was always noisy, chaotic and for Alex it was her favourite part of the day. Although this time she couldn't help worrying what some of Quinn's relatives would make of them being together.

Quinn squeezed her hand to quell her nerves and she looked up at him and smiled. Immy shifted nervously next to Alex and she knew her sister was anxious about seeing Xander again. She was wearing a beautiful red velvet dress that shimmered with small sparkly snowflakes. She looked gorgeous and Alex wondered if it had been chosen specifically to show Xander what he was missing.

Max answered the door and, after giving them all hugs, he ushered them inside and down to the kitchen where the Big Christmas Day Lunch was getting under-way. He rejoined his brothers. Quinn's six cousins when they stood together looked like something out of a Hollywood movie. The Wild brothers, all looked impos-sibly handsome in tight, white shirts and black trousers as they dished out drinks to guests and surreptitiously stole pigs in blankets and other snacks. Archer - Max and Xander's youngest brother - came over to give them all a hug. She knew him from the arts and crafts market, where she used to work before she moved to the Wonky Tree Studios. Jared, Logan and Ryker, the other three brothers, she only knew from the annual Christmas lunch celebrations.

Alex saw Xander look over at their arrival and his mouth dropped as he took in what Immy was wearing. After a moment he moved over to give Immy a kiss on the cheek and wish her Merry Christmas. Alex was also pretty sure she heard him whisper in her ear that she looked beautiful. Alex rolled her eyes. Silly man, he was clearly besotted with her sister and rightly so, she was rather fabulous.

'Ah, you're here,' Violet said, grabbing Zara into a big hug. 'Merry Christmas.'

She hugged Alex, Immy and Quinn too.

'What lovely presents did you get?' Violet asked Zara as she started slicing one of four giant turkeys. There was an older man already slicing one of the other turkeys next to Violet and, while Alex didn't know all the relatives, she wondered if this was Michael, Violet's new boyfriend and Henry's best friend. It certainly looked like the man she'd seen Violet with the other day.

'I got my Christmas wish,' Zara said, excitedly.

Alex stared in horror. They had specifically told Zara not to tell Violet and that they would tell her later on in the day when they got her alone. Alex didn't want to monopolise the Christmas lunch nor was she ready for the whole extended family to know. She tried to intervene but it was like watching a car crash and being powerless to stop it.

'What's that, dear?' Violet said, dishing up roast potatoes into a bowl.

'Mum and Quinn are engaged,' Zara said in a voice so loud it practically drowned out everyone else.

Suddenly you could hear a pin drop, it seemed like every single person there was frozen, listening to what was happening.

Violet turned round to look at Zara, the turkeys forgotten. 'Say again, I didn't quite hear you.'

'Mum and Quinn are getting married, next year, and I'm going to be bridesmaid.'

Violet looked over to her and Quinn to confirm it and Alex nodded. 'Sorry, we were going to tell you this afternoon, discreetly. But yes, we've been in love with each other for four years, we didn't want to wait any longer.'

'Oh that's wonderful news, congratulations,' Violet said, coming over to give them both a big hug. And suddenly Alex was surrounded by lots of other people offering their congratulations too, mostly Quinn's cousins. Although she could see that a few people, aunts and uncles mainly who Alex had barely even spoken to, weren't impressed by it, some of them whispering or muttering between themselves about how inappropriate it was, Alex didn't care. Quinn made her ridiculously happy. He loved her and Zara and that was all that mattered.

But Violet had seen them whispering as she looked

around the room.

'I have an announcement of my own,' she said, reaching out for Michael's hand who now looked terrified as he gingerly approached her. 'This is Michael and we've been secretly dating each other for the last six months. He makes me smile again and it's been a long time since I had something to smile about.'

The whispering and muttering took off at a frenzy but many people came over to meet Michael properly and tell Violet they were happy for her.

Alex looked at Quinn who was smiling.

'Did you know about this?' Quinn said as people gathered round his mum and a very bemused-looking Michael.

'Yes, she came to ask my advice a few days ago about how to tell you. I didn't suggest this big announcement though. Are you OK about it?'

He nodded. 'Yeah, I've always worried about her being alone, I'm glad she's got someone who makes her happy. Dad would have wanted that too.'

Finally as people moved away, and conversation resumed, Quinn went over to his mum. 'I'm happy for you, really I am. And Michael, Dad loved you, I think he would have been happy you two have found each other.'

'Sorry to land it on you this way, but I thought my news might take the heat off you two a little bit,' Violet said.

'It's fine and thank you.'

They moved away to let Violet carry on dishing up the food. Zara ran off to play with Etta, Xander's daughter, and Immy was talking to Xander, so when Quinn suggested they stepped outside into the back garden Alex readily agreed.

Snow was dancing in the air as Quinn opened the back door and they went outside. The garden was quiet and cool, in contrast to the noise and heat of the kitchen. Quinn led her down to the end where there was a fountain, the water frozen in beautiful icicles as it cascaded over the edge.

He turned to face her and kissed her on the forehead. 'My family is loud, chaotic, dysfunctional, rude, judgemental and sometimes just complete pains in the ass. Fortunately, I only have to see most of them once a year, but are you sure you want to marry into this?'

Alex smiled. 'I love you, I love all of you and that means loving your family too.'

'Are you sure? We can always elope?'

'As tempting as that is, Violet would never speak to us again and I'm rather partial to your mum. She makes the best Christmas jumpers and I never want to miss out on that.'

'Oh no, if we elope we'll have to take her with us, and Immy of course, and probably all of my cousins.'

'Not so much an elopement then.' Alex ran her hands up his shoulders.

'Well no, but we can keep it small.'

Inside there was a scream and the sound of a glass breaking.

'And avoid all this drama? I wouldn't miss it for the world.'

EPILOGUE

❄

ONE YEAR LATER

'How about George?' Quinn said, stroking Alex's tiny belly.

It was Christmas Day night and after a long tiring day at Violet's Big Christmas Day Lunch they'd come back to their new little cottage overlooking the sea. Alex was a little bit in love with it. They'd only moved in a few months before and had spent a lot of time decorating and making it their own. Quinn had painted a beautiful mural on Zara's bedroom wall. She'd wanted dragons, her new obsession so Quinn had painted them flying above the sea. But now it seemed they would need to convert one of the rooms to a nursery too.

After selling their house, Immy had moved into the flat above her shop, but Alex still saw her sister every day. They'd chatted a lot over lunch and Immy was ridiculously happy. Alex couldn't help smiling about that.

She focussed her attention back on Quinn.

'Too traditional,' Alex said. 'How about Blaze?' They'd been coming up with ideas for baby boy names for the last half hour and they couldn't agree on anything. So she'd started coming up with more ridiculous ones just to wind him up.

'Oh, I like that.'

'Really?'

'No, I was kidding.'

Alex smiled with relief. 'So was I.' She wanted something unique and special but Blaze was a little too out there.

She yawned and as she was sitting on his lap she leaned into him and rested her head on his shoulder. He grabbed a blanket off the back of the sofa and wrapped it round her, placing a kiss on her forehead, before returning his hand to her belly. She was only just over twelve weeks pregnant. They'd had a scan a few days before and everything seemed normal and healthy but her belly was only just starting to show. Well, in fact you had to look pretty damn close to see it and anyone looking that close might assume she'd just eaten a few too many mince pies over Christmas, but that didn't stop Quinn from stroking it whenever they were alone together. They hadn't told anyone yet, apart from Immy, but they planned to tell Zara tomorrow – so there was no chance she'd be able to announce it to everyone at the Christmas Day lunch.

'How about Clarence?' Quinn asked.

'No. Wasn't that the name of our registrar who married us on the beach?'

'Yes, the happiest day of my life.'

She smiled with love for him. It had been a small affair in the end. Quinn was adamant about not having anyone there who might be judgemental about their relationship. So it was just Zara, Immy, Violet, Quinn's six cousins and a handful of friends but it had been a beautiful ceremony on a secluded part of the beach just as the sun was setting. Clarence, their registrar, had been full of exuberance which had made the ceremony funny as well as joyful.

'I love you so much.' Alex kissed him. 'But we're not naming the baby Clarence.'

'OK, OK, I've got one, and it's not one you could possibly say no to.'

'Go on.'

'Barnaby.'

She smiled in surprise. 'Barnaby. I love it.'

'Thought you might. As we fell in love watching *Midsomer Murders* over the years, it seemed appropriate.'

'It's perfect.'

'OK, now we need a name if it's a girl,' Quinn said.

'Oh, I was thinking about Violet.'

His face lit up. 'I love it and Mum will be over the moon.'

'She has been such an important part of mine and Zara's lives for the last five years, it feels right we name the baby after her.'

'She will be so touched by that. And so am I.'

'Well, now that's decided, shall we go to bed?'

'Nothing would make me happier,' Quinn said, quirking an eyebrow mischievously.

She was almost too tired for that. Almost.

He stood and scooped her into his arms which made her giggle against his lips. They were already in their Christmas-themed pyjamas and were ready for bed, they'd just gone downstairs for hot chocolates with whipped cream and marshmallows and then started talking about baby names.

Quinn walked into their room with those huge windows overlooking the sea; Alex loved nothing more than waking up every morning to that view. He pulled back the duvet, placed her gently down on the bed and then climbed in next to her, wrapping her in his arms.

After a while, she looked up at him. 'Are we not going to make love?'

'I think you're probably a bit too tired for that, besides you know I love cuddling you almost as much as I love making love to you.'

She smiled and put her head back on his chest. She was so blissfully happy right now.

Outside the stars sparkled over the sea. When she was a child her mum would say that if she wanted something badly enough, she was to find the brightest star in the sky and wish on it and maybe it would come true. And while, as an adult, Alex knew wishing didn't make things come true, it was something she still found herself doing from time to time.

She found the brightest star in the sky and thought about what she could wish for. She could wish for everything to stay the same, to live in this perfect bubble of happiness but next year, with a baby on the way, everything would change. She wondered whether to wish to stay this happy forever but, as she looked up at the man she loved with all her heart, she knew that wish had already come true. He was her happy ever after.

If you enjoyed *The Cottage on Christmas Gardens,* you'll love my next gorgeously romantic story, *The Chocolate Shop on Cherry Lane.* You'll get to know more about Quinn's cousin Xander and Alex's sister Immy. It's out in Spring 2026, but you can preorder it now.

A LETTER FROM HOLLY

Thank you so much for reading *The Cottage on Christmas Gardens,* I had so much fun writing this story, creating the wonderful town of Lovegrove Bay and falling in love with the characters. I hope you enjoyed reading it as much as I enjoyed writing it.

One of the best parts of writing comes from seeing the reaction from readers. Did it make you smile or laugh, did it make you cry, hopefully happy tears? Did you fall in love with Alex and Quinn as much as I did? I would absolutely love it if you could leave a short review on Amazon. Getting feedback from readers is amazing and it also helps to persuade other readers to pick up one of my books for the first time.

Thank you for reading.

Love Holly x

❄

Jewel Island Series

Sunrise over Sapphire Bay

Autumn Skies over Ruby Falls

Ice Creams at Emerald Cove

Sunlight over Crystal Sands

Mistletoe at Moonstone Lake

❄

The Happiness Series

The Little Village of Happiness

The Gift of Happiness

❄

The Summer of Chasing Dreams

❄

Sandcastle Bay Series

The Holiday Cottage by the Sea

The Cottage on Sunshine Beach

Coming Home to Maple Cottage

❄

Hope Island Series

Spring at Blueberry Bay

Summer at Buttercup Beach

Christmas at Mistletoe Cove

❊

Juniper Island Series

Christmas Under a Cranberry Sky

A Town Called Christmas

❊

White Cliff Bay Series

Christmas at Lilac Cottage

Snowflakes on Silver Cove

Summer at Rose Island

❊

Standalone Stories

The Secrets of Clover Castle (Previously published as
Fairytale Beginnings)

The Guestbook at Willow Cottage

One Hundred Proposals

One Hundred Christmas Proposals

Tied Up With Love

A Home on Bramble Hill (Previously published as Beneath the Moon and Stars

❋

For Young Adults

The Sentinel Series

STAY IN TOUCH...

To keep up to date with the latest news on my releases, just go to the link below to sign up for a newsletter. You'll also get two FREE short stories, get sneak peeks, booky news and be able to take part in exclusive giveaways. Your email will never be shared with anyone else and you can unsubscribe at any time
https://www.subscribepage.com/hollymartinsignup

Website: https://hollymartin-author.com/
Email: holly@hollymartin-author.com
Facebook: facebook.com/hollymartinauthor
Instagram: instagram.com/hollymartin_author

ACKNOWLEDGEMENTS

To my parents, my mom, my biggest fan, who reads every word I've written a hundred times over and loves it every single time, and for my dad, for cooking celebratory steak every publication day

For my twinnie, the gorgeous Aven Ellis for just being my wonderful friend, for your endless support, for cheering me on, for reading my stories and telling me what works and what doesn't and for keeping me entertained with wonderful stories. I love you dearly.

To my lovely friends Julie, Natalie, Jac, Verity and Jodie, thanks for all the support.

Thanks to my fabulous editors, Celine Kelly and Rhian McKay.

To my lovely agent and the team at Lorella Belli, thanks for all your hard work taking my books to different countries.

To all the wonderful bloggers for your tweets, retweets, facebook posts, tireless promotions, support, encouragement and endless enthusiasm. You guys are amazing and I couldn't do this journey without you.

To anyone who has read my book and taken the time to tell me you've enjoyed it or wrote a review, thank you so much.

Thank you, I love you all.

Published by Holly Martin in 2025
Copyright © Holly Martin, 2025

Holly Martin has asserted her right to be identified as the author of this work.
All rights reserved. No part of this publication may be reproduced, stored in any retrieval system, or transmitted, in any form or by any means, electronic, mechanical, photocopying, recording or otherwise, without the prior written permission of the author.
This book is a work of fiction. Names, characters, businesses, organisations, places and events other than those clearly in the public domain, are either the product of the author's imagination or are used fictitiously. Any resemblance to actual persons, living or dead, events all locales is entirely coincidental.

978-1-913616-68-7 Paperback
978-1-913616-69-4 Large Print paperback
978-1-913616-70-0 Hardback
978-1-913616-71-7 Audiobook

❄

Cover design by Dee Dee Book Covers

Printed in Dunstable, United Kingdom

71508993R00184